PROPERTY

Magdalen Nabb was b— ——
as a potter. In 1975 she —— ——ome
and her car, and moved —— son, knowing
nobody and speaking no—— —. She has lived there ever
since, and pursues a dual career as crime writer and
children's author.

'It takes a writer as good as Magdalen Nabb to remind us
how subtle the art of the mystery can be. She does make it
look easy, though' *New York Times*

'Nabb's elegant writing style and her ability to perfectly
frame a novel enrich this compelling psychological portrait
of a kidnapping . . . *Property of Blood* draws the reader deeply
into other worlds; every word should be savored.'
Washington Post

'Guarnaccia . . . is one of the most endearing and believable
creations in modern crime fiction . . . One of the kindest but
wisest of sleuths, he is an excellent counterpoint to Nabb's
sinister imagination . . . An eerily haunting thriller whose
low-key telling makes its Jacobean plot all the more
disturbing.' *Glasgow Herald*

'A heartrending account of [an] ordeal in the hands of brutal
professional bandits' Susanna Yager, *Sunday Telegraph*

Also by Magdalen Nabb

Some Bitter Taste
The Monster of Florence
The Marshal at the Villa Torrini
The Marshal Makes His Report
The Marshal's Own Case
The Marshal and the Madwoman
The Marshal and the Murderer
Death in Autumn
Death in Springtime
Death of a Dutchman
Death of an Englishman

with Paolo Vagheggi
The Prosecutor

PROPERTY

OF

BLOOD

MAGDALEN NABB

arrow books

Published in the United Kingdom in 2005 by Arrow Books

1 3 5 7 9 10 8 6 4 2

First published in the United Kingdom in 2004 by William Heinemann

Arrow Books
The Random House Group Limited
20 Vauxhall Bridge Road, London, SW1V 2SA

Random House Australia (Pty) Limited
20 Alfred Street, Milsons Point, Sydney
New South Wales 2061, Australia

Random House New Zealand Limited
18 Poland Road, Glenfield
Auckland 10, New Zealand

Random House (Pty) Limited
Endulini, 5a Jubilee Road, Parktown 2193, South Africa

The Random House Group Limited Reg. No. 954009

www.randomhouse.co.uk

A CIP catalogue record for this book is available from the British Library

Papers used by Random House
are natural, recyclable products made from wood grown in
sustainable forests. The manufacturing processes conform to
the environmental regulations of the country of origin

ISBN 0 09 944333 3

Typeset by SX Composing DTP, Rayleigh, Essex
Printed and bound in Great Britain by
Bookmarque Ltd, Croydon, Surrey

For invaluable help, as always, on matters regarding the Carabinieri the author wishes to thank Generale Nicolino D'Angelo.

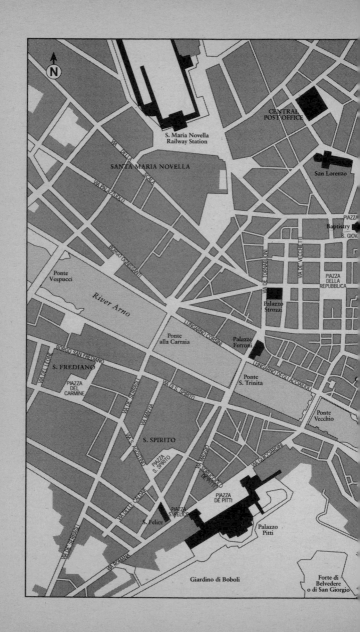

200 metres

To Fiesole

Università

Biblioteca
Marucelliana

PIAZZA DELLA
S.S. ANNUNZIATA

VIA LA PIRA

VIA DEGLI ALFANI

VIA M. SERRI

PIAZZA
D'AZEGLIO

S. Maria Nuova
Hospital

S. Maria
del Fiore
(Duomo)

VIA DELLA PERGOLA

BORGO D. ALBIZI

PIAZZA
GHIBERTI

VIA GHIBELLINA

Palazzo
Vecchio

PIAZZA DI
S. CROCE

S. CROCE

S. Croce

Ponte
Alle Grazie

L. DELLA ZECCA VECCHIA

River Arno

VIA DI BELVEDERE

PIAZZALE
MICHELANGELO

One

'I'll do my best to tell you everything but the things I remember are perhaps not what you need. And then, they took my watch and, because I couldn't see or hear, I often drifted away from the real world and I could have lost seconds or days, even weeks.

'I do remember the beginning, though, because I went over it a thousand times in my head in those first days, trying to work out what I should have done, how I should have reacted. I went over it, reinventing it so that I escaped. I screamed for help, someone happened along, Leo came to meet me – he sometimes did. I passed a lot of time reinventing like that but it didn't change the present any more than it changed what happened that night. I walked Tessie round the block. There was a freezing wind.

I remember it howling and a crash every so often as a tile fell into the road or a shutter broke loose. Tessie kept pulling at her lead, as usual. I never can understand how she can run so fast, scuttling along on her tiny legs – they beat and kicked her until she screamed. I don't want to talk about that.

'I came back into the piazza and was pushing at the doors . . . then . . . nothing.

'I saw in the dark something like the blades of a fan spinning right in front of my nose and the world spinning with it. I wanted to be sick and I couldn't breathe. There was a smell of chloroform and I thought I was in hospital, coming round from an operation. I thought there would surely be something to be sick into but I must have passed out again.

'This is a gap that's serious for you, I know because I don't know how long I'd been in the car when I next woke up. I was on the floor between the front and back seats and my face was pressed against the carpeting. Dust and fluff were in my mouth and nose. Beneath my face I could feel the speed of the car, going straight, probably on a motor-way. Something, I think a leather jacket, was covering me and it stank of sweat and another sour, greasy smell. I wanted to get it off my head because I couldn't breathe but I found that my hands were tied behind my back.

' "I'm suffocating! Uncover my head, I'm suffocating," I cried. A violent blow hit my ribs and I realised that there was someone sitting with his feet on me. I tried to raise my head.

' "You have to let me breathe! Please!"

'He kicked me in the head and said, "The bitch is awake." I heard some fumbling about and a tearing noise, then my head was yanked back by the hair and his voice spoke right in my ear.

' "Don't you ever, ever tell me what I have to do. D'you hear me? You're not in your fancy palazzo now. I'm in charge here, got that?"

' "Yes . . ."

'He put his boot under my chin and pulled my head back against the seat. Then he slapped a broad piece of sticking plaster over my mouth and pressed it hard. He kicked my head back to the floor and covered it even more closely with the smelly jacket. I was panic-stricken. My mouth was full of dirt and the sticking plaster forced me to breathe that unbearable stink deeply through my nose. I lost control and screamed, or tried to, but the screams got no further than my throat and were useless and painful.

'A voice from the front, not the driver, yelled, "What the fuck are you doing?"

' "I've plastered her mouth up. Bitch was making too much noise."

' "You dickhead! Get it off! Get it off! If she throws up after the chloroform she'll choke to death. Get it off!" I heard Tessie whining, then a yelp as someone hit her.

'The fingers fumbling under my nose stank of nicotine. I held my breath as the big plaster was ripped away. A few of my hairs had got tangled in there when he put it on, and the pain as these, too, were ripped away was

3

terrible. I started crying. They ignored me because they were still quarrelling. The one in front was furious.

"You don't touch her unless I say so! I'm responsible for the goods being intact and what I say goes."

'I tried to clean the fluff and grit from my tongue using my teeth and spitting. I breathed through my mouth to avoid at least some of the smell of stale sweat. The arm I was lying on had gone dead but I didn't try to shift my weight. I was afraid of the pain that would come with a return of feeling and afraid of the boot crashing down on my ribs again.

'I was still fairly dozy from the chloroform but, although I might have suffered less, I couldn't let myself fall asleep again. The feeling of suffocation, the darkness, my inability to move would have made dropping into sleep a sort of dying. I decided to be still and quiet so the man above wouldn't hurt me and to listen for clues about the length and direction of my journey. None came. After the row about the plaster they remained silent. What had I thought? That they'd say, "Oh, look, there's the turn-off for such and such a place?"

'Just miles and miles of road passing below me. The weight of their silence above. The smell. Once I thought, "This is too ridiculous to be true. It's a nightmare. One of those nightmares when you can't move. I just have to wait and in a little while I'll wake up in the real world where these people don't exist."

'The nightmare didn't end but the car journey did. I felt through the floor of the car a different sort of road, a

4

road with curves and junctions, then a rougher country road. The car stopped. When they tumbled me out into the cold night air I was grateful for the sheepskin coat and the comfortable fur boots I had worn to take Tessie out . . . I'm sorry.

'Please don't be distressed by my crying. It's not even crying, really, just accumulated pain and tension unloading. As if my body were crying, not me, if you can understand that. You see? I can smile at the same time, which shows it's only a physical reaction. I have every reason to be happy now, haven't I?

'It was then that they kicked and beat Tessie and one of them picked her up and threw her body away.

'We were walking. I couldn't see at all. This was real darkness, thick, oppressive darkness that confuses your senses, makes you lose your balance. We were battling against the icy wind, too. I was pushed and pulled along. It wasn't a long walk that time, first on the stones and grit of the country road, then on soft earth and big slabs of stone, then on tufts of short grass. I didn't see anything but I felt the changes through the rubber soles of my boots. Then we started climbing. It was difficult to keep my balance since my hands were still tied and the blackness around gave me no points of reference. Once I stumbled and, unable to save myself by throwing an arm out, I crashed into the man in front of me. He swore and kicked back violently so that it hurt even through my boot and unbalanced me even more so that I fell. I was pulled up by the hair.

' "On your feet, Contessina. Move."

'As I tried to get up, I realised that I urgently needed to pee and that, as a result of the anaesthetic or perhaps the cold, I could do nothing about holding it.

' "I need to pee."

'They pushed me a little to one side. "Do it there."

'My sheepskin coat was an encumbrance and I was wearing trousers with a zip fastener at the side. "I can't! My hands!"

'They cut me free but it was too late. I was already wet and perhaps only half of it went on the grass. After that, I was cold, my legs were wet, and I thought, "Whatever it is that's happening to me, I can't survive it. These are the things that will destroy me, not kicks in the ribs." But the uphill walking was so difficult that I was forced to concentrate just on keeping my balance, and once I got back into the rhythm of the climb the wetness warmed up and probably even started to dry. I know it sounds strange, even impossible, but I remember that in the midst of all my fear and misery I teased myself, saying, as we do to our children, "Why didn't you go before you came out?" and I wanted to giggle. I expect it was just nervous strain. The children . . . I can't wait to see them. Will it be long?

'We stopped that night in a cave of some sort. I was made to crawl a long way in until we reached a part where it was possible to sit or kneel but not to stand up. Kneeling, I could feel the roof of it with my head.

' "Feel to your right. There's a mattress."

'I felt it. I could smell it.

' "Crawl onto it and lie on your back. Now reach behind your head and find the things that are there."

'A plastic bottle of water, a plastic bedpan, a roll of toilet paper.

' "Now give me your right hand." I felt a chain being wrapped around my wrist and padlocked. Then the chain's weight down the length of my left leg, where it was wound round and padlocked again, the noise of more length of chain being attached somewhere in the cave. To an iron staple in the wall perhaps. But why so tight? What could I have done if it had been just a bit less tight? Where could I have gone? Surely there was no need to block my circulation like that.

' "Hold out your left hand."

'He put something into it, something cold and wet and heavy, like a dead thing. I shuddered. He closed my hand over it and pushed it up towards my mouth, his nicotine-smelling fingers right under my nose. "Eat."

'It was meat of some sort – I think perhaps boiled chicken since it was so wet and slippery. It smelled strongly of garlic. I'm a vegetarian but I knew better, even then, than to protest. It would certainly provoke another blow and some verbal abuse and, besides, if I wanted to survive, I had no choice but to eat whatever came my way. I bit into the cold, slithery flesh and forced myself to chew it. I chewed two lumps of it but I couldn't swallow. I tried but I had no saliva and trying to force it down made me retch.

' "I'm sorry. I'm so sorry. I can't swallow. It's not the food – it's very good – perhaps it's because of the chloroform. I just can't swallow. I'm so sorry." Like someone at a dinner party refusing second helpings. "I couldn't possibly but it was wonderful – no, really. . . ." It was a long time before I was offered anything else but there was nothing I could have done. He made me drink some of the water. I couldn't open the bottle with one hand – later I learned to turn the screw top with my teeth – so he opened it for me. I took it from him – though even that was difficult to manage with one hand, the bottle being soft plastic and full – so I wouldn't have to smell his fingers again. Then I thought it odd that Nicotine Fingers was the only one with me. Had the others, whoever drove the car and the front-seat passenger who'd said he was the boss, gone away? I think they had because after I'd drunk the water I heard him fumbling about for a bit and then, without another word, his footsteps went away from me and I heard the rustle of his clothing as he crawled towards the exit. I remained tense, straining my ears, terrified of one or all of them returning, of more blows, of their raping me, chained as I was. Of their discovery of my shameful wetness, of their finding me as smelly as I found them. I may have lain like that for hours before I realised that they weren't coming back. Nobody was coming. This was forever. They could ask for a ransom at their leisure, and if I stayed here tied up they need take no risks of being seen bringing me food. There was no reason why anyone should ever find me.

'I didn't cry. I think we cry to attract help and comfort, don't you agree? That's why babies cry, after all. They can't move about or speak, they can't control their lives, order food when they're hungry, change themselves when they're wet. They can only cry, but they cry in the knowledge that someone must come, the faith that someone must come. Well, I had all of a baby's problems. I was wet and cold, lonely and hungry. I did even start a feeble cry but it petered out. No one came. There was no one to hear, not even an imaginary person who ought to hear. I was buried alive and the world would go on without me.

'I didn't protest about dying. We all have to die. I protested against not dying my own particular death, my body carefully disposed of. I wanted people to say goodbye to me. I wanted a grave with flowers on it. We don't like thinking about death but, when we're forced to, as I was, we do care how we die just as we care how we live. It's the last thing we do and it should surely be an appropriate finale to what we did in life. I had a lot of time to think, you see, but these are not the things you need to know though you sit there so patiently listening. I'm cold . . . Do you have another of these blankets? They're from the cells, aren't they? – Oh, I don't mind. After all, I'm an ex-prisoner myself. Thank you.

'That was the longest night. I didn't sleep at all. I still had that sensation of falling asleep being an acceptance of death. If I had to die in this cave I would remain vigilant. I would live as hard as it is possible to live chained up in darkness. My brain, after all, was functioning, and they say that starvation alerts the brain even more and that it is a happy death, ending in a sort of euphoric delirium.

'Still, the darkness oppressed me. It was that complete darkness that occurs only deep in the country. It isn't just an absence of sufficient light to see by but an imprisoning force with a life of its own. It makes you hallucinate after a while. Your brain invents information because it receives none. Worms of dancing light, strange shapes that loom up at high speed so you want to dodge them. Total silence, too, plays the same tricks, making you invent noises, voices, anything to fill the void.

'I wanted to order my thoughts, to think over my life and say goodbye to it. I suppose I was trying to regain some sort of dignity, but those tricks of the brain made it impossible, leaving me tormented and confused. Fighting to breathe, too. How big was this cave? How much air was available to me? Had they blocked up the entrance? Death by suffocation was the worst thing I could imagine. I'm not really claustrophobic but, for instance, I'm not much of a swimmer because I could never bear my head being in the water. My son used to laugh at me because I swam with my head bolt upright like a duck and he'd swim along behind me in imitation.

'It was fear of suffocation that made me move, pushing myself into a sitting position with my left hand and then feeling around me. That helped, to know I could cut through the imprisoning blackness with my hand. I could feel the wall of the cave behind my head where the water and the other things were, I could touch the ceiling, but in front and beside me there was space. I shuffled forward, following the direction of the chain, pushing with my free left hand. Not only was there space, I could sense a faint current of air coming in from outside. If air could get in, then light could, too.

'I shuffled back on the mattress and lay down to think. I became calmer. Filling my head with thoughts and images of my own choosing kept out the hallucinations created by the black silence around me. Doing something, examining the space around me, had calmed me down. I did more things. First I used the bedpan, holding it rather clumsily with my left hand, then dried myself with the toilet roll. I pushed the bedpan away to my left and reached for the bottle of water. That was difficult and I spilled a lot on the mattress but I managed to drink some. Although I was very cold, my mouth was hot and dry and my lips chapped, as though I were feverish. The water was so good, so good and satisfying, delicious like a fine white wine. I drank to occupy myself but found I was thirsty after the walk and the long hours of fear. Swallowing the water gave me so much joy, its taste – and its meaning. If they'd left me here to die, would there be water? Would there be a bedpan and even toilet paper? If you find it hard to understand how a sip of water could fill me with joy, how much more difficult to understand how eagerly I waited for the return of my kidnappers. And, as if to celebrate this happy thought, dawn came. I saw the pale shape of my own hand, then ghostly boulders

11

around me, the huge iron staple I was chained to, the way out. It didn't get really light so far inside the cave but if there was enough light to see by, it meant that outside the day must be bright. I was full of energy then. I shuffled to the back of the mattress and with a flat stone from the floor I wrote something on the wall – something I knew Leo would understand and know for sure it was me – I did it low down so I could hide it with a little pile of stones.

' "Lie down!"

'I froze.

' "Lie on the mattress face down!" I did as I was told and someone crawled into the cave.

'My head was lifted and I heard tearing and cutting.

'Big plasters were pressed onto each of my eyes, then a long, wide strip from temple to temple, carefully pressed and modelled round my nose. It wasn't Nicotine Fingers and I recognised the voice of the one who had shouted, "I'm responsible for the goods being intact." I tried to feel his hand – the size of it would give me an idea of his general size – and he hit me a blow that sent my face deep into the mattress.

' "Don't try playing the policeman with us! And don't move unless you're told to move. And, if you've any sense, you won't let yourself cry with those plasters on. It'll burn you till you scream."

'They knew their business. He unchained me. I wanted to turn over and massage my wrist and ankle where the chain had almost stopped my circulation but I didn't dare.

' "Get on all fours. Follow me."

'I crawled out of the cave behind him and someone waiting there dragged me to my feet. The freezing wind attacked me, almost throwing me off balance, a wind whose cutting edge was at my face but whose low, menacing moan was miles away. I sensed an infinite space around me. I smelled snow, and even behind the sticking plaster I could feel a dazzling light.

' "Jesus fucking Christ!"

' "Now what do we do?"

' "Shut up! Just shut up!"

'The one in charge was angry, panicked even. I recognised his voice easily but I wasn't sure about whoever had said, "Now what do we do?" The driver from last night, perhaps. He hadn't spoken in the car. The accents were Florentine, strong and rough.

' "You've made a mistake, haven't you? You don't want me – I'm not rich enough—"

'A slap across the face. "Keep your fancy mouth shut. Give me your left hand." I held it out. "Feel that – I said feel it! Don't drag on it to help yourself. Just keep your hand on it as you walk. If he stops, you stop. When he walks, you walk. Move!" He prodded me with what I guessed was the barrel of a gun.

'I felt the rough canvas of a rucksack which the boss in front was carrying. I tried to do as I was told and walked with my left hand touching the rucksack very lightly. I felt the snow crunch under my feet. I knew we were very high up, not just because of the snow but because the wind's

13

low-pitched whine came from far away below us, not above. We were on a stony track which sloped away from us steeply on our right and, because it was so narrow and my boots weren't suitable for such rough ground, I stumbled on those stones that stuck up out of the dry snow. How could I help saving myself by clutching at the rucksack?

'Immediately I was kicked from in front. "Don't drag on me, you stupid bitch!" The one behind pulled me up and thumped me in the back.

' "On your feet! Don't drag on the rucksack and don't try falling as an excuse to touch one of us or you'll get this across your face." He pushed the barrel of the gun against my cheek and then put my hand back on the rucksack. "Walk!"

'I hadn't fallen on purpose, I hadn't! But I didn't dare speak in case another blow came. I wanted to talk. I wanted to ask them why they were doing this to me. I wasn't rich enough for this. Why wasn't it someone really rich who'd never had to struggle, who'd had it easy? The sort of person these types felt they had a right to hate and punish. I wanted to say, "Not me! Not me!" I wanted to tell them that I had been poor and had to struggle to bring up my children and that I'd worked so hard, for so many years. Didn't I deserve at least a few years of tranquillity between the problems of poverty and the problems of riches? It was so ridiculous that I should be kidnapped before even having time to finish paying my debts.

'But I didn't dare and what difference would it have

made? They'd labelled me a rich bitch and I had to stay labelled for the benefit of their consciences. That's true, I promise you. You wouldn't believe how they preached at me over the weeks, how they justified their greed and cruelty.

'Anyway, I didn't dare speak so I walked. My body in the sheepskin became overheated with the effort but my head and especially my ears ached with cold. I couldn't feel my hands any more so it was difficult to tell whether I was touching the rucksack half the time. I tried for a while to keep my right hand in my pocket but I needed it for balance, sensing the abyss to my right where my boot kept slipping down off the path. Each time I stumbled they hit me and cursed me. We walked all day, and it seemed to me that almost all the time we were climbing. We never stopped for a rest, and I knew that they were nervous, afraid even. Something was wrong. That remark they'd made when they got a good look at me that morning . . . Perhaps I was right. They had made a mistake and didn't want me at all. Perhaps they would make me walk in circles for miles and then leave me somewhere near civilisation. After all, I hadn't seen any of their faces. I couldn't identify them, they were safe from me.

'Still without stopping, the one behind reached over me and took something from the rucksack. He put a plastic bottle into my right hand.

' "Can't we stop? I'm afraid of falling."

' "Walk." I sipped at the water and at once air broke from my stomach, making me dribble. It was so long since I'd eaten. He gave me a slice of rather stale bread and a lump of Parmesan cheese. That tasted good, especially the cheese, crunchy and salty. But when I tried to swallow what I'd chewed, more air came up and my stomach just didn't seem to want me to swallow anything, tightening up the way it does when you want to vomit, or are trying not to. I kept trying, unable to believe that my psychological state could override my basic physical needs. Surely it should be the other way round? In the end I left a bit of chewed food in my mouth and waited until it became so sodden that it was bound to be washed down with my saliva, bit by bit. I got through six or seven mouthfuls like that and drank more water when it was offered. I had to try and keep my strength up. I was sure now they'd made a mistake and were going to let me go. I told myself I must be super-obedient. I was careful to keep my left hand flat and touching the rucksack very light. I kept my head even lower than before and trod carefully so as not to stumble and anger them, especially as I might have to walk a longish distance alone at the end when they let me go and didn't want to be slowed down by any injuries.

'I stopped when Rucksack stopped. I heard him step off the path to go and pee. The other pressed the gun into my back in his absence. I don't know where he thought I could run to but I stood quietly with my head down until Rucksack was back in front of me again and Gun put my hand back in place and went to pee, too. It was only then that I realised fully that Nicotine Fingers wasn't with us. I made a sign that I needed to go and pee, too.

' "Do it here. On the left." The ground on the right still fell away from us steeply and I couldn't have kept my balance. I was able to hide myself with my coat and tried hard not to wet it. Sightless as I was, I felt all the fears we have as small children when this emergency happens. The fear of prickles, nettles, broken bottles. There was nothing except short, prickly grass and powdery snow and the icy wind creeping into my exposed warm body. At the thought that they would release me, my brain became alert and began working furiously. We must be climbing a hill or mountain and, since it still fell away to our right, we hadn't changed direction. We weren't simply going in a circle then. I decided that we must be crossing the hill and that at some point we'd turn in a circle, big and gradual enough to confuse me, and start down again. You can imagine my joy when we did start going down. I was right. They were going to dump me and I wanted to cry for joy! It was all a mistake, and tonight I would be home, having a hot shower, sitting in my corner of the sofa with Leo and Caterina close to me. I would watch television – I could telephone my friends – ring Patrick! Would he be over here already? He would, he'd have caught the first plane out of New York if he'd heard. Would he have heard? . . . My own bed, my own lovely quiet room. None of this had any meaning. It was a mistake, it was nearly over.

'Rucksack stopped. This was it. As I waited for instructions I imagined a road close by, perhaps a service station or one of those bar-shop-restaurant places you get out in the country. I prepared what to say to them, afraid they'd think I was mad, appearing like that out of nowhere without even money to phone. And, of course, there might have been nothing in the papers yet . . . How long exactly had I been missing? It seemed like weeks to me but—

' "Here?"

' "The rifle. Not that piddling thing."

'My ears prickled, my heart started pounding. It was Rucksack who'd spoken. They weren't going to free me, they were going to kill me. I didn't panic. I felt nothing except a great wave of sadness and I began to turn my face up. I wanted to face the sky, even if I couldn't see it. Gun smacked my head down and Rucksack said, "Go on."

'Some fidgeting, then a bolt was pulled. I waited, my head down. Gun fired. Something hot rolled down my face and I felt a splash on my boot, then another and another.

'The crack and whine of the rifle shot was still loud in my head. Another shot echoed far away.

'Rucksack said, "All right."

'Gun placed my hand back on the rucksack and thumped my back.

' "Walk."

'They hadn't killed me. They hadn't released me. They had given a signal and the signal had been answered. They had signalled with guns. We were so far from any civilisation, any hovel, any human being, that they were

18

able to signal with guns. The blood was dripping from my temple because he'd hit me there, probably with the pistol. "Walk." The nightmare was going to go on.

'After that, the terrain became more difficult. For a long time we fought through scrub where thorns pierced us, and I heard Rucksack using a machete. Otherwise we couldn't have moved forward at all. The last part of the journey was the worst of all. It must have been an area of completely impenetrable scrub in which a tunnel had already been cut. We had to crawl for hours, and my legs and back burned with the pain of this unaccustomed strain in such a position. Brambles tore at my head and face, hands and knees. A thorny twig pierced deep into the palm of my hand and stuck there. I had to stop.

' "Please, I can't see to—"

' "Shut up! Move." He whispered it, as usual. It seemed like it was out of fear. Why? First they fire guns, then they whisper. What is there to be afraid of here? I rid myself of the twig, leaving the thorn still embedded, and we crawled on. Soon I felt Rucksack getting to his feet in front of me. We must have come out into some sort of clearing. Gun pushed me forward and another pair of hands got hold of me, chained my wrists together, and pushed me to the ground against a tree trunk. I felt the chain pull as he wrapped it round the trunk and I smelled a different person, the stale, fatty smell of a butcher's shop, one of the reasons I never ate meat. Steps crunched away from me and I sat still as a mouse, listening. I was tensed up and, being unable to touch or see, my brain was

19

concentrated a hundred percent on hearing. The voices were subdued at first. I suppose they didn't want me to hear what they said but a quarrel broke out and I heard Sardinian accents. I couldn't understand the quarrel but I knew I had been right and that Gun and Rucksack were afraid of the men here. When it was over I heard the crunching and dragging away through the tunnel of thorns as Gun and Rucksack left.

'Someone approached and began unwinding the chain. Finding my hands free, I started to rub my sore wrists but the chain was pulled tight round my ankle and I heard a padlock snap shut. A voice whispered, "Turn to your right and get on all fours."

'By this time I had learned to obey quickly so as to avoid being hit. My hands and knees ached and smarted already from the crawl through the tunnel but I didn't protest. These were new people and might be more violent than the others.

' "Crawl forward. There's a tent in front of you. Crawl into it and lie down. Don't pull yourself up by the tent pole or you'll have the lot down." It was all whispered, but not like Rucksack and Gun when they were afraid – this was just to disguise the voice. I felt angry. I wasn't so stupid as to pull on a tent pole. But then I touched it by accident as I felt my way forward and he kicked me hard in the back of the thigh. He must have been wearing heavy boots, and the pain in an already suffering muscle was acute. Yet the tears that came to my eyes were because of the injustice of it. At once I felt my eyes burning and I gasped. I'd forgotten the warning. I tried to swallow the tears and transform my upset into anger. I hadn't pulled on the tent pole. It wasn't my fault. What was I supposed to do if they hit me no matter how hard I tried to do right? I lay down in the tent and felt him crawl in beside me.

' "Take your boots off." I did as I was told thought it wasn't easy in such cramped conditions. "Give me your left hand." I felt the chain pull tight and another padlock. My wrist was chained to my ankle. Butcher. I hated him because he had kicked me unjustly and because the chain round my wrist was much tighter than it could possibly need to be and it hurt me badly. Even so, I prayed he would take the burning plasters off my eyes, but he didn't. Why? If we were so far from help that they could fire guns, how could I possibly escape? I was inside a tent and could have no idea where I was and they would surely have ski masks on. As if he could read my thoughts – how many times had he done this before? – he whispered, "You can take the plasters off yourself."

'I was glad he wasn't going to touch me. I held my breath, terrified by the thought of my eyebrows and eyelashes. I tore the long strip off and lifted a corner of one of the underneath ones. I tried to do it quickly and close to the skin. Pain is a strange thing. Women have their legs waxed, for instance – and the pains of childbirth can be devastating but it's the reason for the pain, after all, that counts. That same level of suffering inflicted on us as torture or punishment would be unbearable. Once I had ripped those plasters off and seen my eyebrows and lashes embedded in them, I understood that I was going to have to develop a new way of dealing with pain if I wanted to survive.

'Butcher wore a black ski mask as I had expected. He was big and filled the small tent. He whispered, "All the stuff you need is behind your head." He threw my boots out, crawled out after them, and pulled down the zip.

'Once I was alone I sat up very carefully, without making a noise. I had been told to lie down but once they were out of sight, my fear and subjection waned. I looked for my watch but they must have taken it from me in the car while I was unconscious. The tent was small and low and I could only sit up in the very centre of it. There was no mattress, only the plastic floor, but there was a sleeping bag and an old flowered cushion. I picked up the cushion and sniffed it. All my life I've been over-sensitive to smells. As a child I would come home from playing with a friend and ask my mother, "Mommy, why does Debbie's house have a funny smell?"

' "What smell?"

' "I don't know . . . I don't like it."

' "All houses have an individual smell."

' "Ours doesn't."

' "Yes, it does. You're too used to it to notice." Patsy's house had a warm smell of cakes and ironing. I loved it there.

'The cushion had a dusty smell but nothing offensive. I was grateful for that since I would have to sleep with my head on it. Behind me, as Butcher had said, there were piles of things: a package of eight rolls of toilet paper, one of twelve plastic bottles of water, a packet of thin, cheap paper napkins. Next to me, to my right, was a bedpan and an already loosened roll of toilet paper.

'There were noises outside. I stopped breathing and listened. They were working, chopping and moving things. A rustling noise above me made me look up and I understood that my tent was being camouflaged with brushwood. No doubt they had living arrangements of their own to hide, too. It all sounded very near and I imagined the clearing as being quite small. When footsteps crunched towards the front of the tent I lay down. The zip went up.

' "Slide forward to the entrance." A hand pushed a tin tray in. There was bread on it and, to my dismay, the chicken with two or three bites taken out of it. Rucksack and Gun had brought it with them! It seemed incredible but at once I felt guilty. The rich bitch. Even supposing I ever ate meat, a partly eaten quarter of yesterday's chicken was something which I would have thrown out without a thought and which in hard times I would have made into a soup or risotto for the three of us.

'Despite my feelings of shame and my determination to force the stuff down so as to survive, I didn't succeed. My stomach sent up spurts of air and remained closed. Afraid of punishment, I did as a child might do: I broke off most of the slippery cold chicken and tried to hide it in a bit of toilet roll in the tent. Then I took the thick piece of hard bread and kept it to suck on slowly with sips of water. It wasn't much but I didn't see what else I could do.

'A hand slid the tray out a little way and a voice whispered, "Clean yourself with a drop of water and the napkins and pass them out." I took this chance to suck out the thorn and clean the worst of my scratches. The cool water was very soothing to them. Only as the tray disappeared did I think I might have got away with hiding the broken meat in these napkins. The tray was gone. It was too late.

' "Use the bedpan and push it out. Then pull the slack of the chain in so you can get in the sleeping bag. Get a move on, we've a lot of work still to do."

'I did as I was told. The zip went down.

'It was very difficult to get in the sleeping bag. I managed by pushing my chained leg in first but even then, my thick coat slowed me down. After a long struggle, I got my arms out of the coat, pushed it down the chain, got into the sleeping bag and put the sheepskin coat on top. The zip opened and the bedpan was pushed back in. I was so exhausted by my struggle with the sleeping bag and by the day's walk that I fell asleep without a moment's thought for my situation.

Two

'My foot was grabbed through the sleeping bag and shaken roughly. I woke up, still groggy. The smell of the tent, my aching limbs and an over-excited feeling confused me. Why was I so distressed if I was on a camping holiday? Then the excitement became recognisable as fear. Outside the tent there was a lot of activity, chopping and dragging.

'A loud whisper: "Get out of the sleeping bag and come forward." The zip only opened a little bit. It was daylight now so they wouldn't let me see out. But I had to get out. Otherwise, how could I . . . I struggled out of the sleeping bag and shuffled forward on my bottom.

'"Listen! Are you there? I have to get out to go to the bathroom." Laughter. Two of them.

' "Use the bedpan. And hurry up." '

'I was panic-stricken. "I can't! It's not possible lying down." '

' "Push your legs out." '

'They were going to give me my boots. Thank God for that. I pushed my feet through the small opening and screamed as a stick or spade handle or something crashed down on them. As my feet recoiled there was laughter.

' "Use the bedpan." '

'It was difficult to manoeuvre the bedpan with one hand, difficult to use the right muscles lying down. More difficult because every muscle was stiff and aching from yesterday's walk. I thought of yesterday and the cave where it would have been easier but where I hadn't felt the need. And now I was afraid. Afraid of my own smells, afraid of being punished for some inadvertent wrong-doing. Thank goodness there was plenty of toilet roll. If only I'd remembered then about the chicken . . .

' "Have you finished?" '

' "Yes." '

' "Push it out." '

'I laid a piece of clean paper on top of the faeces and pushed the bedpan out. Then I waited, alert and frightened, for laughter, comment, punishment. Nothing happened for some time and then the bedpan was poked back in. It was clean and smelled of bleach.

'The zip opened and a black-hooded head appeared.

' "Come here. Put your head down." '

'I shuffled forward and lowered my head, cringing for

fear of another blow. Someone crawled in with me. He must have been small because I barely had to move to one side for him. A new smell, oily. Was it his hair? When he touched my face his fingers were small and bony, his nails thick and sharp. Fox. He pulled a ski mask over my head, back to front so I had no eye-holes, and rolled it up to free my mouth. It stank and the long hairs of the rough wool went up my nose.

' "Please . . . please uncover my nose. I feel I'm suffocating."

' "Shut up." He crawled out.

' "Come to the front." A different voice. I shuffled forward. "Get hold. Be careful. If you spill it there'll be no more." He took my hands and curved the one chained to my ankle around a big tin cup. In my left hand he placed a spoon, squeezing my hand and directing the spoon into the bowl.

' "It's milky coffee with some bread in it." I tried to fish for the bread but, blind as I was, it was hopeless and he had to help me. His hand was big and warm, and when he guided the spoon to my mouth his smell was pleasant. A smell of new-cut wood. Perhaps he had been widening the clearing with an axe or machete. Perhaps it was his job, he was a woodcutter.

' "You have to hurry up, we've still got a lot to do." He spooned the warm, soggy lumps into my mouth and it was hard to keep up with him. Do we feed our babies like that when we're in a hurry, wanting to get everything cleared away, needing to get to work, to the phone, to the bathroom? And we expect them to go on gulping without a pause, mechanically so that they protest, spit some out, hit at the spoon. I didn't do any of those things. I wasn't hungry but at least this was easy to swallow. I tried to keep up. He tipped up the bowl and I drank the last part.

' "Go back inside and clean your mouth. You can take the mask off." The zip went down.

'I was glad to get the smelly mask off and to blow my nose to try to get rid of the hairs. Then I waited, listening to the activity outside, the whispering voices.

'The zip went up. I smelled at once that it was Butcher and tensed up with fear.

' "Move over, I have to get something from the back." I shrank away from the big black ski mask as it came towards me and he crawled past me to take a blue polythene bag from the back of the tent where all the stores were. Coming out backwards he stopped. My heart started pounding as I saw what he was looking at. I must have fallen asleep with the piece of bread in my hand and there were crumbs and lumps of it in the top of my sleeping bag and on the floor of the tent. The black head turned towards me and he threw the bag he was holding aside. There was nowhere to hide, no way to defend myself except by shielding my face with my one free hand.

' "Filthy! Filthy! Filthy! Bitch!" A blow to the side of my head accompanied each word. Then he got hold of my hair and dragged my head close to his to be sure I could hear every loud whispered word. Fat and stale blood. I stopped breathing. "We're not your fucking servants.

You've spent your life with some poor bugger going round behind you cleaning up the filth you leave but you don't do it here! We already have to clean your shit up—"

' "That's not my fault!" I couldn't stand it any longer. What was the use of being submissive if he beat me anyway? "You brought me here and you chained me up! I could have gone outside in the woods. It's not my fault!" I thought he would kill me then but another black head poked into the tent.

' "What's going on?" Woodcutter.

' "Nothing."

' "Come out of there. I'll do it." Do what?

'The head retreated. Butcher gave me a push. "Get it cleaned up, every last crumb, slut!"

'He crawled out. I started cleaning the bread crumbs up with a paper napkin dampened with mineral water. I knew that Butcher wanted to hit me, whether because he thought I was rich or for some other reason, and that he would always be looking for excuses. How stupid that he should look for excuses when I was chained up and helpless, anyway. Or was it because the other two didn't agree with it? I remembered the ones in the car.

' *"Don't touch her unless I say so. I'm responsible for the goods . . ."*

'Who was responsible here? I had to keep calm and work these things out. They had to keep me alive if they wanted money for me. A blow to the head, a neglected infection, food poisoning, so many things could kill me. I had to collaborate, stay alive. I hoped Woodcutter was responsible. He had ordered Butcher to get out, so he might be.

'The zip went up. A black hooded head poked in. I knew at once it was Woodcutter.

' "Move over. I have to come in." He crawled in beside me and lay on his right side, facing me. I tried to see his eyes but it was so gloomy in the tent and the eye-holes of his ski mask had been sewn to leave the thinnest crack. He was a big man, muscular, not fat, and his voice sounded young. There was a gun in a holster at his waist.

' "Lie on your back. I have to do your eyes."

' "No! Oh please, no. It's so dark in here, and I promise never to peep out—"

' "Be quiet. It's in your own best interests. If you see anything, you're dead."

' "But I'm always in here. I can't possibly know where we are and you all have masks on."

' "It's a pain wearing a mask all the time. You'll be safer if you don't risk seeing anything."

'He was opening the polythene bag that Butcher had pulled out. He began ripping at a broad roll of cotton strapping.

' "Lie still, blast you!" He yelled this at me. I was lying still, hardly breathing. Why did he yell? The noise frightened me after all the distorted whispering and yet his anger didn't sound real. Then he whispered, "Believe me, you're safer like this. Look, hold these squares of gauze over your eyes." He placed them in position and I held them while he cut the plasters. One piece over each eye, covering the gauze, then long, broad strips from temple to temple, centred on my eyes, then above, then below, centred again. He pressed them hard to model them round my nose and with each successive layer I felt blinder and blinder, for no logical reason since I'd been blind after the first.

' "I'm warning you – don't touch them! Don't ever touch them!"

'I hadn't moved a muscle. Why was he yelling at me? "I promise, I . . ."

'He put a finger over my lips and whispered, "If you ever feel them coming off, tell me. If they see you trying to peer over or under them there'll be trouble. Now I have to do your ears."

'I was dismayed. To be deaf as well as blind might be more than I could bear. I was afraid of going mad but not afraid of what he was going to do. I suppose I thought he'd put cotton wool in my ears and more plasters on top. I felt him change position.

' "You have to lie with your head on my knees." He pulled me forward and I lay on my side, curled up and with my head in his lap. I heard the zip go up.

' "Here." Butcher. I felt safe because Woodcutter was between us with his back to the opening. "You've to use these."

' "We can't use them. She'll never stand the pain, you can take it from me. She'll go off her head and we'll never cope with her. There's no need."

' "Boss's orders."

' "All right. Give them here." The zip went down.

'Woodcutter bent his face close to mine and I could feel his skin. He had taken his mask off. He whispered, "Feel these," and placed my hand on what was in his. I understood.

' "D'you know what they are?"

' "Yes." They were the hard rubber earplugs that divers use.

' "I'm not going to use them because the pain would kill you but you pretend I have, understand? You don't hear anything, *anything*. Now lie still."

'I lay still. He stuffed a bit of cotton wool into my right ear and poked it deeper and deeper with his finger until the pain was so terrible I tore my head away.

' "Keep still. That's cotton wool. You want me to use those hard plugs instead?" I kept still. He went on pressing until he seemed to have screwed into my brain and my outer ear was full. I heard him fish for other things in the bag and the sound of a cigarette lighter. Then a pause.

' "Keep still. I'm going to drop hot wax from this candle onto the cotton. If you move an inch I'll burn you. I shan't be able to help it."

'The wax fell. *Plaff . . . plaff . . . plaff.* The soft noise moved through my head in waves, stones thrown in a pond. *Plaff . . .* Then more layers of cotton wool, its soft rustle as loud as the sea. *Plaff . . . plaff . . . plaff . . .* and more cotton and wax and more . . .

' "Turn over."

32

' "Oh, please . . ." I was no longer tense. I felt as weak and helpless as a baby and I began to cry like one.

' "Don't cry! Not with the plasters on!"

'I had forgotten, and now the skin under my eyes, my cheeks, and temples burned under the sticking plaster as though I were crying acid.

' "Turn over. Breathe deeply and you'll stop crying." And again he poked deep into my ear, holding me by the neck this time so that I couldn't jerk away from the pain. *Plaff!* The wax came again, and when both ears were covered I was in another world. I had to learn to live in the dark with two big seashells clamped permanently to my ears, with the constant, insistent roar of the sea in the black night. Out of the night an invisible hand came to get hold of mine, and Woodcutter's voice murmured, lower than the noise of the waves.

' "Give me your hand. I'll have to take this ring off." Patrick's ring! My most precious possession! "Please don't. Oh, please not this ring!"

' "It's for your own good. You'll see. Now, remember where everything is. Here's the bedpan and toilet roll on your right. Water and paper napkins behind your head. I'm taking the padlock off your hand now so you'll manage better. Your coat's here on your left. Get in your sleeping bag and lie still on your back until you calm down. Here, I've pulled the loose chain in for you. We'll only chain your wrist to it at night and free it in the morning."

'Why? There was no night now except that it was

always night. And what morning could there be – I remembered that morning, the bread crumbs, the bits of chicken.

' "Listen! Are you still there?" My voice roared in my head. I was a sea monster. "Please listen to me . . ." I told him. I knew I was like a child telling tales but I had to do it. He had to get rid of the chicken for me because I wouldn't be able to find it now.

' "I've got to go. There's a lot to do. The others'll be back any minute—"

' "You've got to listen!" The others weren't there! I had to make him help me. "In a bit of toilet paper somewhere on the right."

'He found it. I got in my sleeping bag and he put his face close to mine to tell me, "The tent has to be kept clean. It's for your own good." Everything here was for my own good. "Do you want rats coming in? Do you know what rats can do to you while you're asleep? They pee on you because their pee is an anaesthetic. Then they can gnaw away at you without waking you up. I've seen them do it to horses, gnaw great lumps out of their legs. The tent has to be clean. And don't worry about those two dickheads. They're pissed off as hell because they should have brought us your daughter and there's a row going on with the boss. They'll calm down. Lie down until it's time to eat."

'A rest before lunch. Rules of hygiene. For my own good.

'I lay still but my burning face and the roaring pressure

in my ears gave me no rest. The only distraction from the pain was the thought of Woodcutter's admitting there had been a mistake, the thought of my Caterina's being here in my place. It wasn't a mistake in the way I had thought, a mistake about my financial condition. They had simply mistaken me for Caterina because she usually takes Tess round the block at night and we have the same long hair. And to think that for years Caterina had been trying to talk me into having mine cut. She was convinced it would suit me better and look more chic for someone my age. But I never could decide to do it. My hair's been long since I was about fifteen. Now I was thankful I hadn't done it. A twenty-year-old beautiful girl would hardly have been safe from their lust, which I could trust I was. Caterina had never formed a lasting relationship and, though she never talked about it, was probably still a virgin. An experience like this would destroy her future. She was so fragile. Any mother would rather suffer herself than have her child suffer. And I've always been strong. If it was possible to survive this experience I would survive it. Already I had discovered that keeping my head still, though it didn't stop the roaring, reduced the pain. That was thanks to Woodcutter. I had also discovered that sometimes he was alone. I must try and work out their timetable. When he was alone I could try and talk to him. I would have to be careful not to ask questions. I must try and make him understand that I was not as rich as they must have thought but that whatever I had would be paid. I had fought all my adult life to make myself and my children safe from poverty and there was no safety. Now all I wanted was to live. I had to try and eat and I had to appear perfectly docile so as to convince them – or at least Woodcutter – to let me out of the tent for a short time each day to move my legs. I could try, if it was possible to keep my head still, to exercise my muscles while lying in the tent, the sort of exercises I did when I was pregnant. If I didn't move I could develop an intestinal blockage, which would be fatal.

'The zip. It sounded different now, through my sea-shell ears, a low, swishing whirr like fabric running through a sewing machine, but I still heard it. Just in time I remembered to pretend I couldn't. I didn't know who it was. Someone grabbed my foot through the sleeping bag and shook it. I sat up. My hand was grabbed and I was yanked forward so that I lost my balance and fell forward on the side of my outstretched arm. I imagined I was to come towards the opening and so I scrambled out of the sleeping bag as fast as I could, which wasn't very fast because of the chain on my ankle, which I had to pull out with me. I felt my way forward on my knees and someone slapped my hand away, then forced it to touch the tent pole and slapped it away again. Did they think I was as stupid as they were? I knew enough not to grab the tent pole. When I reached the opening I was pushed into a sitting position and my legs were stretched out in front of me. It was freezing outside. I thought of my fur boots but didn't dare ask for them.

'A cold tin tray was placed on my legs and my right

hand guided to the food on it. The little claw-like hand of Fox. I understood that now I was blind and deaf I could sit half out of the tent to eat and not dirty it inside again. This was a great relief to me. I felt a bread roll, smooth and hard, a chunk of Parmesan cheese. How could I get this down without appetite and even without water to soften it? My hand was taken again and the neck of a wine flask put in it. Terrified of spilling it, I lowered my head towards it rather than lifting it. The wine was acidic and strong. I didn't like it but, rough as it was, I could tell it was home-bottled because the tattered straw smelled of old wine, vinegary, reminding me of our cottage in Chianti. We take our flask round to our neighbours, who fill it and pop the old cork back in. Healthy country wine would do me no harm and would help break down the dry food. The bread roll was impossible to manage. I couldn't bite into it because to open my jaw much increased the violent pain in my ears. I tried to break it in my fingers but it was too stale. Something cold and sharp slid over the back of my right hand. I stopped moving. The bread roll was taken from me and returned in two pieces. The knife blade slid along my throat. Fox. I could smell him. I understood that he was teasing me, playing with me, and I refused to react, otherwise he would amuse himself constantly like that. I sat dead still and, when the knife didn't touch me again, I began to eat. Tiny bits at a time, each with a sip of the sour wine to help with the painful chewing.

'When I couldn't manage any more I touched the

ground beside me and felt a flattish carpet of twigs and dead leaves. There was no snow there and I was sure that this space had been hacked clear in the undergrowth of a wood. The chain on my ankle, tight and heavy, would still be tied to the tree trunk and there must be at least one other tent or a shelter of some sort for my captors. All that activity and their complaints about there being so much to do must have been related to their covering everything with the hacked-out brush so that we wouldn't be visible from above. I slid the tray sideways onto the ground and waited, not daring to move until somebody told me to. My legs and feet were frozen but I breathed deeply the good fresh air and then listened. Nothing penetrated the roaring inside my head and I was glad enough to crawl back into the tent when someone pushed me and to seek the warmth of the sleeping bag for my cold feet.

'I supposed, since I'd just been fed, that it was now afternoon, an afternoon that stretched in front of me, an aching, empty distance, without sight or sound. I had to learn to live inside my head and to call on a lifetime of sounds and images that were stored there. I had to learn not to cry. I had to learn to eat out of duty and without hunger. I had to learn not to admit hearing those few things I could hear and not to react to deliberate torment. I had to learn to accept pain and immobility quietly so that I wouldn't go mad. I had to learn to be passive when I had always been active. I had always thought of myself as a fighter but now I had to lay down my arms. If I wanted to live, I had to stay quietly inside my body and just be.

'That afternoon I thought for a long time about what would be happening at home. Would they have called the police or the carabinieri? Had they received any message about me? Did the newspapers know? I thought of the anxiety and excitement we'd all been feeling because of the show coming up in New York. Now that had been replaced by this new anxiety. Now perhaps my children would have to face a future of being poor again. We had no choice but to pay whatever we could. How could I have let this happen? In a few seconds, all our lives compromised. What should I have done to prevent these total strangers overturning our world that I had constructed so carefully and thought I could control?

'The minutes dripped steadily away until the afternoon was over and I felt my foot shaken again. I knew exactly what to do and the ritual was soon completed – the same tray, the same roll, already cut, the cheese, the sour wine.

'Back in the tent, I began to arrange myself for the night. There was a sort of comfort in concentrating on the completion of small acts, rendered newly difficult by the absence of sight and hearing and the presence of the chain. I drew in the slack of the chain to allow my entry into the sleeping bag. I closed the zip of the bag. I arranged my coat over my legs and, still sitting up, managed to dab my hands and face clean with paper napkins and mineral water. Each thing accomplished was a small victory. I drank some water from the bottle and was careful not to spill any, which was easier now it was more than half empty. This small, familiar act, a drink of water before sleep, was comforting. I pulled my coat up further, pushed myself deeper into the sleeping bag, and turned on my side.

'I managed to smother the scream down to a choking groan and turned on my back, gasping. I hadn't yet dared touch the area round my ears for fear of hurting myself and I had no idea that those stone-hard constructions were so big. The pain caused by putting my weight on one of them when I turned over was indescribable and seemed to penetrate right through my brain to the other ear. How could I ever sleep if I had to lie on my back, afraid to move even by accident? A great surge of pure rage against these people grew inside me, hard as stone in my chest, hard as the stones in my ears. God damn them for doing this cruel, senseless thing to me who had never harmed them. If I ever got free I would find a way to kill them. If I had the strength of a man I'd kill every one of them with my bare hands.

'The zip whispered! I lay still, hating whoever it was who now crawled into the tent alongside me. A face close to mine, a hand whacking the packages behind my head. A shouting voice.

' "That'll teach you to keep your noise down!" Then a whisper that touched me and came through my undersea world: "What's going on! You mustn't make a noise or they'll plaster your mouth up!"

' "My ear . . . I turned over."

' "Well don't. I told you, lie on your back." Another

whack at the packages. "That's enough!" They were out there. He was pretending to hit me for their benefit.

' "I won't be able to go to sleep on my back and I'm afraid of turning over in the night by mistake."

' "You won't. I know you won't. Just lie still and you'll fall asleep. Do you understand?"

' "Yes."

' "I've got to go." I felt a hand brush my head and he whispered, "Goodnight."

' "Goodnight." He was sliding back out of the tent. I heard the zip. I was alone. And because this man who had chained and blinded and deafened me, had reduced me to the status of an animal for his greed, had said that one word, Goodnight, the stone in my chest dissolved. For that one word I forgave him. One human, civilised word was enough to keep me alive and hoping. My anger left me and I felt my whole body go limp. I let out a long, liquid breath that rattled in my chest and throat as though I were dying. I wasn't dying. I had learned my first lesson. I was crying without tears.'

Three

There was silence in the small office. Beyond the closed window you could hear the moan of the mountain wind in the waving tops of the cypress trees and the occasional crash of a forgotten plant pot or a loose shutter. The heating was on but the icy fizzing air made itself felt even within the massive stones of the Palazzo Pitti. The quality of the light was enough to suggest yellow and purple crocuses sheltered in sunny Florentine gardens and a glitter of snow on the dark northern hills. Salvatore Guarnaccia, Marshal of the Carabinieri, his solid, black-uniformed figure immobile behind the desk, was conducting the silence. It was his strongest professional weapon. The thin young woman opposite him was still with the tautness of violin strings and silent because she was too nervous to speak. What she was nervous about had yet to appear. Her name was Caterina Brunamonti. She was the daughter of the late Conte Ugo Brunamonti. That much, at least, had been offered. She was wearing plain, very expensive-looking clothes and large, very real-looking diamonds in a ring on her long white hand. She looked twenty or little more. Having given him her name, she was now waiting for the Marshal to help her. The Marshal, in silence, observed her. She didn't look him straight in the face but held her head turned just a little away, her brown eyes fixed on him obliquely. This attitude – her long fair hair, the almost invisible brows and eyelashes, and the white hands lying stiffly in her lap with the diamonds exposed to view – made her look like one of the portraits in the gallery next door, the sort that are all stiff lace frills and beaded bodices. Their fingers were always white and pointed like that. They didn't look like real people and neither did Caterina Brunamonti, so you'd hardly expect her to speak, really. She was so wired up she seemed ready to short-circuit if the Marshal didn't prompt her. The Marshal didn't prompt her.

'I had to come here! It's the right thing to do, whatever Leonardo says, and I wouldn't want to do anything illegal!'

'Quite right,' said the Marshal blandly. His brain was filming every fleeting expression, his ears recording every word but listening for the ones she didn't say. He kept his expressionless gaze fixed on the map on the wall behind her just to her left. Nervous people stop talking if you stare them in the face. If you let your eyes drift, they come after you, seeking your attention. 'Leonardo . . . that would be your . . .'

'My brother, and he's wrong. I'm the right person to decide. I'm more practical than he is and I've been reading up on these things. It's best to call in the carabinieri.'

'I'm sure you're right.' It was a map of his Quarter and he scanned it idly, looking for Piazza Santo Spirito. He knew where the Palazzo Brunamonti was. He didn't know everyone in this area personally but he knew that. 'And now you've called us in.'

'I'm worried about my mother. She's . . . something might have happened to her. Leonardo . . . I don't think you're listening to me!'

Which was understandable since he'd picked up the phone without so much as a glance at her and connecting himself to Headquarters across the river.

'Captain Maestrangelo.'

The young woman shot to her feet. 'What are you doing? I just wanted to talk to you . . .'

Now he did stare at her with bulging, solemn eyes. She sat down and was silent, turning her head to its watchful position as before.

'Your mother has a fashion house, if I'm not mistaken.' Many years ago, the fashion shows which still bear its name were really held in the Palazzo Pitti. The security measures involved in giving the workforce access to the galleries were a problem the Marshal wasn't sorry to be relieved of when they moved on, the men's and children's wear to the Fortezza over on the other side of town, the women's wear to Milan. A long time ago, but he remembered the Contessa Brunamonti, not because hers had been among the better-known houses but because she was remarkably beautiful.

He pulled out his notebook. Someone much more important than he was would have to take her statement. 'What is your mother's name?'

'Olivia Birkett.'

He spoke as he wrote. 'Olivia Birkett, widow of the Conte . . . was it Ugo? Brunamonti . . .'

'She never used the title, except on our label. My mother was a model before she married.'

'Born?'

'Sixteenth May, 1949, in California.'

'When did you see your mother last?'

'Ten days ago, but—'

'Hello? Hello! No, no. I must speak to him personally. I'm sure the Colonel will understand. It's urgent. What? Yes. Yes, I'll hold.'

'Please wait!' Her white face had turned deep pink and her brown eyes were alarmed.

'It can't wait, Signorina. You should have reported your mother missing immediately. What on earth persuaded you and your brother to wait all this time? And what are you doing here? You should at least have called 112. Hello? Yes, I am still here . . . Tell him it's Guarnaccia at Pitti. Thank you. No. He'll call me back.' He hung up.

'You haven't answered my question. Why have you come here?'

'It wasn't me, I've told you, it was Leonardo. He doesn't want the police or carabinieri involved in this case . . . He doesn't even know I'm here now. I wanted to call you in last week so, whatever happens, nobody can blame me.'

'Ten days ago. At what time?' The moment for urgent action was long gone.

'At night, almost midnight.'

'And your brother's afraid she might have been kidnapped, is that it? He thought he could deal with this alone? He's afraid of your assets being frozen?'

'Yes, but I don't agree. We should be trying to find her and whoever kidnapped her, otherwise we're aiding and abetting criminals. Besides, they can still kill the victim even if you pay. She could be dead already.'

'Why are you so sure something has happened to her? People do often disappear because they want to and for many other reasons.'

'Her dog had to be taken for a walk round the block before bedtime. Usually, I did it because she and my brother always work late. I'm an early riser because I think you should work when you're fresh. But that night I'd already showered and was in my room so she took Tessie, and when she didn't come back Leonardo went out to look for her. He found the broken-off handle of the dog lead in the courtyard. Her car was gone. She always left the keys in it because she tended to lose them otherwise and, since the entrance doors which give on to the courtyard were locked after eight at night . . .'

'Except, perhaps, when the dog was being taken round the block for ten minutes?'

'They're very heavy doors for a woman to manage. She'd been thinking of having a normal door cut into them but it would spoil them. Olivia always said that if thieves wanted to get in they'd get in and if you locked your car it only meant the window would be smashed if and when you got it back.'

'She's right. Can you describe the car, tell me the licence number?'

'I've written it down.' She opened a leather shoulder bag and gave him a sheet of paper from it. He looked at it and placed it by the phone.

'What about the dog? What sort of dog is it?'

'Very small, sand coloured.'

'Any particular breed?'

'No. It was a mongrel bitch. She rescued it from the dog pound. She was rather sentimental about animals and thought it ridiculous to spend money on fancy breeds when so many ill-treated dogs needed homes.'

'You disagree?'

'Only because it's a health risk. They can have leukaemia or even AIDS these days. I took the dog to the vet and had it checked. I'm the one who tends to think about these things. I'm very practical.'

'I see. I take it no contact has been made?'

She shook her head. She was still very flushed and her

eyes were glittering as though about to overflow with tears. The Marshal felt guilty. He felt he'd been clumsy and the ethereal appearance of this delicate young woman whose long white hands lay motionless in her lap as she cried made him feel even more of a bull in a china shop than usual. Of course, he could never have imagined that the matter was so serious. 'You're quite sure your brother doesn't know you're here? If he has any reason to suspect you he could have had contact and kept it from you.'

'He hasn't moved from the sofa by the phone since it happened but I've been there all the time, too.'

'The phone in your own home?'

'Yes, of course.'

'Hm.' There had been no contact in that case. 'You haven't explained why you came here.'

'I went to your Headquarters in Borgo Ognissanti first. I couldn't call from home. Leonardo never moves from the phone, day or night. The guard at the entrance there stopped me and asked me what I wanted. I could hardly tell him, out in the street. I just said I had to report something and he sent me to that window just inside where you report thefts and things. I'd been there before once when my car was stolen. They offered me a form to fill in and I told them I wasn't there to fill forms in, that I needed to talk to someone who could advise me. They sent me here.'

'Hm.' He could hardly blame his colleagues. They were constantly beset with time wasters and troublemakers and she wasn't very forthcoming even now.

'I was nervous about doing this. The others were so against it.'

'Others?'

'My brother and Patrick Hines. Patrick's a lawyer. He manages our affairs in New York. He came over as soon as it happened, and now he's in London trying to hire a private investigator from a big agency there. He'll be furious that I've been here. They'll both be against me when they know what I've done but it's the right thing, isn't it? The proper legal thing to do?'

'Of course. You mustn't worry. It's done now and they'll have to accept it. It will be all the better if they can be convinced to collaborate rather than just tolerate our presence but, either way, they're going to be too concentrated on your mother's situation to be worrying about you.' The phone rang. Before picking it up he said, 'Would you mind sitting out in the waiting room a moment?' She got up, her eyes still fixed on him obliquely. She was tall. 'Do you have to say it was me? Isn't there some other way you could have found out?'

'Please . . . I'll be with you in just a moment.'

He waited as the door closed behind her.

'Guarnaccia?'

'Yes, it's me. Something serious, yes. The Contessa Brunamonti, missing since about midnight ten days ago. Took the dog out – on a regular walk round the block, leaving the main doors of the palazzo open the way people do when they go out for ten minutes. Handle of the dog's lead found in the courtyard . . . Yes, the same

49

thing every night. Asking for it. Palazzo Brunamonti in Piazza Santo Spirito. We can't rely on it, no. This has come from her daughter and she's not that convinced . . . Could change her mind at any minute. There's a brother and a business lawyer, American, who want a private detective in, so . . .'

As the Marshal hung up, a sigh escaped him. According to statistics, the 1991 law permitting a magistrate to freeze a family's assets in kidnapping cases worked, the average number of cases per year having been reduced from twenty-one to five. Statistics didn't tell you the rest – the increased difficulties the law created for investigators when families didn't report the kidnapping quickly, the cruelty inflicted on the victim when money was longer in coming, the alienation of the victim, who would fail to release vital information on being freed. Professional kidnappers were adapting their methods to accommodate the new law and choosing victims who were sufficiently well-connected politically to get at least part of the ransom paid by the State under the clause allowing 'payment for investigative purposes'. The Marshal doubted whether the Contessa Brunamonti would be consoled by the thought of being one of five rather than one of twenty-one. You can't add people together. You can't add one person's pain to another's. It doesn't mean anything. Getting up from his chair, he hoped his superiors would decide to go along – at least for the moment – with the daughter's request for secrecy. It would make very little difference to the first stages of the inquiry, and it wouldn't help if they lost the only collaborator in the family. He opened the door and looked out into the waiting room. It was empty. 'Lorenzini!'

His young Brigadier appeared.

'Did you let that young woman out?'

'Yes. Should I not have—'

'Never mind. Have Di Nuccio and young Lepori left?'

'Just.'

'Well, I hope to goodness they remember everything I said last night. Did they eat something?'

'I think so.'

'And take a supply of water? I told them. There isn't a bar for miles.'

He zipped up his jacket and pulled his hat low, ready for the wind, grumbling as he stumped down the stairs. 'You'd have thought a royal family could afford its own bodyguards. I don't know what the army's coming to . . .'

The winter sun was every bit as bright and strong as the Marshal had imagined and he came out under the great iron lantern of the archway fishing hurriedly for the dark glasses which would prevent his sensitive eyes from streaming. Safe in a darkened world, he could enjoy the feel of the sun on his face and the morning smells brought to him by the fierce mountain wind. Sunshine or no sunshine, once he came out of the shelter of the Pitti

Palace onto the open slope in front of it, that icy wind bit at his ears and made him thankful for the solid weight of his black greatcoat.

The traffic passing through the piazza at the bottom of the slope was noisy and ebullient, as the Florentines, inspired by the brilliance of the day, wanted to drive *allegro con brio*. The result was decidedly *staccato* since the junction with Via Romana and Via Maggio snarled up every few minutes to a chorus of horns. It was to avoid this confusion to his left that the Marshal crossed the piazza and continued straight ahead, cutting through the high buildings by a narrow alley lined with parked mopeds but empty of cars. He went into Piazza Santo Spirito at the corner by the church. There was no need for it. He could have crossed the river and gone straight to Headquarters. He knew what this business was going to entail and he knew his commanding officer. A case like this meant specialists, the emergency intervention group arriving in helicopters from Livorno, probably cooperation with the civil police force. All this would already be under way. It would not involve the Marshal. Captain Maestrangelo, on the other hand, by hook or by crook, would involve the Marshal. Somebody had to hold the family's hand, and that was just the sort of task Maestrangelo would earmark him for. So Guarnaccia walked quietly into Piazza Santo Spirito, sniffing the air.

He plodded slowly between the shops and the market stalls, between the sawing and tapping of artisans and the vulgar shouts of the man who sold cheap underwear, between sawdust and coffee on his left and old clothes and fresh fennel on his right.

'Morning, Marshal.'

'Good morning.'

'Your lad's already been.' A question disguised as a statement. One carabiniere took responsibility each day for the shopping and cooking in their little barracks at Pitti. The Marshal ate in his own quarters with his wife and family. So he must be here on business, no . . . ? The Marshal offered no explanation, so tiny Torquato, apron down to his ankles, woolly hat down over his ears against the wind, turned his attention to the next customer.

'Oh, really, Torquato! This salad doesn't look at all nice.'

'What do you expect in this freezing wind? Were you wanting it for a wedding bouquet or are you going to eat it? It's dark in your stomach, you know. Here, a bunch of parsley and a bit of carrot and celery for your sauce . . .'

The darkness in your stomach was Torquato's standard defence for the few bunches of greens he had been bringing in from the country each day for as long as anybody could remember. The Marshal waited until Torquato was free and then peered down, pretending to examine the limp, wind-blasted lettuces himself, not wanting to draw attention.

Torquato peered up, examining the Marshal. 'It's the Contessa, am I right?'

'What have you heard?'

Torquato shrugged. 'I used to see her most days, and

her staff in the workroom on the ground floor buy their greens here. Only they haven't, not for over a week. Young Leonardo likes a joke, not been seen. And her car's gone from the courtyard, you can see that from here.'

'And what are they saying in the piazza?'

'Kidnapped. Keeping it quiet, are they?'

The Marshal stepped behind the little stall and past the thin hedgerows between tall trees into the centre of the square. Keeping the blank ochre silhouette of the church to his left, he stared across at the Palazzo Brunamonti. The gigantic studded carriage doors of the main entrance stood open, and at the end of the dark tunnel inside you got a glimpse of brightness and colour like a spotlit painting. It was usual for these Renaissance palaces to turn their backs to the outside world and keep their gardens, fountains, statuary, and decorated façades for their owners' exclusive delight. It had always seemed to the Marshal to be a funny way of going on but, then, the Florentines . . . the Marshal had no words for the Florentines though he had lived among them for twenty years.

Olivia Birkett . . . the sort of beauty that stopped traffic. The Marshal remembered her striking green eyes and legs two metres long. He recalled a little boy around her in those days, though not a girl . . . perhaps not born yet. He hoped he'd written the girl's name down because he couldn't for the life of him remember it. Well, Olivia Birkett wasn't a Florentine, so what did she think of it all? A mongrel. A sandy little mongrel. A sandy little mongrel up there behind those brown slatted shutters, looking out on that very private garden. Dead now probably, since they wouldn't have wanted it barking to give the alarm . . .

The Marshal was vaguely aware of a tot in a pink ski suit pedalling her tricycle round and round his motionless black figure as she might pedal round the white marble statue of Ridolfi at the other end of the square or the fountain in the middle.

The Palazzo Brunamonti had a loggia on the top floor. Must have a good view of the piazza, looking down on the treetops, the globular lamps at night, the church. And from those rooms on the top floor left, where all the shutters were closed, you could probably see the river Arno. Three dogs raced, skidding and tumbling, across the piazza, ignoring their owners, who recalled them furiously. The smallest one jumped the largest and a mock fight broke out. A little sandy mongrel . . .

'These days they can have AIDS.'

These days . . . if you make money, you can get kidnapped . . .

The Marshal sighed and moved off.

'Hey! Watch out!"

He looked down, frowning, as the solid front wheel of the little tricycle bumped up against his shiny black shoe. The child, encountering the expressionless stare of his black glasses, turned and pedalled furiously away towards a huddle of red-nosed shoppers.

'Gran! Gran!'

'Come here and let me tie that scarf. We've to get to the baker's yet.'

He crossed the Santa Trinita Bridge. The river was full and the fierce wind burned his face, took his breath from him. The hills upriver beyond the Ponte Vecchio were capped with snow and the horizon reflected it, pearly pink and violet below the deep blue of a winter sky swept clean of its leaden pollution.

Captain Maestrangelo's hand was warm and dry. 'Guarnaccia. Let me introduce you to Substitute Prosecutor Fusari who's in charge of this case.'

A thin, elegant man rose out of a deep leather armchair amid a cloud of blue smoke, a wicked half-smile flickering over his handsome face, like a theatrical demon.

The Marshal held out his hand, hardly registering the man in his surprise at finding him there at all. Prosecutors summoned people to their offices on these occasions. Then he absorbed, the face first, then the name. Virgilio Fusarri, an alarming man indeed. Last time they'd met on a case he had alarmed the Marshal by being 'Dear Virgilio', friend of the family, the last thing you wanted with a dead body in the bath next door. It had been all right, though. And years before that . . .

'I know you.' Fusarri looked at him keenly. 'Don't tell me, I'll remember when it suits me. Right, Captain, let's sit down and get on.'

'Yes. I've got a call out to all stations for the car. We

56

can assume they'll have changed cars once out of town but it's the first point at which we can pick up the trail, always allowing for attempts to mislead us. Of course, ten days is a long time and far too late for roadblocks and for a useful examination of the point where she was taken. The family . . .' He looked at the Marshal.

'The son found the dog's lead in their own courtyard . . . It looks like they slipped in while she was out with the dog. She didn't lock the main doors, as a rule, for these ten minute turns round the block. The daughter, a young woman of about twenty, could have been the intended victim since she often walked the dog. She is collaborating – at least for the moment. The son I haven't seen yet. Then there's' – he had to check his notebook for the foreign name – 'Patrick Hines, a lawyer.'

Fusarri pulled a face.

'There's worse,' warned the Captain. 'The Marshal tells me he's bringing in a private detective.'

'Oh for God's sake.' Fusarri leaned forward to stub out his pungent little Tuscan cigar in the big glass ashtray on Maestrangelo's desk. 'Dog been found?'

They both looked at the Marshal, who examined the hat lying on his knees. 'They wouldn't want it running home to give the alarm. They wouldn't want it making a noise wherever they're hidden, either.'

'So?' Fusarri was lighting up again. They could barely see each other.

'I'd say they'll have thrown it out on the motorway, or on some fast road, or beaten it to death out in the country.'

'Could we find it, Captain?'

'It's not impossible. The hunting fraternity might help.'

'Good. The first thing we want is the car.'

'We'll soon find the car.' Maestrangelo looked at the Marshal. 'Tell me anything you know about the family.'

The Marshal told. Sometimes he addressed himself to the hat on his knee, sometimes to a huge dark oil painting to the right of the Captain's head. He wasn't happy about telling anybody anything at this stage because all he had in his head was a series of unconnected pictures, some real, like the stiff-fingered girl, some imaginary, like the sandy little bitch behind the shutters the Palazzo Brunamonti. What could he say?

He said, 'They'll need careful handling. They're not agreed among themselves.'

'They never are. So handle them carefully,' the Captain said.

'And this private investigator.'

'I,' Fusarri said, 'will handle him.' He leaned back, waving a space in his personal cloud, and flashed an amused look at the two of them. 'I remember you now,' he said to the Marshal. 'We met at my dear friend Eugenia's house, did we not?'

The Captain stared at the other two in amazement at this evidence of the Marshal's high-flying social life. Then he remembered there had been a body in the bath in the story and everything settled into place again.

Fusarri drew on his cigar, frowning. Then he pointed

the thing at the Marshal. 'There was something else. Years ago. Maestrangelo?'

'The Maxwell kidnapping. Your first, I think. We worked on it together.'

'Yes. And the Marshal here came into it somewhere along the line. The girl was American, wasn't she? Were you brought in because you speak English? Something of that sort?'

But the Marshal only avoided his piercing eyes and murmured, 'No, no . . .'

'There was something. I'll remember. Right!' He got to his feet. 'Helicopters?'

'Special Operations Group on standby in Livorno.'

'Dogs?'

'Also on standby. Until I know where I'm looking.'

'Which will be?'

'When I know whose job it is. That will determine the territory.'

'True. You'll need some of her clothing. I imagine that's something we can leave to the Marshal here. I shall get their telephone under control and their assets frozen – I'd like such information as is available on what those assets are, if your investigators would be so good – you haven't mentioned a planner, no ideas on who might have set the victim up?'

'None. Somebody, of course, with access to information about the family's finances and habits. My men are already working on that.'

'I should have thought the Marshal here'd be our man

for that if he's going to babysit the family.' For a second his sharp eyes caught the Marshal's and he said, 'I'm beginning to remember now,' and turned back to the Captain. 'And we await a contact. I assume you'll tell me you haven't the men available for this and that it's going to have to be Criminalpol but I'm not calling the civil police in on this yet. Until you do know where you're looking, I'm of the opinion that you're best left in peace with the help you know and trust in your Investigations Group here.'

'Thank you. I appreciate that.'

'And here's something else you'll appreciate: I rather think I'm not going to be able to find room for you at the Procura. I have this feeling that all three listening posts are about to be occupied so that you'll have to use your own room here. I apologise, of course.' He didn't look at either of them but stared brightly at the wall.

'I . . .' Unable to find suitably camouflaged words of gratitude, the Captain changed the subject. 'The press . . .'

'We use them. Not vice versa. Be nice to them. Make an effort to toss them some little printable nonsense each time you talk to them. Try and get the family to be nice to them. There'll come a point when we'll need them. Who is it, Maestrangelo? We're on Sardinian-controlled territory here in Tuscany as far as kidnappings are concerned, I know, but who is it? You're so damn cautious but you must have an idea.'

'I have two. Giuseppe Puddu and Salis. Francesco Salis.'

'Both wanted men?'

'Yes. Puddu escaped as soon as he was out on parole last year. Salis has been in hiding for over three years.'

'I'll expect to hear from you tomorrow then.' Fusarri stubbed out his fifth cigar and left.

The Captain opened the window.

'Well, Guarnaccia? What do you think?'

'I don't know how I'm to manage, not if this royal guard duty business keeps up – and I've two men out looking for a couple of witnesses who didn't turn up in court this morning. Call from the Procura . . . jack-of-all-trades we're expected to be. Lorenzini's alone now and what I'm saying is, if something happens . . .' He stopped, remembering that something had.

So damn cautious . . .

And Fusarri was so damn quick. He talked too fast, for one thing, coming as he did from the North. He was unorthodox, too. Maestrangelo didn't like that, the Marshal knew. Unorthodoxy was one of the seven deadly sins, and not the least of them, as far as he was concerned. That business about tapping the phone! The rule was that they should listen at the Procura, which meant sharing the room with other forces, all of them ready to muscle in on your case and take the credit where credit was available. A much-hated arrangement but that was the rule. No officer could ask for what Fusarri had offered, and Maestrangelo was a stickler for the rules. He'd take it because it was too good to refuse. It left him speechless, though. Fusarri's speciality was leaving people speechless. And the idea of the Captain tossing – what was it? – 'printable nonsense' to the press. The man known among the journalists of Florence as 'The Tomb'. Printable nonsense indeed. The Marshal himself wouldn't be up to providing it either. How the devil should he know which nonsense was printable? No, no, they could make up their own, the same as they always did – unless the young Brunamontis could help with personal titbits, photos and so on, though, from what little he'd seen of the sister he couldn't imagine her gossiping with journalists. Perhaps the brother, if he came round to collaborating . . .

'Two ideas,' the Captain had said. Even before kidnappers showed their hand, one thing was obvious. There had to be a known professional kidnapper in hiding from the law running the show. The new law had made kidnapping a lengthy and difficult business, effectively eliminating all but the best professionals. And professional kidnappers didn't drop from the sky, their careers were known and documented so that, unless they were in hiding, they could be checked on. Two ideas. Two wanted men, each with his own band of associates and, most important of all, his own territory where he could operate without risk.

Back on his own side of the river with the church bells ringing out midday, the Marshal gravitated to Santo Spirito as the market was packing up. He would have been happy to take up the same position as before, staring at the brown shutters whilst working out how best to approach the son of the house, but the sharp eyes of Torquato made him change his mind and sent him instead into the ice cream bar next to the Brunamonti entrance.

'Morning, Marshal.'

'Giorgio . . .' Sheltered from the wind and sunshine, he removed his hat and black glasses. 'A coffee.' Giorgio and he were old acquaintances. The bar had moved up market in recent years and, in addition to its famous ice cream, served fashionably light lunches to students and professional people of the area. Giorgio kept the place clean of drugs and himself on good terms with the law.

'It's true, then, that something's happened to the Contessa?' Giorgio was a Florentine with 'no hairs on his tongue', as the local saying went. In Sicily, where the Marshal came from, you didn't see or hear things, let alone remark on them, and this sort of opening still nonplussed him.

'The Contessa . . .'

'Brunamonti. My landlady, apart from anything else. They own this whole block, you know.'

'I didn't know.'

'The whole block. We all know something's up. She hasn't been seen in ten days. Dog neither. And they're preparing for a big show – New York – which would normally mean Leonardo working until all hours and coming in here for an after-midnight snack. No sign of any of the family. Staff from the workrooms haven't been in for their lunches in a week and now you're here for the second time this morning. Your coffee. A drop of something in it?'

'No, no . . .'

'Suit yourself. Freezing weather.'

'Yes. It's nice and warm in here, I must say. I wonder if we could have a quiet word as you don't seem to be too busy.'

'No problem at all. Good half hour before we start lunches. Come in the back. Marco! Bring the Marshal's coffee. I don't think you've been in here, have you?'

'No. It's very comfortable.'

'Have a seat.' The small round tables with white cloths were set for lunch. The Marshal sat on one of the grey plush seats which ran round all the walls. It was warm and comfortable indeed.

'You must know a fair bit about the family . . .'

'Me? Well I've been here twenty-nine years. The old Conte was alive in those days – father of the one who died ten years or so ago, a real good-for-nothing he was but his father was what they call a character. "The Professor", they used to call him. He insisted on that because he had a doctorate in philosophy. "Conte" he wouldn't stand for, "Doctor" he didn't care for. "Professor" it had to be. Took one coffee on his morning walk and always wore a hat – trilby in winter, panama in summer . . .'

For a long time the Marshal didn't speak at all. People often began by asking him things but they were usually just as happy telling him things. Most people prefer talking to listening. The Marshal accepted questions and then waited quietly as now, his dark glasses in his pocket, his hat with the gold flame on his knee, his gaze fixed at random on the walls covered in designs for the façade of the Brunelleschi church outside. At one point, mis-understanding the concentration of his gaze, Giorgio launched into the story of how the municipality had asked all the artists in the city to design a façade for the blank silhouette left by the architect and how, one hot summer night, these designs had been projected onto the church. What a night that had been! Of course, in those days, with a Communist mayor—

'What was his name?'

'The Communist mayor? Gabbuggiani. Before your time, I suppose, but it was mostly the idea of . . .'

'The late Conte Brunamonti. The one whose father called himself "the Professor", the one who was no good.'

Back on course, Giorgio told all. There was plenty of it, too. The way the Marshal saw it, if somebody went missing from the family photograph – whether kid-napped, murdered, or lost – the only way to give the missing person a clear outline and a shape was to fill in the rest of the picture. The empty space remaining was as much as you could know about the victim. The Marshal very much wanted to know about this victim. To his Captain he would have said it would help the investi-gation. To himself he would say it was because people don't recover from being kidnapped on the instant of their release and always need help. The real reason was a little sandy mongrel. He couldn't have explained that to anybody.

So he listened to the story of the Conte Ugo Brunamonti, husband of an American model, son of the Conte Egidio Brunamonti, known as 'the Professor', born with a silver spoon in his mouth, died of starvation.

He had been, by all accounts, a beautiful child, fair-haired and brown-eyed, but odd. Odd in precisely what way nobody was still alive to say. He had studied at a Jesuit college and been expelled for unspecified vice. He had taken up art, bought a gallery to show his work in, and invented the Brunamonti sculpture prize, which he first awarded to himself and then to his failed artist friends. This prize, like many others of its ilk, was still awarded annually. It was a heavy bas-relief medal in a blue velvet box, the cost of reproduction covered by the competition entrance fee. An elderly princess with a pretty villa, a decent income, and mild pretensions to an artistic salon gave a supper party in her garden each June after the award ceremony. A big party which people willingly attended, though often ignorant of the motive, because the garden was even prettier than the villa, and the terrace where supper was served on a velvety June night was perfumed by roses and lit by moonlight. However, the only member of the Brunamonti family who could work up enough sense of family duty to attend this party each year was the daughter. The son had never been seen there. Of course, this could be because the daughter had dabbled a bit in art herself at one time but that was some time ago and she'd gone on attending, so only family feeling would explain it. No, she'd never won the prize.

He had been a very handsome man, Ugo, there was no denying that, and it was easy to understand how he'd dazzled that nice young American woman, what with his looks and his title and his fine old property. She had once told Giorgio – oh yes, she came in the bar, too, now and again for a late-night snack when they were really busy just before a show, usually with Leonardo and perhaps a designer – that the oldest building where she came from was the gas station. Whether that was true or just a joke, Giorgio couldn't say. Anyway, she married him, right there in the church of Santo Spirito. A passage still leads from beneath the palazzo to the sacristy of the church – they were Guelphs, the Brunamontis, and had to keep off the streets when the Ghibellines were on the ascent.

After the wedding, it was trouble all the way. She brought a decent amount of money with her but you can imagine . . . The art dabbling had been harmless enough but it was followed by stock exchange dabbling and that ruined them. Good money after bad, hers after his. She always was an optimistic, enterprising type and deserved the success she achieved after what she had to fight against. She kept finding ways to keep them afloat, leasing out various parts of the palazzo and renovating a number of dilapidated Brunamonti properties and renting them to tourists.

Unfortunately, the Conte never ran out of exciting

new ventures to invest in and newly discovered talents to be expensively developed. One was Renaissance music, I remember. He set up a group and bought all the antique instruments. Funny thing is, I believe they're still going – started doing rather well once they'd got rid of him. Couldn't play, you see, thought he'd pick it up as he went along, being a genius. And so it went on. When there was no other way to get money he began borrowing on the palazzo. And all the time there were other women – not that he was a cheery philanderer. It was always some complicated romantic affair that would have a business or artistic angle to it, or both, and would end tragically, leaving another loan on the palazzo for his unfortunate wife to pay off. That's what made her go back to work as a model, and then he left her. A Contessa Brunamonti doesn't go out to work. It disgraced him publicly.

She must have got control of the Brunamonti finances at some point and stopped the bank from lending him any more money, which couldn't have been easy because they must have liked the thought of getting their hands on the property at the end of the day. After that, the Conte went downhill very rapidly. A few friends lent him money but that didn't last, and when he was destitute an ex-mistress took him in and looked after him until she became ill and left to go back to England, where she came from. He stayed on in her flat, and it was the landlord who, after a year of not being paid and getting no answer to letters, calls, or doorbell, broke in. They say he'd been dead for quite some time. His body was emaciated and had been gnawed at by rats as well as maggots and ants. There was no food at all in the flat. He didn't die in his bed either, but at his desk, with notes and plans for yet another brilliant scheme in front of him.

It never got into the papers but the woman who went in to clean up the place brought his few belongings to the Contessa and among them was an unopened box delivered from Pineider, the fanciest stationers in Florence. It contained headed letter paper and envelopes and elegantly engraved visiting cards announcing in English 'Count Ugo Brunamonti, Exporter of Fine Italian Wines' and gave the number of the little flat he died in and a U.S. number which turned out to be his mother-in-law's. She knew nothing about it, of course, since no such business existed. The Contessa paid the stationer's bill and the amounts outstanding to the landlord. That wasn't the end of it. For months afterwards more bills kept arriving: tailor, shoemaker, wine merchant – he hadn't drunk his imaginary wine – and even a year's rent on an office he'd taken and long since abandoned. The Contessa not only paid the rent but sent her maid round there to make sure the place was clean before giving the keys back. No doubt 'clean' included clean of any other evidence of his folly. It was pathetic. A good enough room with a view of red rooftops and a slice of the cathedral dome. A desk and a chair, a telephone, unconnected, a leather desk set that had been the Professor's and which the maid brought home.

What was really incredible was that there were a lot of

offices in that building, and all their occupants had seen Brunamonti going in and out on a regular basis until about a year before, keeping real office hours in a real office and running an imaginary business. This was before the wine – an antiques business it was, that time. There was a brass plate on the door. That would have been the period when he was still living with his ex-mistress and no doubt she believed he was going out to work every day. He was always very plausible and kept his good looks until she left him to starve. After his death, relieved of the Brunamonti burden, the Contessa – who never used her title again except on dress labels – soon made her fortune in the fashion world. She was talented and hardworking, and the banks, who for years had watched her rescue the family estate against all the odds, had absolute trust in her and backed her all the way. By now, the *Contessa* label was well known in Europe, America, and Japan.

'So, are you going to tell me what's happened?'

'Oh yes. I'll be back. I'll just go up there and have a word if you'll excuse me . . .'

As he went out through the front part of the bar, a waiter was lining up carafes of red wine on the glass counter. The unmistakable smell of roasting pork with roast potatoes and aromatic herbs awoke the Marshal's appetite with a sharp pang. He glanced at his watch and then, hat in hand, went next door and entered the Palazzo Brunamonti.

Four

He plodded slowly along the dark carriageway, past a boarded-up porter's lodge, until he came out into a cloistered garden where a fountain played quietly and winter jasmine flowered on the ochre walls. Sheltered from the mountain wind, yellow and purple crocuses made splashes of colour around the stone base of the fountain and sparrows hopped among them chirping cheerfully. An idyllic picture. The Marshal looked upwards. All but two of the tall brown shutters were closed on this inner façade, too. It seemed to him too quiet.

'Can I help you?'

He turned. Beyond the cloister to his left a plump, grey-haired woman stood holding open a glass door. He walked towards her.

'Perhaps you could tell me which entrance to use . . . I'm looking for Leonardo Brunamonti – I should say Conte—'

'No. He's never used the title. He's not well, I don't . . .' She looked back at the long room behind her. 'You'd better come inside.' He followed her. It was a very high-ceilinged room that had perhaps been built to house carriages rather than people. The spent light from the courtyard was ideal for the Marshal's sun-allergic eyes but the many people at work there had individual spotlights on their sewing, cutting, and the draping of models. The atmosphere was that of a beehive in production, emphasised by the whirr of sewing machines. One by one these slowed and stopped as they saw the Marshal's dark silhouette in the doorway. He didn't know what their reaction to his presence was, only that it was unanimous. They stared as one person, breathed as one person, there was no mistaking that. A planner . . . someone who knew the family's finances, their movements. The Marshal would have staked his life in that instant that this person wasn't here. As to whether he should be in here himself, well, he'd had to ask directions, hadn't he? It wasn't his job to question these people. Somebody more important, of a higher rank – even the Prosecutor himself – would do that. The Marshal didn't question them.

'I'm Signora Verdi, Mariangela Verdi. I want to tell you right away that we don't know what's going on but whatever it is we're here to help.'

'Thank you.'

'You needn't thank me. It's Leonardo we're here to help, not you.'

'Is there a difference?'

'We don't know because we don't know what's going on, do we? Or are you going to tell us?'

She broke off to take delivery of a parcel. 'Excuse me . . .'

'Please . . .' He watched as she undid the small package. It contained what he assumed were dress labels. They were white with *Contessa* embroidered in gold italics and Florence in the bottom left-hand corner.

The Marshal couldn't help a mental comparison with the engraved letterhead and visiting cards of the crazy husband, the Conte Ugo Brunamonti, exporter of imaginary fine Italian wines.

'May I . . .?' He picked up one of the labels.

'Help yourself. It just shows how behind we are when these arrive before we're ready for them instead of our having to kick up a fuss to get them delivered. They used to be silver on black but some cheap imitator copied them and our designs so we've had to change. It ought to have been Contessa Brunamonti in my opinion, instead of just Contessa – they could hardly have copied that – but her ladyship wouldn't have it and that was that.'

'A little long, perhaps,' murmured the Marshal. He was surprised that she seemed to expect him to have an opinion on the subject and even more surprised at the tone of that 'her ladyship', which was little less than venomous. A disagreement over labels would hardly

73

warrant such a tone. Had his instinct been completely mistaken about these people? He made a mental note to talk to the Captain about it once they'd been questioned. Something was seriously wrong here.

How many of them were there in the room? So many pairs of eyes fixed on him, a smell of new cloth and sewing-machine oil, a smell of his childhood and his mother's rattly old treadle machine.

Let me pedal for a bit, please . . .

You'll break the needle.

'I'd be glad if you could direct me . . .'

'I see. You're not going to tell us anything.' She led him back out.

'An officer will be coming to talk to you all. I'm not in charge . . . These stairs?'

'Take the lift. Second floor.' She pressed the call button for him and went away.

On the second-floor landing where the floor was of glossy white marble, he was faced with double doors and a brass bell push. A Filipino maid in blue and white answered his brief ring. She was crying already, and when she saw his uniform she broke into howls of dismay and ran off without showing him in.

The tall, fair daughter was immediately before him – what the devil was her name? He'd forgotten to check. She appeared to be trying to block his way, and her face was white with apprehension. The legs and feet of a young man, wrapped in a plaid blanket, were just visible sticking out over the edge of a white sofa some way behind her.

The Marshal made a negative sign to the girl, hoping to convey the idea that he wouldn't give her away but she didn't move from his line of vision and it crossed his mind that she was hiding her brother from him rather than vice versa.

'Signorina . . .' He was willing to pretend he didn't know her but he stood his ground. 'I beg your pardon for this intrusion but I'm looking for Brunamonti, Leonardo Brunamonti.' She didn't stand aside, even then, so it was by edging round her that he saw the young man on the white sofa untangle himself from the rug and sit up very slowly. At the floor by his feet lay an airman's leather jacket. The Marshal felt sure it had been lying there since he came back on that fateful night. Yes, he was right. That was surely the handle of a dog lead sticking out of the pocket.

Leonardo's face was a shock. It was to be expected, of course, that he would not have slept, would be distraught, but his face had a greenish pallor, his skin was dry, and black rings circled his eyes, which he seemed barely able to keep open. In fact, after attempting to see the Marshal, he dropped his head into his hands and mumbled, 'Shutter . . .'

Only one inner shutter was open in the long room and the girl went then and closed it, leaving the thinnest possible crack of light by which they could see each other. Even that wouldn't have been possible had not the room been almost entirely white. The Marshal found this whiteness odd but there was no time now to wonder why. He went and stood before the sofa. Leonardo was evidently as long and thin as his sister. He peered up between his fingers and murmured as though afraid of the slightest movement of his face. 'Why are you here? Who . . .?'

This couldn't be just stress. That woman below had said he wasn't well, and the possibility that this was an abstinence crisis crossed the Marshal's mind at once.

'Have you been sitting by the phone for ten days?'

No answer. He dropped his head further and pressed his fingers to his temples as though to prevent it from bursting apart. His voice seemed to come from another world.

'How did you find out?'

'An informer. There's no point in your worrying about that now and you needn't fear that anything we do will put your mother's life at risk.'

The phone rang and Leonardo almost screamed before he grabbed at it.

'Patrick . . . I can't . . .'

His sister took the receiver from him.

'Patrick? He can't talk, he's too ill. I know he should. I've told him. I can sit by the phone. Patrick, listen, the carabinieri have found out – I don't know – an informer or something. There's somebody here now. I think you should talk to that agency and cancel everything. She's my mother, Patrick, and Leo's in no condition . . . When? I'll pick you up from the airport. I'll pick you up!' She replaced the receiver. Her brother was lying down again, holding, with splayed fingers, a corner of the rug over his face.

The Marshal indicated an inner door. 'Could we . . .?' He almost tiptoed out behind her. Whatever the reason for it, the young man's pain was a palpable presence that hung heavy in the shuttered white room where the air could not have been changed for days.

'I'll take you to my room. We can talk there.'

This room, when they reached it, seemed amazingly large for a single young woman. It was probable, of course, that all the bedrooms in such a palazzo were as big as this. Even the massive carved bed was lost in such a space. Facing the door, two broad steps led up to a high window with pale shiny curtains looped back in front of the shutters.

'We can sit here.' A long oak desk with a round leather chair in front on which she sat, remaining bolt upright, her hands posed in her lap. This time, though, she seemed a little excited and began twisting the diamond ring round and round her long finger as she talked.

'Please sit down. I don't think he suspected me, do you?'

'No, I'm sure not.' The Marshal sat down on a high-backed carved armchair that felt like a throne. 'He's much too distressed to care, I'd say. He also seems to be ill.'

'It's nothing. I mean he's not what you could really call ill. It's migraine. He gets it when he's under stress. He can't stand light or noise so it's no use trying to talk to him. I can tell you everything you need to know.'

He noticed that she made no apology for having disappeared from his office when he'd asked her to wait. Perhaps she hadn't understood and, in any case, though not reduced to a rag like her brother, it must be remembered that she must be equally upset. No doubt she had a stronger personality. She was certainly coping better.

'Surely there's something your brother could take for the pain?'

'There is but it's a really strong cocktail of painkillers and the doctor comes to inject him with it. The trouble is it knocks him out completely for about fifteen hours and so he won't do it. He won't leave the phone. He wants to stay awake, which is ridiculous since I'm here.'

'Yes. But try and persuade him. There's no point in either of you sitting by the phone. Nobody will contact you here because of your phone's being tapped.'

'The phone's tapped? Already?' Round and round went the diamonds, flashing bright as her feverish eyes.

'I'd say it will be before the day's out and, for all the kidnappers know, it could have been done days ago. That's a very elegant desk set. Was it your father's?'

'Yes, and my grandfather's before that. My father left it to me. You might expect he'd have left it to Leonardo but I was his particular favourite. All the furniture in here was my father's. This was his room.'

The Marshal could well imagine that the wife wouldn't want it after what he'd put her through, but the daughter, according to Giorgio, had a sense of family duty. Now he knew why the whiteness of the drawing room was odd. A room in a Renaissance palazzo should look like this one, with furniture of the period. The other was clean-lined and very modern looking. Among the many expedients for her own survival as well as that of her two children, no doubt the sale of antique furniture had played a part. Poor woman, it must have been a long time before she could afford all that modern white stuff.

'Signorina, it is most likely that your mother's captors will make contact with you and your brother by having your mother write to you. The letter will almost certainly be sent to a close family friend – This man Patrick . . .?'

'Hines. He's flying in from London tomorrow evening. I'm picking him up from the airport.'

'Yes. But would he normally be arriving now? Would your mother expect him to be here?'

'No. He wasn't to come over for the Milan show because there's so much to do over there for the New York fashion week.'

'She won't write to him then. Her closest woman friend?'

'I don't know. She had a lot of friends but I was always telling her she never gave them any time because of being so taken up with her work. They invited her to lunches and on outings all the time but she never was very sociable. She practically wore a furrow between her office and the workrooms downstairs. I felt it couldn't be good for her health to drive herself so hard. I don't know which one she'd write to – and what if whoever it is gives the letter to Leonardo instead of me? Then we won't know what's going on.'

'We'll cross that bridge when we come to it. I hope to have talked him round by then. In the meantime, there are two things you and he must do together – when he's well enough: Think of three questions to which only your mother can know the answer. You'll understand, I'm sure, that we have to know your mother is alive.'

'She could be dead already, couldn't she? That's what you mean.'

'Don't distress yourself. It's very unlikely. They know they have to furnish this proof so it's in their interest to keep her alive and well at this stage.'

In the hope of distracting her from the idea of her mother's being already dead, he said: 'That's a beautiful photograph of you on the wall. They all are. We'll soon have you relaxed and smiling like that again, you'll see. Is this you on the horse?'

'Yes. I don't ride any more. That photograph there in my ballet dress is my favourite. It was taken last year. I had to give up dancing because of the demands of university.'

'It's a very striking picture of you. Signed, too, I see.'

'Yes. By the photographer. Gianni Taccola's very well known in Florence. He used a set of photographs of me in an exhibition of his and gave me this one as a present. He used the word you used – striking – and he said it was lucky I had no ambitions to be a model like Olivia because nobody would use me. People would notice me instead of the clothes. A model has to be quite good-looking but she's got to be a mobile coat hanger more than anything. I did a little modelling to help Olivia out but I really didn't care for it – We can't manage! We won't be able to manage without her!'

'No, no, no. You won't have to manage without her. We'll bring her home. Try and keep calm now. You've been doing so well and we're going to need your help.' So much for trying to distract her. 'And now I need you to give me a piece of her clothing, something worn rather than laundered. Will you do that?'

'Certainly.' She rose and went towards the bed head, where she pressed a bell. After a moment, the Filipino maid tapped and came in.

'Yes, Signorina,' she said, sniffing loudly. Her cheeks were still wet and she made no effort to control or conceal her weeping.

'Take the Marshal to my mother's room and give him what he asks you for.'

The Marshal frowned. 'It might be better if you came, too.'

'I want to see how Leo is.'

'Of course . . .'

There was nothing to do but follow the weeping maid, who led him to the end of a polished dark red corridor and up two grey stone steps into the end bedroom. As he expected, it was a room full of light and air. Here, too, there were photographs, a wall almost entirely covered with them, in silver frames and all of them of Leonardo and Caterina. There was one of the two of them together as small children. The Marshal examined it closely. He had never in his life seen such beautiful children. It was little wonder the Contessa had had them photographed so often. A black-and-white enlargement stood out among all the colour. The daughter in a gauzy ballet frock, her slippers and coiled plaits of hair shining, the rest as insubstantial as a shadow. It couldn't have been taken that long ago, either.

'Is the signorina a dancer?'

'Long time she is dance. Stop now. Must study exams. University.' The maid pulled a face through her tears.

'Yes, it's a shame,' he agreed, looking once more at the lovely photograph, 'but, of course, these days all young people need qualifications . . .'

The maid, if she had understood him, didn't answer.

The winter sun shone in between high muslin swags, and the big, new bed had a pale, silky cover. Perhaps the smooth emptiness of that bed so long unslept in was too much for the maid, because she burst into even louder howls.

'My signora! My signora! Oh, what will happen to me now?'

She was so small that, with her short, straight hair, she seemed more a little girl than the young woman she must surely be, and the Marshal automatically placed a comforting hand on her head and stroked it.

'Come on now, come on. It's going to be all right.' He

had enough experience with such things to check at once. 'You're not worried about your documents and so on, are you? If you are, I can try—'

'No!' She all but screamed at him. 'My signora do everything for me and do my work permit. *Everything!* I cries for my signora because they kill her!'

'No, no . . . We're going to bring her home. Now listen to me: We have special dogs who will help us find your signora and you must help the dogs by giving me a piece of clothing for them. Do you understand?'

'Yes, Signor.'

'Something the dogs can sniff at and then . . . do you understand me?'

'Yes, Signor.'

The Marshal sighed. He understood that she would answer 'Yes, Signor' if he asked her to jump out of the window and would then continue to stand rooted to the spot as she was doing now. He also understood that this sort of thing was why his Captain had sent him here. He'd try once more and if he failed, he'd try and send her to fetch the daughter back.

'What's your name?'

'Silvia, Signor.'

He gave her his big white handkerchief.

'Thank you, Signor.'

'Unfold it. Dry your eyes.'

'Yes, Signor.' She doubled it up, put it in her overall pocket, and dried her eyes with hand and sleeve.

'Now then, Silvia, your signora's clothes. Clothes . . .'

He looked around him but there wasn't a scrap of clothing in sight.

Silvia opened one of a long line of gold-and-white wardrobe doors. This was progress.

'My signora hundreds of clothes,' she wept proudly. 'Hundreds . . .' She went on opening and suddenly yanked out something long, frothy, and very transparent.

'This one when Mister Patrick come from States. My signora very sexy for Mister Patrick – oh, my signora . . .' She collapsed in tears again, remembering reality. The transparent frothy thing fell from her small hands.

The Marshal picked it up. It was obviously freshly laundered and of no real use to him.

'Laundry,' he said, getting a grip on her shoulder. 'Where is your signora's laundry? Her washing?' She had probably washed every scrap after ten days. She looked unhappy about it but led him into the bathroom, all white and gold and very large.

A laundry basket! He opened it without much hope but a couple of lacy scraps of underwear lay at the bottom. He helped himself.

Silvia was horrified and a crescendo of 'My signoras' followed him as he returned to the bedroom, slipping the underwear into a polythene bag from his pocket. He felt almost as bad about it as she did. A total stranger pawing her signora's intimate clothing – unwashed intimate clothing – with his big clumsy hands! He was glad to get away from her tears and squeaks of protest and find his own way back to the white drawing room.

Leonardo was talking very quietly into the phone, his free hand holding his forehead. His sister was perched on the arm of the sofa beside him.

'All right. I'll come down.' He hung up.

'Leo, you can't possibly. It's ridiculous! I'll go down.'

But he picked up his jacket and put it on cautiously as if any sudden movement would increase his pain. He stroked her arm gently, calming her. 'They need me. I'll be all right.' He got to his feet and, seeing the Marshal, said, 'I'm sorry . . .'

'Please don't worry. I can see you're in no fit state to talk to me. I'll come back when you're better – but, excuse me, surely your sister's right. You can't be thinking of going anywhere?'

'Only down to the workroom. Otherwise they can't get on. Will you walk down with me?'

'Of course.' If only because he'd probably need to hold him up. The Marshal had never seen anyone look that ill and be on their feet. Yet he started, albeit unsteadily, down the broad staircase.

'Don't you want the lift?'

'Sorry. The noise, movement . . . I can't.'

They made it down the stairs but as they crossed by the fountain the young man stopped, swaying. The Marshal steadied him.

'My mother . . . oh, God, I don't know any more what's best . . .'

'It will be all right. If you'll let me talk to you. If you'll trust me.'

But the Marshal realised he was talking to himself. The young man's deep-set eyes were blank. He could no longer hear or move.

'Help me . . .'

'I'm here to help you, believe me—'

'No. Ambulance.' He doubled up to vomit into the grass and in silence laid himself down very carefully on the broad stone ledge of the fountain.

'And how is he now? Have you heard? Open that flask, Salva, will you, since you're standing there.'

Teresa passed him the bottle opener and the Marshal grasped the neck of the straw flask. 'I rang the hospital just before I shut the office. They say he's out cold and will be until tomorrow.'

'Poor thing. I never heard of migraine being that bad.'

'He was blind when the ambulance men got there and had no feeling in his hands or feet. They thought it was something worse but, luckily, his sister had explained to me.'

'What's she like? Get out of my way, Salva, I want to get to the sink. Is she beautiful like her mother?'

'Sort of beautiful, but different.'

'What did you say her name was?'

'I didn't. I can't remember. Do you remember the Contessa then? You were still living down home in the days when the fashion shows were here.'

'Seen her at the hairdresser's.'

'What?'

'Oh, don't panic. I haven't been spending your entire salary on the sort of hairdresser she must go to. No, in the magazines – one in particular, I remember, did a big feature on her, a sort of famous people at home thing, you know. I remember one photo of her dressed in beige cashmere, very casual, and a little dog curled up beside her on a white linen sofa in a room that was all white. I remember thinking two things: one was that she must be older than me and yet she looked like a model, just perfect.'

'She was a model once.'

'And then I thought I can just imagine what our two would do to that white room. Call them, will you? It's ready.'

First thing next morning the Marshal called the Santa Maria Nuova Hospital from his office. Leonardo Brunamonti, they told him, was still sleeping but would probably be awake for the doctors' rounds at eleven after which he would leave. The Marshal decided to be there with the excuse of driving him home and that, in the interest of privacy, he would go in his own car so as not to take a driver.

If the young man was surprised to see him, he was not nearly as surprised as the Marshal.

'I wouldn't have known you.'

'I'm all right now. Once I've slept, it's all over.' The cadaverous creature of the day before was now a handsome young man with large greenish brown eyes, and if his expression was still troubled it was also alive with sincere gratitude. 'I ought to knock myself out the minute my vision starts going, before the headache even begins, but I couldn't . . . you understand.'

'Of course. It's too late now but, as I told your sister, your vigil was pointless. Nobody will ring. My car's right here. I hope I wasn't taking a liberty, coming for you like this, but I'd like to talk to you . . .'

'I'm glad you came. The truth is, it was Patrick – Patrick Hines – who really insisted on our going it alone. He's American and doesn't trust the authorities here. Excuse my saying so but—'

'Don't worry. It happens.'

'His feeling is, you see, that a private detective would be working only in our interests but that your first priority is arresting the kidnappers.'

'It's true in part,' admitted the Marshal, 'but you can't imagine we'd consider a case successful if we lost the victim.'

'No, but you'd maybe take more risks . . .'

'When you meet Captain Maestrangelo you will not be able to imagine him taking a risk. Oh, nobody's going to object to your bringing in your man as long as he collaborates with us. Can I just ask you to talk to the Captain and the Prosecutor first? Does that seem reasonable?'

'More than reasonable. To tell you the truth, it's a relief to me. I don't see how we could have managed alone.'

'You couldn't. Nobody can. If you've seen cases where they appeared to, it is only an appearance.'

'I suppose so. Can I ask you a favour? Would you stop a moment? I haven't had a breath of air for ten days and when I get back I'll have to go straight to the workroom. I don't want to waste your time . . .'

'You won't be.' He might have recovered from his headache but he was still too distressed and distracted to notice that the Marshal had taken a very long route, climbing the Viale Michelangelo although he was permitted to drive through the centre of town. He felt he had Leonardo Brunamonti's full attention and couldn't be sure he would keep it once this Hines fellow appeared on the scene. He parked below the statue of David and they got out of the heated and sun-warmed car to gasp at the icy blast that hit them.

They walked along by the marble balustrade in silence. Below them was spread a tapestry of red roofs and glittering white marble, and the river, smooth and full, was a deep olive green. Huge, brightly coloured tour buses were parked in the piazza and tourists leaned on the balustrade to steady their cameras, the wind flattening their furs and reddening their noses.

The Marshal pursued his usual policy of interrogation. That is, he kept quiet. Leonardo breathed deeply for a while and then his gaze drifted up to the right and the dark snow-speckled hills on the horizon.

'She hates the cold . . . She was always telling us about her first years here, how she suffered from chilblains and had no idea what they were – you can imagine, coming from California. It's the floors – stone, marble. In America the houses are carpeted . . . They'll keep her somewhere sheltered, won't they?'

The Marshal avoided his earnest gaze. 'It's in their own interests to keep her alive and well. They have to prove it. You'll hear from her before long.'

'It's just that – I've never followed these things that closely but I've heard of people kept in holes – hear from her? They'll let her write or something?'

'Write, yes . . .' He didn't correct the 'let'. His eyes, too, were drawn towards the northern hills, their sharp contrasts softened by his sunglasses. Dark, inhospitable hills. Some people thought them beautiful, going on about wild orchids and asparagus, impenetrable woods full of boletus mushrooms weighing kilos, truffles and bristling pigs. Such vast, savage landscapes, such picturesque flocks of sheep, such coolness in midsummer.

And the Marshal would say with a frown, 'No, no . . .' He had no words to express his dismay. You could stand there beneath that statue with the riches of civilisation spread at your feet and tourists from all over the world posing for photographs and giggling as the wind whipped strands of hair across their faces, and up there on those hills there could be a woman chained up like an animal. If she was lucky, her life would be merely permanently damaged. If not, pigs left no scraps unless you counted kneecaps, which they didn't bother to chew and which went straight through them. The Marshal didn't like those hills, or the Aspromonte in Calabria, or the Barbagia in Sardinia. He didn't want to be cold in summer, he didn't find the bleak poverty of the shepherd's life picturesque, and the impenetrable woods that sheltered wildlife also sheltered bandits. He didn't like it one bit.

'No, no no . . . ,' he would say. With a frown.

'It's so cold. I suppose because I haven't eaten . . . Can we get back in the car?'

As the Marshal started the engine, he sensed the young man shaking. He must be frozen.

'I'm sorry . . .' It wasn't the cold that was making him shake but dry sobs. 'I'm sorry, it's just . . . complaining about the cold after five minutes when she . . .' He couldn't go on.

'Don't try and talk. It's true you need to eat—'

'No. I want to talk to you. It's been so awful – the silence, the waiting. I'd like to talk to you.'

The Marshal let him talk. Instead of taking him home he took him to Borgo Ognissanti, where the Captain, about to go to the Prosecutor's office, stayed with them a while, sent someone to bring them drinks and sandwiches, and then left them the use of his office.

Leonardo talked non-stop for two and a half hours. He went over that night of his mother's disappearance repeatedly, hoping, as we all do, to make the outcome other than it was, saying, 'I knew she was tired, I could have taken the dog out for once . . . My sister was showered and ready for bed' or 'I actually thought of going down with her. I was working on a design and needed a coffee to keep me going so I could finish that night. It's something we often did at that hour, you see, so I might easily . . . If I'd—'

'Don't torment yourself. It's bad for you and no help to your mother.'

'She should have been in the country. We have a little cottage, you know, not too far out or she'd never get there. She always tried to get a couple of days' break before the Milan fashion week, once everything was running smoothly, so as to be fresh for the show itself because it's really hectic, nerve-racking. Only this year, because we're going to New York for the first time in April, she didn't go. I should have taken on more responsibility. She should have felt able to leave me in charge. If she'd gone this wouldn't have happened.'

'I don't think that's true. They could have been waiting their chance for days and would have gone on waiting.'

'But why? Why us? We're not rich enough.'

So here came the inevitable. There had yet to be a kidnapping where the family admitted being as rich as the kidnappers knew they were. They did their research and the magistrates did theirs and the polite veil was drawn before the public eye as undeclared money was discreetly withdrawn from off-shore accounts. Mistakes were made, of course, but, by and large, kidnappers know their business.

'My mother's business is successful – if you knew how she's worked, the years of not breaking even, borrowing and borrowing. She's made it now but she's ploughed it all back to go for the foreign market. It's possible, even probable, that there'll be no profit this year. Do you know what came into my mind this morning as I was waiting for the doctor's visit? The murder of Versace. Do you remember that day, the TV news? He was well known, of course, but it was only when people saw that house of his in Miami that they realised just how much money he'd made and it was a shock. Immediately there was gossip . . . Mafia . . . money laundering . . . God knows what . . . Do you think that could have sparked this kidnapping, drawn attention to the fashion world? And the Gucci murder? Such sums were mentioned . . .'

'It's good,' said the Marshal carefully, 'that you should give that aspect some thought because it will help us to trace the origins of the kidnapping.'

'Does that matter so much – from the point of view of saving my mother, I mean? I realise it's important to you.'

'It's important for both. If we know who set it up we'll know whose job it is and where he can operate, where his territory is.'

'I see. Even so . . .' Leonardo got up from the deep leather armchair and began wandering around the room, distractedly staring at the paintings, the line of tasselled calendars, the medals, the immaculately tidy desk. 'We're not Versace, we're not that famous – nowhere near – we make nothing in comparison.'

The Marshal had to tread carefully. If he lost the son's

confidence now, the arrival of Hines and a London detective would be the end.

'Well, Versace, they say, started with nothing . . .'

'And my mother started with debts! If you knew anything about my father . . .' He stopped rambling round the room and faced the Marshal. 'You mean our name . . . is that . . .'

'The property. This is something you should discuss with someone more competent and, besides, until a ransom demand comes through you don't know how much they've found out about you. What you could be thinking about is where such information came from. It's an unpleasant thing to ask you to do but I have to ask it. List everyone who works for you in any capacity, who knows about you, who frequents the house for whatever reason. Start with your own girlfriend if she's new.'

'No. No, she's American and lives in Switzerland.'

'The last one, then. Did you quarrel? Did you leave her?'

'No. She left me. They usually do because I work day and night. No quarrel. I can't believe—'

'If you want to save your mother, make that list. Your regular workforce, your accountant, your gardener, anyone previously unknown to you showing a recent interest in your family. Everyone. Don't be afraid. They'll be checked on discreetly. They'll never know. The name Brunamonti wasn't picked out of the phone book with a pin. Do you understand me?'

Leonardo sank into an armchair and rubbed at his eyes

as though forced to look at his world in a new way. 'All right.'

The Marshal barely had time to decide whether to take the young man home or to suggest he walk and get some air when a carabiniere looked in and, excusing himself, asked the Marshal to pick up the telephone as Captain Maestrangelo wanted to speak to him.

'I was hoping you were still there. Is the son with you?'

'Yes. He's here.'

'You might bring him with you. We've found the car.' He gave directions as far as the point where someone would meet them and rang off.

'We've found her car.'

Five

During the journey, which they made in an official car with a carabiniere driver, the Marshal sat in the back with Leonardo in case he still wanted to talk. Whether he was always that way or it was the effect of shock, Leonardo had no happy medium: either he opened his heart in a flood or he was silent. True, you wouldn't expect him to make small talk, but the Marshal, who had been in so many similar situations, still found him remarkable. There wasn't much traffic at this time of day – it was early afternoon by now – and they were soon out of the city, leaving great palaces and marble façades for a ribbon development of terraced houses, narrow, overused roads, and factories. A jeep belonging to the local force escorted them on a country lane leading away from the built-up area towards the hills. Despite the bright sun in a pure blue sky, the ditches on either side of the ochre-coloured lane were still partly crusted over with ice. At the foot of a steep tractor path the jeep stopped and the driver suggested they join him since it would be difficult for them to go any further by car.

They climbed aboard. The Marshal kept a close eye on his companion, unnerved by his collapse of yesterday, but he seemed calm and had some colour in his face. He looked much younger. He turned away now to look out at the hills to the right and the Marshal's gaze followed his. No matter how bright the sunshine, no matter what the weather, these hills always looked black and inhospitable.

They hadn't gone far up the steep track before the jeep pulled over into a field and stopped. Prosecutor Fusarri was already there with the Captain and a group of local men. Behind them, the Contessa Brunamonti's black car, partially obscured by boulders and branches, was being photographed.

'They've ripped the number plates off,' the Marshal observed, 'but does it look like your mother's car?'

'Yes. What does it mean? Is she . . . ?' Again his gaze turned to the dark, snow-powdered hills.

'It doesn't mean anything except that we've picked up the trail. That's always easy enough. They change cars in some quiet spot. She could be in these hills or at the other end of the country. Stay in the jeep and keep warm until they've finished work and then they'll ask you to take a look inside.'

It took time. No one expected to find any useful fingerprints but the car had to be checked for them, even so.

The Captain and the Prosecutor were deep in conversation, and the Marshal stood at a respectful distance, frowning. The car had been backed part way into a cave in the hillside. There were many such caves in these hills, some of them only big enough to hold a man, some big enough to hide a battalion.

The Marshal looked around for the carabiniere who had brought them. He couldn't find him but he spotted Bini, the Marshal in command of the local station, and went over to ask, 'Whose land is this?'

The local man lowered his voice. 'Salis, Francesco Salis.' It gave the impression he was afraid of the notorious bandit hearing him. 'I've told the Captain there but he knew already, of course . . . been in hiding a good three-and-a-half years now.'

'How long have you been here?'

'It'll be seven years this coming September.'

'You know him then.'

'I know him all right, but there'll be no laying hands on him until the day he decides to come down. They say he can crouch double and run, and I mean run, crashing through the undergrowth like a wild boar. They once got on his track with the dogs but only one dog could run after him at a time through such a narrow space. He turned and shot at them until they gave up. Helicopter above never saw a thing. No, they'll not get him unless he comes down. And it doesn't look like he'll be coming down now, does it?'

'And if he gets a ransom payment?'

'He'll be out of the country before the rest of them release the victim. Believe me. I know him.'

'Guarnaccia!'

The Marshal excused himself and joined the Captain.

'Guarnaccia, get the son to take a look inside, will you? How are things . . . Is he cooperating?'

'For the moment. It's the arrival of the others I'm worried about. He's so frightened and confused he'll lean on me now but . . . Well, finding the car will help.'

'I'm glad to hear it since it won't get us much farther. We need to find more than the car.'

They found more. Not in the car. There was nothing to be seen there, though the forensic labs would certainly come up with evidence for what they already knew but would have to prove in court: human and dog hairs, for instance. They found a great deal more in another cave higher up the hill. Plastic water bottles, bits of food, a filthy old mattress, and, behind that, something written on the wall in English.

gone swiming

Leonardo, brought to examine it, crawled out of the cave, stood up, and was silent. He turned his head away from the Marshal's inquiring gaze, muttering, 'Sorry . . .' and moved away from the group for a moment. Fusarri, an unlit cigar in his mouth, raised his eyebrows and, holding the cigar between his teeth, looked from the Captain to the Marshal.

'I take it his reaction means he's sure his mother wrote it. I wouldn't have thought myself that handwriting done with a stone could be recognisable, which must mean the words convey some message to him. They don't to me. Captain?'

'No, but . . .'

'Come on, now, Maestrangelo. Your English, as I remember, is excellent.'

'It's good enough to know that there's something wrong with the spelling.'

'Really? You mean it's a fake? Done by the kidnappers perhaps? It's odd enough, after all, that they didn't scratch it off since it wasn't hidden.'

'It's odd enough that they didn't clear the place out altogether. They might have had reason to leave in a hurry, I suppose, but . . .'

Fusarri removed the cigar and waved it. 'This whole setup's a fake? But the car's real.'

'Yes. And the son's reaction is real. Marshal?'

The Marshal went over to where Leonardo was sitting on a boulder, staring up at the hills as though unable to drag his gaze away. It was with difficulty that the Marshal gained his attention.

'She was here. That was a message for me. She was right here . . .'

'It's not written correctly, is it? We were wondering if,

in fact, it had been written by her captors. They might be trying to confuse the trail by creating a false hide-out.'

'No, it's . . . No.' He took a deep breath. 'It's because . . . It's a message to me. When I was a child I went to Italian schools and spoke Italian with my father as long as he was with us. My mother always spoke to me in English and tried to teach me to read and write in English, too. She read to me a lot . . . I'm afraid English spelling was beyond me. I'm not too hot at it even now, to tell you the truth. When I was about thirteen or fourteen I did a swimming course in the afternoons, and if my mother was down in the workshop I'd leave a note in the house to remind her. That's what I always wrote, no matter how often she corrected me, so that, in the end she began pronouncing it the way I wrote it and it became a private joke between us. She was here. If I'd come to you at once . . .'

'Don't torment yourself.'

'You're right, I know. "If only I'd known." The most useless phrase there is. Tell me what to do.'

The Marshal gave an inward sigh of relief and explained to him about the three questions he must prepare with his sister, the phrase his mother had written being a perfect example of the sort of information they should ask for.

'And what do we do with them when we've prepared them?'

'You'll be told.'

'By them, you mean?'

'Yes.'

*

Francesco Salis, born in Orgosolo, Sardinia (official occupation: shepherd, real source of income: kidnapping), had been on the run from the law, as the local force knew and records confirmed, for three and a half years. The Captain needed to know everything there was to know about Salis, his fellow criminals, his previous convictions, his habits, his money-laundering possibilities, and any white-collar prison contacts who could link him with the Brunamonti family or their business. He had a good man on his investigating team, a Sardinian himself and a veritable bloodhound, who was destined to work a lot of extra hours in the next few weeks. The Captain himself, who had worked every hour God sent every day of his military life, worked even more without noticing it. Prosecutor Fusarri managed to make himself available at any time of the day or night without appearing to be working at all.

The Mashal went to see Signora Salis.

He took the local man, Bini, with him. Bini told jokes. He told them incessantly. Goodness only knew where he got them but they weren't very funny. There weren't that many of them, either, so that by the time the jeep had gone three kilometres further than the point where the car was found he was repeating himself.

'I bet you've never heard this one: Why is the city of Florence like a woman's body?'

'What? I'm sorry, I . . .' Guarnaccia, miles away, deeply worried by something he couldn't quite put his finger on, came to with a start. One of the problems of living in

102

Florence was that you got bombarded by Florentines with a mass of complicated information you didn't want and the rest of the time you got bombarded by visitors with requests for that same information which you didn't remember.

Bini, not fussy about a response, rolled right along.

'Then lower down again there's the bottom fortress . . .'

Before picking him up in the nearby village square, the Marshal had drunk a politic cup of coffee in the Bar Italia, and the barman, after saying his say about Salis, had brought up Bini's name.

'Heart of gold, always ready to do anybody a good turn, generous to a fault. I won't hear a word said against him but he'll bore you to death. It's awful really, when you think about it, that we all prefer an entertaining rogue to a saint who keeps repeating the same dull jokes.'

The Marshal wasn't an exceptionally patient man but he was, as good luck would have it, an abstracted listener who had never in his life followed the plot of a film. And since Bini wasn't fussy about feedlines they went along quite comfortably.

'There's the place.'

They were at the edge of Bini's village on the brow of a hill, looking down at a pale ribbon of road that wound through a narrow valley, little more than a trough between steep slopes really, and up to a tiny village on the crown of the next hill. The Salis place was to the right of the road in the middle of the trough and was the only building there.

On reaching the dismal-looking house, they parked the jeep in the yard, where there was a washing line, an empty dog kennel, and a beaten-up car with its roof, back, and licence plates cut away, a makeshift such as farmers often use for moving bales, barrels, or dead animals.

The Marshal was surprised by the age of the woman who reluctantly admitted them, thinking at first she was Salis's mother since she was grey-haired and looked sixtyish. Her teeth were bad and her clothes stained. Ransom money went to buy land, sheep, even bonds made out to the holder. The kitchen looked as if it had been furnished from a rubbish tip and probably had. They sat down at a Formica table and were given strong red wine in kitchen glasses.

'You're wasting your time here. He has nothing to do with this.'

'This what?' It was Bini who did the talking. The Marshal listened to what the woman didn't say.

'I have my eyes and ears.'

'The car's on your land. And a used hide-out.'

She didn't answer that.

'When did you last see him?'

She shrugged.

'Don't tell me he isn't in touch with you.'

'He hasn't come down in a year.'

'So who's taking food to him?'

Another shrug. 'I don't hold with it, if you want to know.'

'With what?'

'This kidnapping business. At least not when it's children.'

'It's not children, though, this time, is it? Still, you get little enough out of it, that's true.' Bini looked about him. The kitchen was imbued with the smell of years of cheese-making but was severely clean. 'It's no life for you living in this place alone. Don't you ever think of going home to Sardinia? You must still have family there.'

'They wouldn't have me if I left my man. He's my husband and this is our land. What about you? You haven't much to say.' This was, of course, directed at the Marshal, who cleared his throat and looked at the plastic flowers on the washing machine.

'I was thinking the same as my colleague here. It must be a hard life for you. Have you sold his flock? I notice there's no dog outside.'

She gave a start and then glared from one to the other of them. They couldn't get another word out of her and soon gave up trying.

Back in the jeep, Bini told a couple of jokes while the Marshal thought about the woman's life in that isolated farmhouse until he was interrupted.

'If you don't mind my saying so, you'd have done better not to mention the dog. You'd think, wouldn't you, that with the trouble he's already in he'd have more sense than to do a job that could send him down for good.'

'It might make him a lot of money. He hasn't much to lose, I suppose. Has she sold his flock then?'

'Right away. No shepherd boy will work for them, not now. She had no choice.'

It wasn't late and it had been another bright, windy day but the sunlight had already gone in this valley so overshadowed by the nearness of the high black hills.

When they drove past the track where the car had been found, the Marshal's ill-defined worry surfaced again. A car was bound to be found, no point in the kidnappers' worrying about that, but they could have left it to be found near a motorway going south, or at least on somebody else's land.

'Bini, I can't help thinking that setup's a fake. Salis, they say, is a professional and not a fool.'

'Losing his grip in his old age, perhaps. He's nearer sixty than fifty, you know. And then, over twenty years in Tuscany . . . must have lost his Sardinian instincts. Anyway, the car and the message are real, aren't they? It's beyond me. Need a bigger brain than mine to make sense of it.'

The Marshal, with an even humbler opinion of his own brain, having already collected and stored most of the information necessary to the understanding of this contradiction, dropped the matter.

'I hadn't thought he was that old,' was his next remark, 'though I don't know why really.'

'It's the wanted poster. That photo is from when he was arrested in the eighties. Went grey in prison. Hasn't sat for the photographer since, if you see what I mean.'

'No, of course not . . .' Another source of unease welled

up but before it could reach the surface, Bini had slammed on the brakes as a woman stepped into the road and flagged them down.

They were almost back up on the hill where Bini's village began and there were a number of yellow-stuccoed farmhouses along the side of the road, each with its bit of land, a few chickens, a vegetable plot, a tiny red icon light, a dog running out on a long chain from a wine barrel to bark at the passing jeep.

The woman was small and she stood on tiptoe to talk to them through the window of the jeep. As Bini opened it, a waft of sweet wood smoke and a good smell of minestrone scented with rosemary drifted in. The woman was wearing a big apron and a thick woolly shawl over that but, despite the freezing cold and the fading light, she had come out in open-toed house shoes to give corn to her chickens and lock them up.

'I heard you were looking for a dog.'

'That's right. Probably dead but we want to know if it's found, just the same.'

'I was at the market this morning when you were asking around here. I only heard on my way back. Anyway I saw it, over a week ago. It was alive then but it'll be dead by now, I should think. It was all over blood and dragging itself along like it had some broken bones.'

'What did it look like? You must be frozen – shall we go in to your kitchen?'

'I've my hens to see to.' The thick red hand clutching the jeep was turning bluish with cold, and the skin of the fingers was cracked and stained. 'It was a little scrap of a dog, pale coloured. Not the sort of dog you see round here, not a hunter's dog – those are the ones you usually find wandering about lost, especially the young ones. My husband tried to catch it and shoot it, put it out of its misery, but it wriggled away from him and made for the road towards the village. A car hit it and flung it in the air but it got up and scrambled off, yelping. If you look around I reckon you'll find its body not too far from here. We thought it had been run over once already to be in that state but now they say it's to do with this Salis business. What's he done now?'

They thanked her and went on their way up to the village.

As the Marshal got back into his own car, Bini was looking worried.

'I suppose every Sardinian household in the area's going to be ransacked now. It's a bad business and usually it's badly done. Thing is, I have to live with these people when your case is over and done with. There are some good Sardinians round here, trying to lead a respectable life . . . They're not all criminals, you know.'

'What about the endless feuds that always end up with somebody getting knifed if not shot? You must be dealing with that sort of thing constantly.'

'That's as may be but it's a far cry from kidnapping.'

'True, but they'll all know, Bini. Every one of them will know.'

'I'm not saying they won't. All I'm saying is there are ways and ways of going about things. A case as big as this one, that's going to mean the police, not just us – and they don't have to live here when it's over. They won't get anything for their trouble, either, if they behave badly.'

'No. No, they won't. There's nothing I can do about it, Bini – unless . . . This Prosecutor, now, is not the usual type. He'd be the man to talk to.'

'You're joking? A Public Prosecutor wouldn't listen to a nobody like me.'

'This one would. This one even listens to me.'

The following day, the Prosecutor listened to a great many people, including the Marshal and Captain Maestrangelo. He then decided to call a press conference. Naturally, word had already got about, and journalists had been hanging around outside Borgo Orgnissanti Headquarters and the Public Prosecutor's office. The local paper, *La Nazione*, had already carried an article by Nesti, one of its most seasoned crime reporters, of the sort that consists almost entirely of questions – Why is the Contessa Brunamonti missing just before the big fashion shows? – and statements of fact without comment – Missing car: The staff of the *Contessa* fashion house refuse to comment – and so on.

So Fusarri decided. 'We need them on our side. Have you advised the family, Marshal?'

'I had a talk with the daughter by telephone yesterday

evening with the excuse, as you might say, of telling her the news about the dog.'

'Excellent! I knew we could rely on you. That's just the sort of thing she can toss the journalists to keep them happy without getting on to any touchy areas. If she lets them take the odd photo we're home.'

'I suggested that. They're both very attractive.'

'Splendid. You're going there today?'

'Every day, as long as they'll let me.'

'Make the suggestion about the dog story if she seems in difficulty. I'm leaving them to you until we know of a ransom demand or, if it should happen first, this American shows up with a detective.'

'I'm afraid that is what's going to happen first. Tonight.'

So the Marshal made a point of being there in the afternoon. With the two of them he discussed the formulation of the three questions which would demonstrate that their mother was alive.

'Once there's contact you'll be agitated and anxious for action. You had better be ready too early than too late.' He suggested that photograph albums of their childhood might jog their memories as regards odd little details that no one outside the family would know. They came up with a request for a description of the daughter's first party frock, designed and hand-sewn by her mother, the title of the first English book which Leonardo had read alone and the period design planned for their New York show on which Leonardo was still working, the drawings having been seen by no one but her.

'You're sure about that? What about Signor Hines – is it Hines?'

'Yes, but he doesn't know. I wanted to finish the drawings first. But surely he—'

'No one but your mother must be capable of answering. No exceptions.'

'That's all right.'

Before the Marshal had time to pass on the Prosecutor's advice about the dog story, the journalists were at the door.

The ever-weeping Silvia went to answer, and Leonardo stood up and turned to his sister. 'Will you? Marshal, if you'd come into the studio for a moment . . .'

The Marshal followed him. The studio was untidy. The walls were covered in plans and inked sketches, none of which appeared to have anything to do with dresses, as far as he could see. Not that he knew anything about these things . . .

Leonardo reassured him. He didn't design clothes, he designed the shows, the themes, the lighting, the music. He chose the venues, which could be anywhere these days, from a private Roman villa to a warehouse on the London docks. He also did similar design work for other events requiring spectacular presentation.

What he wanted to discuss with the Marshal was their financial situation. He had likewise thought that he should be ready too soon rather than too late. From being the devastated, wordless sufferer who had been carted off in an ambulance the other day, he had become concentrated, intelligent, determined. He had obtained information about the law governing the freezing of the family assets and understood both its uses and its elasticity. He was well aware that no member of the family could be prosecuted for breaking this law, and that clause seven, paragraph four of the new law permitted the payment of ransom for investigative purposes. Rightly assuming that this could involve marking the notes or intervening during the consignment, he declared himself agreeable to the former and opposed to the latter as being too risky for his mother.

He had prepared figures. He had had a visit from their banker. He explained that he and his sister had inherited two-thirds of the Brunamonti estate on their father's death. They each had a certain amount of money in long-term investments which, given the emergency, he could get access to quickly. A number of apartments which the Contessa had renovated and rented to tourists in long-ago hard times could be sold to the bank and would produce a substantial sum which he hoped might meet the ransom demand. If the worst came to the worst, they would have to raise money on the Palazzo Brunamonti itself. He and his sister were in a position to do this, since they owned two-thirds and had power of attorney whilst their mother held one-third and the usufruct.

The Marshal, who had never had anything more than his pay and whose father had left him a sick mother, nevertheless knew enough not to ask what that substantial sum might be or in which country their money was invested. It was his information that the Contessa had bought out her husband and gained complete control of the estate well before her husband's death but he made no comment on that either. Nor did he write anything down. Information like this was as elastic as the law governing its use.

'This is certainly an emergency situation' was all he said as they stood up to return to the white drawing room.

He had every reason to be satisfied with the timing of his visit. As they went back through the drawing room, the journalists, photographers, and Caterina were on their feet. She was very elegantly dressed in something longish and must, the Marshal thought, have given her face a bit of touching up because she looked much less pale. Under the circumstances, a compliment would be out of place so he contented himself with a kindly look and a murmured word of thanks for her cooperation under cover of the general move to the door.

'You're doing very well. You're very patient.' It hardly seemed necessary to make the point about the dog since she was evidently on top of the situation.

'They still want to take some shots down in the workshop. I'll follow them. I have to put something else on first.'

'Of course. It's very cold out. You'll need something warmer.'

There were too many of them to fit in the lift so the

Marshal walked down the stairs together with one of the journalists, Nesti, whom he had known for years.

'How's it going?' Nesti asked.

'We don't know much yet . . .'

'No.' Nesti lit a cigarette, his fat face sullen. 'We don't even know whether this is supposed to be a kidnapping or a career opportunity.'

They had reached the bottom of the stairs and Nesti went back to his colleagues without another word. The Marshal didn't understand him. They had known each other too long for Nesti to imagine his having any ambitions beyond his present rank. And this Prosecutor Fusarri, odd as he was, was known to have private means and to find his job a source of interest more than anything. The Captain, it was true, was ambitious. He had spoken at considerable length at the midday press conference about already having made considerable headway in the case and – this in very discreet terms – being determined that the carabinieri had the means at their disposal to deal with it. But, ambitious or not, the Marshal had a great respect for his seriousness and integrity. Nesti was pretty sound, as journalists go, but this time he was way off beam. If the Marshal had gone home vaguely uneasy yesterday evening, tonight he was thoroughly distressed.

'What's the matter with you?' was his wife's first remark, without even looking up from the cooker where she was tossing bread crumbs in olive oil.

'Nothing.'

Teresa sighed. He always turned up in the kitchen when he would be most in her way, and in all the years they had been married she had never given up trying to throw him out. The kitchen wasn't especially big and he took up a lot of room. However, the years had taught her that if he got out of uniform and showered before presenting himself, he was looking for a hug and a chance to sniff and taste whatever was for supper. The black, silent form she saw looming out of the corner of her eye meant trouble.

'Is it this Brunamonti case?'

'No. Yes. I don't know.'

She slid the fried bread crumbs into a bowl and went to the cupboard for olives and pasta.

'Do get out of my way, Salva.'

He shifted a few centimetres and stuck again.

'Why don't you go and watch the news?'

No answer.

'We're having *spaghetti alla mollica* . . .'

'Where are the boys?'

'In their room doing their homework, supposedly. You might as well call them. The water's boiling. Salva, please! You fetch up here like a beached whale just when I'm trying to get supper on the table. You could open a flask of wine at least . . . Have I put glasses out? I have . . . Out of my way. I don't know what gets into you. It's like talking to a wall when you're like this. Remind me to get spaghetti when we go to the supermarket. It's three for the price of two this week. Are you opening that flask or not?'

He stood drinking in the comforting sound of her voice and felt better.

'Now where are you going?'

'I thought I'd watch the news. What's for supper?'

By bedtime, as he checked that the shutters were secure against the wind, he was more himself. Spaghetti and red wine are great restorers of the soul. Even so, as he lay enjoying that most tranquil five minutes of all, stretched peacefully between the covers, as Teresa pottered back and forth, folding things and putting a little cream on her face and reporting on the children, some nameless unease was still twitching inside him. It wasn't anything big but something niggling. It wasn't clearly defined but formless and prickly.

'You know, Totò is really quite a lot cleverer than Giovanni, it's his attitude that's the trouble.'

He just couldn't put his finger on it . . .

'Pride has a lot to do with it as well, if you ask me. Giovanni knows he's slow and doesn't mind plodding along and asking for help when he needs it, whereas Totò likes to think he can get by without studying at all and it won't do. He's going to have to make an effort between now and June.'

'It's only February . . .'

'For goodness' sake, don't say that to him! A bit less arrogance and a bit more hard work is what's wanted. He's got to get it into his head that he has to study the same as everybody else.'

'Yes . . .' The same as everybody else. Was it the

unorthodox behaviour of Prosecutor Fusarri . . . no, hardly that. Even so, the knot of discomfort that made itself felt all the more now that he was lying quietly in bed seemed to have its origin in something to do with that train of thought . . . the Prosecutor, Captain Maestrangelo, Nesti.

Nesti – that remark about a career opportunity was really annoying but Nesti had only appeared on the scene today and whatever was wrong had been wrong before that. Right from the start, really. He oughtn't to feel so uncomfortable. He'd done all he had to do. Most important of all, he'd established real contact with the son. If he could do the same with Signor Hines he'd feel on safe ground.

'You won't forget, will you, Salva? You know what you are . . . you'll have a talk with him tomorrow?'

'Yes . . . yes. I'll have a word tomorrow.' Include him, tell him details about the car, the hideout, Salis, and the old Sardinian band – of course, that was something that might well be considered as a separate issue from what Fusarri had called babysitting. Out of his province.

'Salva, are you listening to me?'

'Yes, I'm listening.'

'What was I talking about?'

' Totò.'

'Oh . . .'

All his teachers used to say when he was a schoolboy, 'What was the last thing I said?' Absentminded though he was, he became an expert at dredging up the key word of the last sentence still hanging in the air when his ear was pounced on.

Ashamed of himself, he turned and pulled her close to him. 'I'm sorry. Tell me again.'

'What's the matter, Salva? You only get like this when something's really disturbing you. What is it?'

'I don't know, I really don't. It's nothing I can put my finger on, that's the trouble.'

'Kidnapping's a terrible crime. The thought of that poor woman . . .' She shivered. 'Who knows what conditions they're keeping her in, and in this freezing weather. There's such a wind.' They were silent a moment, listening to the moaning of the mountain wind, the soughing of the cypress trees in the Boboli Gardens, and the occasional bang of someone's unfastened shutter. 'It makes you realise just how lucky we are, safe and warm in our beds. Of course it's worse if it's a child – well, I think so anyway, and I'm sure any woman would rather be taken herself than have her child taken.'

'I suppose so, yes. Tell me again about Totò.'

They talked until late and he felt much better as he settled to sleep. It didn't last. At three in the morning he was tossing about, muttering, half asleep and dreaming. He was getting near to pinning the problem down. It was the missing dog, that was it! And the photographer . . . the photographer came into it somewhere. It was too late now. Nesti and his photographer had gone home long ago. He tossed and worried for a long time until he came to a solution so obvious it was absurd. They had their own photographer at Borgo Ognissanti, for goodness sake. He did the mug shots in his tiny studio, went out on scene-of-the-crime shoots. If anyone should have known that mug shot of Salis was out of date, he should. At this point, the best thing was to take the dog there. The photo, when it was developed, was odd, not what you would have expected. The dog's head hung down instead of resting back against the support that keeps heads straight for mug shots. Of course, it was badly injured and couldn't help it. There was a lot of blood round the mouth. Still, the shot was done, that was the main thing. The Marshal strained his eyes trying to read the name and number propped in front of it. He couldn't see so well because he was tired – no wonder, since it was the middle of the night and the wind still howling . . .

'Write it down.' That would be best, if he could find the light switch, get his notebook . . .

'Salva!'

'What?'

'You're hitting me in the face! What's going on?'

'Nothing, nothing . . . just had to write . . .'

He was asleep.

Six

'I've given up my course at university. I went to see the assistant professor this morning and told him. He was very nice about it but upset, too, because I'm one of his best students, probably the best he's ever had, but he understood when I told him we were going through such a difficult time.'

'But surely you'll go back after . . .' It was difficult for the Marshal to find a suitable ending to that sentence.

'How can I think of that? We don't know what's going to happen! If Olivia's dead, if she doesn't come back, I'll have to take over everything. I won't be able to think of my own studies.'

'But your brother . . .'

'Leo won't do it. I'm talking about the administration

of this house and of the rest of the Brunamonti property. Leo's very artistic but he thinks of nothing else, sitting over his computer drawings until all hours. He's always asleep during the hours when business has to be done. It will all fall to me.'

'Well . . .' The Marshal's eyes strayed to the large black-and-white photograph of her in her ballet dress over the desk. 'It's a very great pity, a very great pity indeed since you gave up your dancing to study. Could you take that up again? Even now . . . some exercise, some distraction, it would do you good. It doesn't help and it's bad for you to be shut in here the whole time.'

She turned her head away and observed him with that sideways glance, her erect body perfectly still as she spoke.

'Classical dancing isn't about exercise and distraction. The best pupils are skimmed off and put into the professional course, which means lessons five days a week plus rehearsals when there's a public performance in preparation. I had to give up, as many others did, because of the demands of university. The ballet mistress, who was once a prima ballerina herself, was furious about it. It's understandable, of course. She's trying to set up a company, and when she's trained someone for years and they leave . . . She barely speaks to me if I see her in the street now. But I couldn't have made a career of it. It would hardly have been suitable for me. And now, because of this, I won't be able to study either.'

'You mustn't be too pessimistic. It may take time but I'm sure you'll have your mother home again. How did you get on with your visit to the Prosecutor's office this morning?'

'He hardly spoke a word to me. He was only interested in Patrick and that detective he insisted on bringing from London. They're staying in the same hotel. Personally, I see no need for it. Patrick normally stays here.'

The Marshal, remembering the frothy, transparent white garment and weeping Silvia's remark, had assumed that was so but made no comment.

'But the Prosecutor did explain that he's set up a television spot on the news for you both?'

'Yes, he did. Patrick's going to be with us but the Prosecutor said Leo and I should do the talking. I thought a plea for my mother's safety would be better coming from me. I don't know what I should wear. I want to get it right and Leo's no help at all.'

The Marshal was no help, either.

'Oh well, I'll ask Patrick.'

She wore black. A very simple black suit. No jewellery except the usual ring, which she twisted incessantly as Leonardo Brunamonti spoke. Then the camera focused entirely on her. She turned her head sideways with a little jerk and eyed the camera with that alarmed, sideways look, as though it might attack her.

'Poor young thing. She's too upset to speak,' Teresa commented, joining her husband on the sofa for the late news and handing him a cup of camomile tea.

Patrick Hines's shoulder was just visible in the frame as he must have tried to rouse her to speech. The interviewer was thrown but tried to recoup the situation.

'Your brother, Leonardo, has given his message to your mother's kidnappers, begging them to get in touch with you and let you know if your mother is alive and well, which we all sincerely hope she is. But I think you had your own personal message, Signorina . . . ah . . . Signorina Brunamonti?'

The rigid torso, the sideways stare. Silence.

'She's terrified,' the Marshal said. 'I'd be the same in front of telecameras, but she managed so well with the press photographers that I thought she'd be all right.'

'You don't have to speak, though, do you?' Teresa pointed out. 'Not for a photograph . . . Look, they're going back to the brother.'

Leonardo begged whoever was holding his mother to treat her well and respect her as they would their own mothers. Patrick Hines was shown briefly as a friend of the family's there to help, which effectively eliminated him as the recipient of the ransom note. No carabinieri appeared in the piece but the kidnappers would know enough to assume this could have been set up by the Prosecutor. In fact, eliminating him was what the Prosecutor had in mind. He didn't care for this private detective idea, though the detective himself he rather liked.

'I assure you I intend to operate within the law,' the detective said, 'and that my presence will in no way affect your investigation. I should merely be regarded as a friend of the family – or, I should say, a more than usually well-informed friend of the family.'

'Delighted to,' returned Fusarri, 'but in so regarding you I feel obliged to point out that friends of the family, unlike the family, do not enjoy the exemption from prosecution under Law Eighty-Two, which freezes the Brunamonti assets and forbids any unsupervised payment of a ransom.'

'A well-informed friend of the family,' the detective repeated without emphasis. He was a big man, muscular, with short hair, neatly combed. He wore a thick dark blue overcoat, a regimental tie. He worked for a London agency but Fusarri saw at a glance that he had spent years with the Secret Service and said so.

'MI6, yes.' Though peaceable at the moment, there was an edge to his voice that said he would become dangerous if annoyed. Fusarri did not annoy him. He offered him a cigar and made the Marshal step forward and be introduced, happy in his conviction that no amount of years in the Service would prepare anyone to cope with Guarnaccia's bulging-eyed silences.

The newspapers that day ran two full pages on the Brunamonti kidnapping with a picture of Olivia Birkett in her heyday as a model. An article recounted her arrival in Italy for an Italian course at one of the many American schools in Florence and her being approached by a fashion house to model for them. She had never returned to America and, after a few successful years as a model, had married Conte Ugo Brunamonti. The photographs of the daughter, though taken in the white drawing room and the courtyard of the palazzo, were suitably trimmed and focused so as to avoid giving information about the property and general wealth of the family. She was quoted as saying that their circumstances were limited and that she hoped unreasonable demands would not be made which they had no hope of meeting. Asked for a message to her mother she said they were doing everything, *everything*, that it was possible to do.

'That's a lovely photo of her,' Teresa remarked, folding the page to look more closely. 'Is it a good likeness? She looked different just now on the news.'

'Good enough. She'd have done better not to wear that fancy fur coat while saying their circumstances were limited.'

'Mm . . . It's not suited to a young girl, anyway. Her mother's perhaps.'

'Probably my fault. It was a cold day and I told her to put on something warm. Still, even a fur a bit less glamorous would have done – or a loden, even better. Limited circumstances . . .'

'Is she not very intelligent?'

'Oh no. Apparently one of the best students her professor's ever had, though she's decided she has to abandon her studies because of what's happened.'

'That's a shame. Still, she can always take them up again when this is over. Let's hope it ends well. What do you think, Salva?'

'There's no saying. No contact. It's bothering the Captain because he says it's a power game, making the family wait so long to prove they're not in a hurry, have no worries.'

'And is that what's been bothering you, too, for days? Give me your cup . . . I think we should have an early night . . .'

The early night helped. Though he slept undisturbed and remembered no dreams, he had a sense of having been sorting things out during the night. It often happened that he knew he was staring something in the face and not seeing it and this always had the effect of making him grumpy and introverted, at least so he was told. The best cure was a quiet, rather dull day in his own little office, away from officers, prosecutors, and the Brunamonti family, and that was what was on his timetable, for the morning.

At eight o'clock he was behind his desk and by twelve he had received a woman who said she had been threatened by two electricians who had done a bad job rewiring her house and still wanted payment, an elderly man who wanted a reference for a gun permit as he intended to shoot to kill next time some lout attacked and robbed him outside his own door, and a boy whose moped had been stolen. When they had all gone away feeling better, he felt better himself.

'Ah,' he sighed quietly, as one source of anxiety extricated itself from the general unease. An empty dog kennel, *'you'd have done better not to mention the dog . . . ,'* *'with the trouble he's already in . . . ,'* *'no shepherd boy will work for them, not now.'*

The Marshal sat for a while, mulling this over.

A man like Salis, even when he wasn't a wanted man and in hiding, spent half his time on the road, shifting stolen sheep up and down the Apennine trail, trafficking in stolen weapons and vehicles. He kept a shepherd boy, they all did. His wife made the cheese, life went on, and his cover was secure. If he was inside, the same. When he was on the run, the same.

'*Not now.*'

The Marshal tried to reach Captain Maestrangelo and was dismayed to hear that he had gone out to the country to start a house-to-house search and that Criminalpol had been brought in. The Marshal all but hung up before the end of this bad news. It was inevitable, he knew that. All suspect households would be checked for missing members. Somebody was taking food up to the hills and somebody besides Salis was up there guarding the victim. As Bini said, there were ways and ways of doing this checking, and police ways were not carabinieri ways, especially as the carabinieri had to go on living with the country people when the police had gone back to the city.

'And, besides, it's not them,' muttered the Marshal to himself. 'It's not them because it's not Salis. The dog . . .' He'd known the dog was what was wrong but before he'd been able to ask Bini about it that woman had flagged them down and started on about the other dog. And now, where to start? The facts. Get the facts.

Francesco Salis was wanted, as his criminal record

stated, but not because, like Puddu, he'd escaped when on parole. He had served his last sentence, going grey in prison, and as Bini had said, he hadn't sat for another mug shot because they'd never caught him for his latest job. Salis was wanted for the murder of a shepherd boy.

When he got out to the country, the Marshal found Maestrangelo already fraught with repressed anger. It was hopeless. Upset one family and a whole clan turned against you. More than one family had been upset. The Captain felt responsible for what he couldn't control. It wasn't his style of doing things. It also didn't work.

'If I had the men I need . . .'

The Marshal's news was both bad and good. Bad because these householders had been wrongfully disturbed. Good because, far from damaging the investigation, it was exactly the right course – and one it would have been difficult to justify the expense of, had they wanted to do it deliberately. The Salis trail was false, as the Marshal now understood, but this search, carried out in good faith, would serve to satisfy the real culprits and annoy Salis, who might, if they could make contact, be angry enough to help them catch the enemy who had set him up.

They drove back to the village and visited Bini. He didn't tell the Captain any jokes but he did make his complaint about having to live with the people round those parts after this was over. The Captain pointed out, reasonably enough, that the sooner it was over the better for everyone concerned and got him sufficiently focused

128

to give an account of the shepherd boy's murder. Bini could tell them what no official documentation could tell them: who they were dealing with and what their motivation might be.

During the time Francesco Salis was in prison, his flock had first been tended by a cousin of his who had later returned to Sardinia, where he had inherited a bit of land on the death of his mother. His place had been taken by Antonio Vargiu, a nephew of Francesco's, a teenager, newly arrived, as the saying goes, 'on the continent'. This nephew hadn't been on the scene for long before there was trouble. Francesco's wife soon noticed that the boy was neglecting his work and had been seen in the village bar consorting with members of a rival clan. The boy had a heroin habit which he was trying to hide from his own family. He was being supplied by the rival clan and paying with sheep abstracted from Francesco's flock. Stolen sheep, though earmarked, are never recovered, unless incidentally. They do sometimes turn up during the search for a kidnap victim but have been transported so far from home on the trail between Bologna and Rome that their owners are unlikely to be identified.

The Salis clan moved in to punish the boy and his suppliers but all that resulted was a knifing incident in the village bar which failed to put a stop to the trafficking. Salis was released from prison, fully informed. He supped and slept and rose in the misty dawn to take down his rifle from behind the door and aim it at the traitorous boy's heart as he slept in the fold. But the boy was young and agile and fear had kept him alert as he slept. The first shot hit his shoulder as he rolled away and leapt to his feet. He ran out to the farmyard, hoping to escape on his moped. The next shot ricocheted off the moped and Salis had all the time he needed, as the boy tried to kick the damp motor into life, to reload and shoot the boy twice between the shoulder blades.

Before it was fully light he had transported the boy's body over the hills in the back of his old cut-off car and dumped it on the rival clan's land. Given the earlier knifing incident, Bini knew all about the matter and had no hesitation in setting out to arrest Salis. He found a great deal of blood in the yard, a moped, and a tight-lipped wife. Salis was gone and had never been seen since. Francesco's wife didn't hold with kidnapping but she clearly had no serious worries about this one. What she had been afraid of when Bini and the Marshal turned up was that her husband, if found during the resulting searches, would be charged with the boy's murder. So she clammed up when the Marshal mentioned the dog.

'Do you have any proof of Salis's guilt? asked the Captain. 'I mean concrete proof, apart from the blood.'

'I don't have the blood,' Bini said. 'It was August. Before the forensic people got here there was a storm. Sheets of rain that made every ditch and stream overflow and flooded the lanes. No, I've no blood. All I've got is a dog. Like Guarnaccia here, when I went to question his wife, the day of the murder, that was what struck me. The sheep in the fold and an empty kennel. A shepherd has a dog. I said to her, I said, "Where's the dog?" and she said, "It's dead." According to her, her husband had shot the dog, had to put it down because it was sick. I asked her where it was buried. She showed me and I had it dug up. They did an autopsy. The dog had been shot, all right, but it hadn't been ill. And the weapon used was the one that killed the boy. It was the bullet that had ricocheted off the moped, you see. I've got evidence. That dog's still in the fridge at the medico-legal institute.'

'Surely he knew,' the Captain said, 'that you'd find the dog.'

'Of course he did,' Bini said, 'and he couldn't have counted on that storm, either, but he did nothing to hide all that blood. Salis is a bandit of the old school, you have to understand that. According to him, he had the right to do what he did and no reason to hide it. He dumped the body on the Puddu clan because the boy had betrayed him to them and, as far as he was concerned, they could keep him. He'd die in those hills before he'd let behaviour like theirs go unpunished. I know him. He's proud and he's strict in his code.'

The Captain refrained from wishing aloud that Bini had spoken up before. It would hardly have been just. Nobody had confided in Bini that there had been a second suspect, other than Salis, and that this suspect was the head of the rival clan, Giuseppe Puddu, who the year previously had escaped while on parole. All he said was, 'And Puddu? What do you know about him?'

'No, no, Puddu . . . No. A man like Salis you can

follow his way of thinking but Puddu's got involved with all sorts of people, mixed up with Tuscans, money-lenders, mafia, too, in my opinion. No, Puddu forgot he was a Sardinian years ago. It's not a bad thing, is it, that after today's search he'll think he's pulled the wool over your eyes? You ought to ask Francesco Salis what he thinks about Puddu but, as far as I'm concerned, he should be put away for life. It seems to me a bit too easy for some people, this parole business after serving half their time. They plan their next job inside, and the minute they're out the door they vanish and we've another kidnapping on our hands.'

'So it seems,' the Captain said.

The Marshal drove back to Florence, leaving the Captain to call off the search of Salis's territory at the end of the day and explain the new development to the Prosecutor.

So much for the empty kennel. But one dead dog lying in the fridge at the medico-legal institute wasn't the end of it, as far as what the Marshal called his 'day of dogs' was concerned. He paid his regular visit to the Palazzo Brunamonti towards seven in the evening and found Leonardo and Patrick Hines – not, thank goodness, the detective – sitting on the white sofa, bending over something that lay on the floor between them. Silvia the maid, crying rather more than usual, let the Marshal in and disappeared.

'She's come home,' Leonardo said, looking up with shining eyes. 'Tessie . . .'

On the floor between the two men was a basket. The little sandy mongrel lay in it in a state of collapse. Leonardo was gently washing away the encrusted blood from her mouth and giving her water from a dropper. There was gauze round all four feet. She was too weak to lift her head or even open her mouth but as the drops of cool water slid in between her teeth and rolled over her parched tongue, her tiny tail made a feeble attempt at wagging her gratitude.

'She's a mass of injuries,' Patrick Hines said. 'Heaven alone knows how she managed to drag herself home. She couldn't get up the stairs and was trying to get near the fountain. She can't have had a drink for days, let alone food. I found the people from the workroom standing round her when I arrived and they carried her up here on a piece of cloth. She has more than one bone broken, I should think, and the pads on her feet are completely worn away and bleeding.'

The Marshal stood looking down at the little rag of fur and bone, the flesh all gone but the spirit still capable of a tiny wag of the tail. She looked so fragile, so racked with pain, that he wouldn't have dared stroke her with his big clumsy hand. All he could do was ask, 'Doesn't she need a vet?'

'She's too weak,' Leonardo said. 'She needs water and peace and a night's rest before she can be properly examined and X-rayed. It could damage her now. I'm sure she'll live. She's got to live!'

He got up to go and get clean warm water for bathing

the wounds. When he was out of the room, Patrick Hines told the Marshal that the dog's return was a blessing in more ways than one because it gave them something concrete to do for Olivia instead of sitting around helpless. 'And I speak for myself as well as Leo in that.'

'It's very understandable. You'll feel less in limbo when contact is made.' The Marshal, though he regarded Charles Bently, the detective from London, as though he were a creature from an alien planet, rather admired Patrick Hines. He was a tall, well-built man, athletic looking, grey-haired and blue-eyed. He was quiet and he was discreet and, from what the Marshal knew of Olivia Birkett's past, the ideal man for her. It seemed, too, as though his presence there gave the son considerable relief.

Loud sobbing announced the imminent arrival of Silvia. The Marshal and Hines exchanged a glance and the latter murmured, 'Thank goodness she has a married sister nearby. I think she's going there tonight.'

The sobbing girl came into the room and wailed from behind a paper tissue that the signorina wanted to speak to the Marshal. She seemed to expect him to follow her so he did, not to the signorina's room but to her mother's.

The room was bathed in a soft, glowing light from some invisible source, and this time the big bed looked as though it had been slept in. The pillows were bunched at the centre of the headboard and the counterpane flung over the foot. Perhaps the daughter had sought comfort in her distress by sleeping there to feel nearer her mother.

A pile of clothing lay in the centre of the bed, and all the wardrobes and drawers were open. A small, decorated writing desk was also open and a great many papers were strewn on it.

'You can leave now, Silvia. I'm sorry there's nowhere to sit down, Marshal, but as you can see – Silvia, you can go.'

'I am making supper, Philippine supper. Mister Patrick ask me—'

'You can go.'

Silvia's response to what the Marshal supposed to be an evening with her sister to cheer her up suggested that it didn't help. She left the room crying loudly, and a diminishing series of 'my signoras' reached them as she retreated down the long corridor.

The daughter apologised yet again for the disorder. It seemed early to be doing the seasonal changeover, an event which most women dread, with all its hard work of climbing up to high, little-used cupboards and endless trips to and from the dry cleaner's with the winter clothes. The Marshal himself disliked the business because a chilly, rainy spell invariably set in as soon as it was done, necessitating the search for parcelled-up sweaters and an ensuing stink of mothballs.

He was about to comment on this prematurity but stopped himself in time. The wardrobes lining all the walls of the room surely accommodated four seasons, the changeover being a question chiefly of the restricted space that went with a restricted income. The thought also crossed his mind that, pessimistic as the daughter always seemed to be, she was doing something of the sort on the assumption that her mother was unlikely to be with them before winter was over. In this she was probably right. She confirmed his idea by saying, as she moved a fur over to a pile of them at the end of the bed, 'These may as well go into refrigeration since they're not being worn. And there's a lot of stuff Olivia had been intending to take to the Red Cross shop and never found the time. I thought I ought to see to it.'

'It's very sensible of you to keep busy. The little dog seems to be keeping your brother and Mister Hines occupied.'

'Oh yes, I know they're fussing round her but she needs to be taken to the vet. I'll take her tomorrow. What I wanted to talk to you about was this private detective from London. Have you met him?'

'Once.'

'What did you think of him?'

'I . . . well, his Italian's very good and he seems well informed.'

'But what use is he?'

'To us? None at all. He can only be useful to you in dealing with the kidnappers when the time comes.'

'Excuse me, but aren't you here to do that?'

'Yes, I am. But I can't prevent you—'

'Me? My brother and Patrick! Have you any idea what he's going to cost us?'

'I don't . . . It's not something . . .' Surely she wasn't

taking all that transparent white stuff to the Red Cross . . .
hadn't the maid said—

'He's costing a fortune. A four-star hotel, heavy daily
expenses, and a fee you wouldn't believe. I want you to
speak to Leo and Patrick. I've been going through my
mother's private accounts so that I can deal with anything
that comes up. She's been pouring money into her
business in the last year and we just can't afford this
waste. It is waste, given that you're here, isn't it? Surely
we'll need all the money we can manage to get together if
we have to pay a ransom?'

'That's true but I don't think I can—'

'I want you to speak to them. They'll have to agree
that the ransom money's more important. I read all
those articles about kidnapping in the papers today. You
need contacts, informers, phones tapped, men in
disguise hidden out in the hills, not that fat creature
with his greasy hair eating his head off at our expense in
a first-class hotel. It's true, isn't it?'

'Yes, Signorina, it's true. But remember that all those
things are being done for your mother anyway and that if
Mister Hines and your brother feel more comfortable
having this man here too, then they will cope better with
the stress that's yet to come. Try not to upset yourself over
it. As long as, at the end of the day, you have your mother
home, nothing else is of serious importance, now is it?'

'He doesn't even seem to be very intelligent. I've talked
to him twice, and when I saw him this morning he
couldn't even remember my Christian name.'

The Marshal decided to excuse himself before his own intelligence was put to the test. He left her lifting and discarding evening dresses that glittered softly in the diffused light, none too sure of her name – though by now he'd written it down in his notebook – but very sure of one thing: right though she was about the detective's being superfluous, he had no intention of speaking to her brother about it. He couldn't afford to alienate him.

His last call of the day was on his Captain. He found him out of sorts, as was to be expected, now that the powers that be had taken control of the case from him. A lesser man, and there were many such in the army, seeing himself deprived in advance of any credit should the case be solved, would tread water and turn his real attention to something he would get credit for. As it was, though his face was drawn and he sent for a glass of water to take a headache pill while the Marshal was with him, he didn't even take this opportunity of getting his frustration off his chest. The Marshal wondered that he could even find time to receive him, never having understood the calming and supportive effect he had on his commanding officer. It was likely that, had the Captain properly understood it himself and tried to communicate it, the result would have been an uncomprehending stare. Their interdependence was as deep-rooted as it was unacknowledged.

The Captain's news, once the Marshal's latest dog report had been made, was that his men were now working overtime on the whereabouts of all Puddu's associates and, in particular, on any contacts he might have made in prison who could have given him information about the Brunamontis.

'The workforce,' said the Marshal. 'I only glanced in there but I suppose you've . . .'

'Clean as a whistle, all of them. Why? Do the family suspect something on those lines?'

'No, no. I got the impression, just at a glance, you know, that they were very loyal and united . . .'

'But?'

The Marshal examined the hat on his knees, his left shoe, the painting on the wall facing him. 'There's something . . .'

The Captain restrained himself from prompting or questioning.

'I don't know. I felt right from the start that there was *something*, but I couldn't quite . . . and then, you see, there was the business of the dogs and that – but of course it couldn't be anything like that bothering me . . . No, you see, it was right from the start . . . "Her ladyship", they called her, and it didn't seem right to me. I'm not well up in these things – you'd know better – but would you think it the correct thing? To refer to the Contessa as "her ladyship" like that?'

'I would say not, but—'

The Marshal went on, slow and inexorable as a steamroller. 'And in that tone of voice. It was that bothered me more than anything.'

The Captain sat listening, turning a pen slowly between his fingers on the polished desk, well aware that

Guarnaccia in this mood was only using him to bounce images off.

'There's something wrong,' the Marshal declared at last, 'something in the family but you can't fault any of them individually – I'm including Hines.'

'As family?'

'Something the maid said. He and Olivia Birkett are lovers but he's discreet. Some men might act like they owned the place. He's in a hotel, though he spends the day there with the young people, sometimes with the detective chap, sometimes without.'

'But you do feel they're still cooperating? You've no worries there?'

'Yes and no. They're not agreed between themselves, you see, so I do have to be careful not to be seen to take sides.'

Given the Marshal's Sicilian background, the Captain had no worries on that score, but all he said was, 'I've got a couple of men hidden up on Puddu's territory on the lookout for feeders, changes of guard, and so on. Helicopters are going over tomorrow, though they'll see nothing. Puddu's an expert at his job.'

'Useful, perhaps, if the victim hears them.'

The Captain shook his head. 'Timing's wrong. It's something you can do in the first two or three days when your victim's still counting and then in the last few days between the ransom and release. There's a chance then of the victim's remembering the timing and direction, which can help to pinpoint the hide-out. Flying this way and that at random—' He checked himself, and his only other observation was 'Good for public relations. The TV news cameras will be there. No, it's the planner we want, Guarnaccia. Stick to the family, there must be a link, however tenuous. Has the daughter a boyfriend?'

'She hasn't mentioned one and she never seems to go out. The only man she's mentioned, apart from her late father, is a photographer who seemed to think a lot of her, from what she said, and her university professor . . .' Photographs . . . there was something about photographs connected with his irremovable unease. He opened his mouth to speak and shut it again in embarrassment as he remembered his ridiculous dream about a mug shot of the battered dog. Blood around its mouth, which Leonardo had been washing off that evening. But hadn't Nesti been in some way connected with that unhappy train of thought? Nesti had thought the Captain was making a career opportunity out of the case. Well, Criminalpol had put paid to anything of that sort. Besides, Nesti was wrong there, quite wrong, might even say so next time he turned up. The Captain was a good man, a serious man who would do his duty on this case no matter what.

The Captain, seeing that nothing further was to be got out of Guarnaccia that evening, let him go and got on with doing just that.

It was as well that the Marshal was driven back over to the Pitti Palace by one of his carabinieri because he was still lost to the world, running images through his head, stopping them occasionally to check on a detail, rerun the dialogue.

'Her ladyship' . . . 'her ladyship wouldn't have it and that was that' . . . what? Ah yes, the labels with Brunamonti on them. Well, why should she have it? Her own name was Birkett and her marriage hadn't brought her much luck. She'd started work in spite of it . . . A Brunamonti wife doesn't go out to work. Hm. So why that tone of voice? 'Her ladyship.' No, no. It didn't fit. The Captain must find out, somebody competent. What the Marshal could do with was some friend of the family, not too involved, someone who knew all the gossip, preferably a woman because men tended to be hopeless about that sort of thing. Teresa now, if she'd known the family, would have known everything, and here he was, practically living with them and couldn't say whether the daughter – whatshername – had a boyfriend. If it came to that, Teresa might even know! She'd read that stuff at the hairdresser's and wasn't that just the sort of thing magazines would be interested in?

It was. She hadn't a boyfriend. Teresa was creaming her face at bedtime.

'Not as far as I remember, anyway, but that was months ago, you know. She could have found a young man since then.'

'Was her picture in the article, too, or just her mother's?'

'Just her mother's. The article was about her.'

'Which magazine was it?'

'*Style*. A glossy, quite expensive.'

'I'll order a copy. I'd like to see it.'

'Mm. Switch your light out. Have you noticed something?'

'Is it a new nightdress you've got on?'

'Of course it's not. I've had it for years. You are incredible. They should have women doing investigative work, d'you know that?'

'Yes.' After a while he added, 'I'm not an investigator. I just try and help people find their mopeds.'

'And their mothers.'

'That's the Captain's business. I just chat to the family, keep them cooperating. Anyway, what was I supposed to notice?'

'Listen. The wind's dropped.'

Seven

'That morning, for the first time, my face wasn't cut by the icy wind the moment I put my head out of the tent. I had become used to it and even looked forward to it because it was a contact, a presence I could feel, a strong, exhilarating touch that penetrated my isolation in a dark undersea world. And then the freezing cold made me glad to crawl back into my prison and snuggle into the residual warmth between my sleeping bag and coat. But that morning when I crawled out, there was a sense of emptiness. The air smelled quite different, earthy and damp. It was much warmer. After the morning routine, I sat at the entrance of the tent with my legs outside and my boots on. This was a recent victory. I had been so careful and quiet and obedient that I was given my boots each morning and the chain padlocked over them so that I could go outside instead of using the bedpan inside the tent. I followed my chain, pulling it taut until I reached my tree and they brought the bedpan. I don't know how to make you understand what that meant to me but, believe me, it gave me back the sense of being a human being which I had been losing. I took with me wads of toilet paper and wet paper napkins to clean myself and my hands. If it didn't bother me much to do all this in front of whoever was guarding me, that's probably because I couldn't see anything or hear much and so felt enclosed in a private world. Afterwards I sat with my feet outside the tent and had breakfast. They had never given me milky coffee with bread again, the one thing that was easy for me to swallow, after the first two or three days. I suppose they couldn't be bothered feeding it to me, and the one time I had asked them to let me try alone I spilled almost all of it. I remember it rolling down my neck and slopping onto my chest. I had no other clothes then. It was only much later that they brought me a tracksuit.

'So, that morning, it was the rubbery bread and hard Parmesan again that was still so difficult for me to get down. The worst of it was that I couldn't spend long trying to chew it because they wanted to get on and would take it from me. Even so, it was a luxury to sit almost outside the tent and breathe the clean air. I was careful not to turn my face to the sky, searching for the morning sun, because this was seen as "detective work" by them and the one time I tried it my head was slapped down.

145

'Another victory: the heavy chain on my ankle was always kept much too tight and after some days I was pretty sure there was a wound there. I asked Woodcutter to look at it one morning and he brought something to put on it next day. He also put plastic tubing on the chain – like you use on a bicycle – and some padding and plasters on my ankle. Why couldn't they just keep it less tight? It was ridiculous. I decided then that the next things I would try for were an apple or something, anything fresh to eat – I needed vitamins – and a little piece of soap. I had waited my chance and talked to Woodcutter when he was alone. Up to now I had only requested the apple. One thing at a time. Soap was less important.

'I had worked out, by this time, that there were usually two of them present in the evening but that Woodcutter was there most often. I also knew, though he never came near me, that there was a boss of whom all of them were afraid. I knew this because sometimes when I asked Woodcutter for some new concession he would speak with his lips to my bandaged ear and say, "Can't. Boss's orders." I was quite sure he was telling the truth.

'I worked out other things, too. For instance, my hearing, adapting to the plugs, began to discern things and recognised their new, muffled quality.

'*Plaff! Plaff! plaff!* A noise like the wax falling into my ears, but distant. Hunters! No wonder my captors hadn't hesitated to signal each other with rifles. Remembering our arrival here on hands and knees, I realised that they were probably hunting wild boar and would certainly

146

have a pack of dogs with them. I spent, or wasted, hours imagining their coming across this hide-out by accident, led by curious dogs. I invented a dozen scenarios which resulted in my being saved. I even decided the precise moment at which I could risk calling out, "Help me! I'm here! Help me!" But my real world overturned the invented one each time for two reasons: The first was that should they spot this encampment, even see my armed captors, they would surely think it was a group of other hunters and move away to a patch of their own; the other, which is more difficult to explain, was that I had promised good behaviour and silence to Woodcutter as a necessary requisite of my survival, which he guaranteed in turn. Had the hunters discovered me in the first few days I would have screamed my heart out. Not any more. They had subdued me. I had given my word. I would remain silent. *Plaff! Plaff! plaff!* On those days they were edgy, all of them, including Woodcutter. After a while I recalled that hunting was prohibited on Tuesdays and Fridays. I have never hunted but we have a small cottage in the country and I only ever let Tessie run around free on non-hunting days. I've known so many dogs shot, some by accident, some on purpose. Non-hunting days were the ones when I would take care to sense the period when Woodcutter was alone, partly for the human comfort and partly so as to gain more small concessions.

'It was about the time when I understood about the hunters that there was an improvement in the food. Woodcutter explained to me that when the mistake of taking me instead of my daughter was discovered, there had been a lot of quarrelling and economic difficulties. He didn't give me any details, for obvious reasons; he just kept saying, "It's a right cock-up."

'Then, at some point, the boss had adapted himself to the new situation and, I suppose, decided to invest a few thousand lire in keeping me alive. I should say in keeping us all alive because my guards ate and drank what I ate and drank, which, for the whole first period, was nothing but bread, Parmesan, wine, and water. Then, one late morning, a wonderful odour of cooking filtered into my tent, and when the zip went up and I presented myself at the opening, my tray held a plate of something hot. It was spaghetti with tomato sauce! The scent which had reached me before was the garlic frying in olive oil for the sauce. Woodcutter placed a spoon in my right hand.

' "I've cut it up for you. It would get stone-cold if you tried to eat it with a fork. The flask is here on your right."

' "Thank you." Spaghetti and red wine! It was inevitable that I wasn't able to eat much, even though the first scent of it had awakened something of an appetite and dissolved the lump of terror that had been blocking my throat. By now, I just wanted to live, even if I had to live like this. I tried desperately to get it all down so as to show gratitude. Otherwise they might not bother again and I had to have enough nourishment. It tasted wonderful but my jaw was soon hurting, my ears in agony, my shrunken stomach protesting.

' "You're an excellent cook," I enthused to

148

Woodcutter, wanting to be forgiven for not finishing the food, not wanting him to sneer at the rich bitch. "The scent of this tomato sauce awoke my appetite for the first time." Did he understand? He didn't sneer at me. He wasn't angry, either, when I explained that my stomach had shrunk and that I'd need time to get used to eating normally.

'As I sat now with my tray beside me, awaiting orders to go in, I smelled coffee. Toasty coffee, hot and fresh on the morning air! I was overwhelmed by feelings of nostalgia for mornings at home, the news on the radio, Caterina's soft tangles of hair, her crumpled white silk dressing gown. The feeling was so acute that I refused the coffee itself, saying to Woodcutter, "You have it all. Just the smell of it is enough for me."

'I really meant it. I was quite content without, but he answered me curtly, "There's enough for everybody. Once it's made, it's made."

'He didn't understand. How could he? The hot cup was put into my hand and I drank. Then he put something else in my hand. An apple! I needed vitamins but I could hardly bear to begin eating it. I sniffed at it, pressed its smooth, cold skin to my cheek, imagined its colour – I felt sure it was a Granny Smith. I nursed it until it became warm in my hands, and thought of my student days in upstate New York where the autumn meant wet fallen leaves along the country roads and barrows from which mountains of crisp, juicy red apples and jars of cider and cider vinegar were sold. How ignorant I was then of the sad realities of the world. I tried to imagine what it would have meant to me if I'd read in the papers of some woman being kidnapped far away in Italy and kept chained to a tree by bandits.

'Nothing, of course. It would have had no reality just as that faraway world of my student days had no reality now. It had the quality of a dream, of something I had observed, the way we observe ourselves doing things in dreams rather than being the protagonist. If I ever returned to the normal world again I would have to put the two broken selves back together, myself before, myself after this episode. In the meantime I must concentrate on survival and that meant on detail, on small victories, on my apple. I ate the whole thing except for the stalk, which I plucked off. I ate the core and chewed the pips, which tasted like almonds. I wanted to do this but there was also an element of show in it. Again, I didn't want to be the rich bitch whose only way of eating an apple was to peel and slice it with silver cutlery in some elegant restaurant. It was true that I had been eating apples that way ever since I married, but in those sunny student autumns we bit into their crispness like children and the juice trickled down our chins. I did this now, though I had to nibble rather than bite because of the pain it caused me to open my jaws. They noticed and they sensed the falseness of my eating the core. Woodcutter was watching me, I could feel it.

' "You don't normally eat the core, what's that about?"

' "It tastes good, the pips taste of almonds. I ate apples

this way as a child and at university, too. I was in a place where they grew wonderful apples."

'When the apple was finished, since nobody had yet told me to go inside, I sat on in the fresh air, thinking about my university days. I tried to remember the names of my fellow students but couldn't, except for two or three. I had lost touch with all of them, with America altogether, in a way, except through my new persona as a businesswoman. So this imprisonment wasn't the only fracture in my life. Leaving America, divorce . . . They happen without our noticing and so we don't try to mend them. Perhaps I should think of trying to put all of my life back into one whole. Perhaps that's the real reason for my wanting to show in New York. I put this idea to one side to look at later during my thinking time in the tent. As long as I was outside I wanted to enjoy remembering my university days. I had very little recollection of studying but I suppose I must have worked occasionally since I got through. It wasn't at all difficult, not like here. My stomach felt a stab of anxiety as I wondered if I'd done wrong in encouraging Caterina to enrol in the Faculty of Letters. It isn't easy in Florence. It's overcrowded, disorganised, long-winded. She has only scraped through one exam out of a possible five in a year and a half so it already looks as if it was a mistake, decided on in a hurry to distract her from the disappointment about dancing . . .

'A tap on my shoulder. Time to go back inside.

'"Thank you for the apple. Not just because it was delicious but because an apple or any other fresh fruit or greens will help me stay healthy, which is as important for you as it is for me, don't you think?"

' "That's enough. Take your boots off."

'The daily routine, morning ablutions, feeding, back inside, an attempt at flexing and stretching my muscles, thinking time, feeding, into the tent again, long thinking time, the chain and padlock on my wrist, sleeping bag, night, never varied. I didn't want it to, unless the variation was my release. In the meantime, the routine was all, my civilisation, my comfort. I greeted Woodcutter in the mornings and said goodnight to him each evening. He almost always answered me. Only occasionally was he curt, usually because of some disagreement with one of the other two or with the mysterious boss. I think eating the apple made me consider, for the first time, what a problem it must be to get supplies to such a remote place. I appreciated having mineral water and paper napkins and now even pasta. I thought, too, that the mystery of their insistence on rules of hygiene while never allowing me to wash myself properly was easily solved. Probably there was no source of water near at hand. An area that did have a stream would be frequented by wild boar and consequently by hunters. Until then I had only considered my own plight but from then on I had a clearer idea of theirs and began to take more notice. Not that my opinion of them on a personal level altered. I was still afraid of Butcher, still aware of the waves of hatred that came from him and his potential violence, which only Woodcutter's presence curbed. The little claw-fingered one I called Fox often tried to play tricks on me and I was determined not to react. I hated the smell of him and especially disliked taking my food from him. Inevitably, my exaggerated gratitude on being given something different to eat was grist for his mill. One evening, as I sat at the entrance of the tent waiting to be fed, he came close and got hold of my right hand.

' "Here's another treat for you, something different to eat."

'I was very wary since he'd done this before and Woodcutter had snatched the food from me before it reached my mouth. That time it had been a packaged square of cream cheese, thickly covered in green mould, he told me later. This time he put something warm in my hand and pushed my hand to my mouth. The distorted noise of his loud sniggers reached me as I recoiled from his penis with a gasp of dismay.

'Then his voice whispered close to my sea-roaring ear, "What's up, don't you like it in the mouth? Want me to lick yours instead?"

'It was one of the rare days when Woodcutter was absent, and I sweated in terror at the thought of what Fox and Butcher could do to me. But I think that Woodcutter was in command and answered directly to the boss for my well-being and they respected this when he was absent. More than once he had reminded me that I should be thankful to him for my being treated decently, and I was. I wouldn't be able to recognise him – you do know that, don't you? Not even his voice, so it was for my own good that I suffered so much pain.

'When Woodcutter was putting the chain on my ankle and was close to me I asked, "Are you going to do my eyes now?"

' "Later."

'What I really wanted to ask him was whether he had brought the newspaper with an article in it about me as he had promised, but I didn't dare for fear of seeming a nuisance. He went away with my boots and I crawled inside and settled down, lying on top of the sleeping bag since it wasn't at all cold. I had discovered that if I put my arms behind my neck and supported my head so that there was no pressure on those great stones in my ears, the pain was reduced to a bearable level. However, a few nights of sleeping in this position caused terrible pains in my shoulders so now I used a toilet roll as a neck support. I had come to look forward to this moment of retreat in the way you might look forward to settling down to watch a favourite TV programme. My entertainment was provided by my own thoughts and memories. I felt there was something luxurious in this, after years of running to stay in the same place, of juggling insufficient money, then later, the pressure to maintain the success I'd achieved. Only once, and that was as a small child, had I had this same feeling. I was recovering from an illness – measles, I think – and had to stay in bed. That special feeling of separateness that comes from lying quietly in your bed and hearing the world outside go on without you, voices you recognise calling to each other on the way to school, cars starting up, the radio and the vacuum cleaner downstairs. I had a colouring book and crayons, a jigsaw puzzle of horses in the snow, and a shiny new book – even in my musty tent I could recreate the delicious smell of the glossy cover and the fresh print – which I couldn't read because my eyes hurt. At such a young age I already appreciated the luxury of those hours so totally my own. I can see you must find the comparison odd given that I was a chained captive in the tent but, apart from the chain itself, was I any freer as a child with measles? And Woodcutter was my nurse, responsible for me, feeding me, sometimes kind, sometimes angry. I tried, at first, to fight against my growing dependence on him, but then I stopped fighting and let it take its course. Most things that happen naturally have a good reason for happening and I believe that if I hadn't accepted it, hadn't allowed myself to trust him, I would have died. The overt reason might have been an intestinal blockage, blood poisoning from the chain wound, whatever. But the real reason would have been that without that contact I couldn't have saved myself. It was that or death and I wanted to live.

'I must have relived everything I could remember of my childhood, good and bad, and my thoughts absorbed me so completely that the interruption for feeding was often unwelcome, especially under the stale bread and cheese regime, as I had no appetite and eating was a necessary mechanical process. I much preferred my mental wanderings. Leo is like me, I think. I know he's always spent a lot of time with his own thoughts, even when he was quite small. Most often he was silent, concentrating on whatever he was drawing, but I would sometimes hear him humming or even talking quietly to himself. He lived a second, very intense life in his imagination, I think. I used to read to him in the evenings in English because at school everything was in Italian. I felt he should know his own literary heritage. So we read *Tom Sawyer*, *Nicholas Nickleby*, *Alice's Adventures in Wonderland*. And we read the *Odyssey* and the *Iliad* and some of the Bible in English, too. They were already so different, he and Caterina, even as small children. He could lose himself in his own imaginative world for hours but Caterina liked company. She liked someone there to talk to and she loved little presents, tiny dolls and miniature china animals. She had such a collection. I felt I ought to read to her as I had to Leo but she only wanted her father to read to her so it was always in Italian. You know the way girls are with their fathers. I wasn't even allowed to be there if she had him! Then when he went she couldn't bear to be left for a moment. No matter how busy I was, she would never do her homework alone, even though she always got angry if I tried to help her. She'd scream at me, "I can do it! But you've got to stay with me!"

'Poor Caterina . . . We make so many mistakes with our children but even with hindsight who can tell what's right? She needed her father and he was . . . what he was.

156

He had little enough time for the children and then we divorced. I don't know yet how it could have gone differently. In my efforts to take the blame on myself I go as far as feeling guilty for marrying Ugo in the first place and so giving my children an unstable father and an unstable life. That's as foolish as you can get, I think, since then they wouldn't have existed – not as their present selves, anyway. Besides, for my sins, I was hopelessly in love with him. He dazzled me after all the fresh-faced dull boys at home. Then, when he'd gone, what could I do to make up to Caterina for her father's absence since it wasn't my attention she wanted? I resorted to tricks, the way we all do sometimes with our children. Little presents I would say came from him. I wouldn't do that if I had my time over again, or at least I believe now it was wrong, but my heart bled for her, so still and silent, waiting for him to come back. I didn't know what else to do.

'It was a relief in more ways than one when he died. She was only ten, Leo fourteen. That was my biggest subterfuge of all, a "will" which gave them a two thirds share in the family estate on reaching their majority. Ugo did actually leave a will but it was all fantasy and I made it a reality by arrangement with our lawyers – the children don't know, so please don't ever tell anyone. I did what I did to protect them from the truth about their father. At least, that's what I told myself then. Now, I suspect my motives. I think I was playing God, reinventing reality. It made me feel good, generous, powerful to give my children such an important inheritance *and* a caring

157

father. But it was the Brunamonti inheritance really, and Ugo cared nothing for that or his children. Vanity . . . vanity and presumptuousness had a hand in what I did. Ugo, you see, no longer owned anything. He had only ever given the estate a thought when he wanted to borrow money on it, and he never gave us a thought at all. I had long since paid him off and got control of the estate. I sold off the smaller properties to launch my business and invested a sum of money for each child.

'Leo went through a bad time – perhaps the worst in his young life – just before Ugo died. They met in some bar in town, or avoided meeting, and Ugo was reduced to a pitiful state. It shocked and frightened Leo. Caterina was spared that, thank heaven, but his death was a terrible blow. She didn't shed a tear, she never does. I feel sure not even this business will have made her cry. It frightens me, what she might be suffering when she's like that. She was too young to understand about the will, and I gave her the only thing I had of Ugo's, a leather writing set that had been his father's. I told her he had particularly wanted her to have it and she has always treasured it. Was I wrong? Was I? Oh, why couldn't he have cared a little for her, whatever he thought of me? I've failed to make it up to her, I'm sure I have – and now I've been the cause of so much stress and made them poor again – I'm sorry, just give me a moment . . . I know I'm not talking sense. I didn't cause it, did I? Did I cause it? I left the main doors open . . . Do they blame me? It will pass if you just give me a moment . . .

'I want to tell you . . . what did I want to tell you? That morning . . . Yes, that morning when Woodcutter changed the plasters on my eyes. He let me take the old ones off and with the gauze it didn't hurt so much. As I was doing it he came close and explained why it was necessary, that after a time, the sweat and the oil from your skin cause them to work loose so that there was a risk of my being able to peer under or over them. He warned me again, for my own good, to tell him if I felt them loosening.

' "You lie still and never mess with them. That's good. Give it here. Be more careful with the square ones over your eyes."

' "I don't mind lying still. I think about things."

' "What things?"

' "Today I thought about my time at university."

' "Lucky for you. I had to leave school at fourteen and see nothing but sheep for years until I started my own business."

' "What sort of business?"

He didn't answer.

' "If you have your own business, then why do this? Is it anger because you had no chance to study? Is that why?"

' "No, that's not why! I do this because I've no choice. I ran away from home at fifteen and came over here to some relations. I thought I could work as a shepherd boy part-time and still go to school. Be careful with that one, the gauze is out of place . . ."

' "Agh!"

' "Give it here."

'I rubbed at the sticky soreness. "And did you go to school?"

' "Did I go to school, like hell. I had to be a feeder for a kidnapping the first year I was over here."

' "But later, when you were older, couldn't you have got out?"

' "You can never get out. They don't let you. It's forever. You make me laugh when you tell your pathetic stories about how hard up you've been. People like you don't know what poverty means—" His voice against my face stopped in the middle of a sentence and there was only the sea roaring in my ears. He was no longer touching me and I felt for him. He slapped my hand away. The zip. I smelled someone new but he didn't come inside. I also felt Woodcutter's tension. I think the man outside spoke. I was sure this was the boss. I kept as still and quiet as a mouse until I heard the zip again and sensed Woodcutter relax. The boss had gone. This wasn't the only visit. I learned to read the tension around me when he was there, but it was the only time I knew he had looked at me. I was soon to find out why he had come. Apart from checking on the condition of the goods, which I suppose was his usual reason.

' "Open your eyes." I opened them. Woodcutter's denim jacket, his square hands screwing up the used plasters, the olive light in the tent.

' "You were scared of going blind, weren't you?"

'It was a relief. At once my eyes were searching the tent. Had he brought the newspaper? He was wearing a ski mask, of course, for this job, but I attempted to look into his eyes.

' "The newspaper. You promised . . ."

'He hadn't brought the whole paper, just the pages with articles about me, the front page and one inside page. There was an old photograph of me on the front page as a model. Another world broken off and floating away from me. Then on the other page . . . I can't tell you how it hit me. They'd got hold of a picture of Leo from two years ago. He was looking back over his shoulder towards the camera, his blond hair rather longer than he has it now, and he was wearing a thick patterned sweater. You could only see a tiny bit of the sweater but I remembered it so well – white, patterned in red and green. The background looked deliberately blurred, though perhaps that was just the newspaper repro-duction. It was taken on a skiing holiday and I kept it pinned to my notice board in the office. How had they got it? And Caterina! My little girl. A big beautiful picture of her. I couldn't tell where it had been taken but it was new. You can imagine how I felt when I recognised the collar of one of my coats. It broke my heart to think of her seeking that comfort. At school, when we were dating a boy, we'd wear his sweater. It was like being hugged and you had the smell of the boy on it. I cried then, though even without the plasters I cried deep in my chest from habit, afraid of tears. I cried so much that when, at last, he took the pages back and put them in his pocket I hadn't read a word. I couldn't, I was too agitated, shocked into reality by the pictures. My beautiful, beautiful children!

'And to think that I had dedicated a part of my quiet thinking time each day to trying to calculate the stage my kidnapping had reached. I imagined Patrick's arrival, I thought of the ransom demand – would they phone? I wondered how much they would ask for and longed to discuss this with Woodcutter because I was still convinced their information must be wrong and I was perfectly willing to tell them my real possibilities, which they could then check for themselves. I calculated how long it would take to get the money together, wondered how they arranged these things. I was sure that, after all this time, I must be near to being released and that kept me determined to eat and try to keep well. But I had no information, and now the newspaper was back in his pocket and I had missed my chance. Yet there was no point in my asking for another chance. I was still crying, almost howling, and could still not have read the article.

' "Signora, calm yourself. You must quieten down." The black masked head moved back from my ear and I tried again to look through the narrow slits into his eyes.

'I stopped crying obediently.

' "Why did you call me signora?"

'He didn't answer me.

' "It's because I can see you, isn't it?" He had also addressed me in the formal third person, the way we would have spoken to each other in the real world. Until

162

then, he had always used the informal *tu*. I tried to take advantage of this suddenly acquired human dignity.

' "Please, allow me to see for a while longer."

' "I intend to. You're going to write a letter."

'I remembered other kidnappings vaguely with letters full of polemical or political nonsense sent to all sorts of people – once it was the Archbishop of Florence. Was this what they wanted from me, imagining that I had influential friends?

' "I don't know anybody important, if that's—"

' "It doesn't matter. Choose a friend. Someone outside your family whose mail won't be checked. And someone who won't go to the cops or it'll be the worse for you. Here. Write it on here and copy from this one the boss has prepared. His is just notes. You've to write it in your own way."

'It was a ransom demand. A ransom demand! And all this time I had imagined they'd have phoned, that everything would be under way, the money organised, a matter of days to my release.

' "You can't mean you haven't been in touch with my family before now? Surely it's more risk for you the longer you wait?"

'He only laughed. "Write."

'What else could I do? I wrote. I followed the notes given to me by the boss, and my disappointment, my despair over all the wasted time drove me to say spitefully, "I can see why he wants me to write it in my own words. He can't spell or put a sentence together, can he?"

'As if this had not crossed his mind before, Woodcutter snatched the notes from me, and I could see that he didn't know how to answer me, that his own Italian wasn't up to seeing the mistakes. Satisfied at this little triumph over them, I took the notes back and read to the end.

'"Here. Get on with it." His voice was angry now because of what I had said. He pushed a thick magazine and a sheet of lined paper into my lap and gave me a cheap plastic pen. The light was feeble. There was a sort of window of transparent plastic in the tent but we were under trees and the tent was covered in brushwood anyway. I hoped I would be able to see well enough to write. I soon found that I couldn't but I wrote, anyway. I was writing blindly, the little light serving only to keep me more or less within the lines. I was excited and nervous at the thought of communicating with my children, with the outside world, and I think this feeling took over from my horrified dismay on discovering that no contact had been made before.

My dearest Leo and Caterina,

I am allowed to tell you that the contents of this letter have been decided for me and that only one paragraph at the end can be my own. They'll read the whole thing, of course, before this letter goes to you. I am in the hands of professionals and, consequently, if you want to see me again, stick precisely to the rules given you. The first rule is be careful how you deal with state-employed murderers, i.e., police and carabinieri. These squalid cowards are two-faced, double-crossing worms and *you must avoid them*, otherwise you, my own children, will be guilty of murdering me. You must be even more careful of public prosecutors who have no interest in anything other than their own careers and who don't care what happens to me or to you.

Don't put your trust in a lawyer, either, because in a situation like this they would take money from you, further their careers, and still be at the service of the state-employed murderers, and that can only lead to my death. I have already suffered terrible tortures and am so destroyed by pain and grief that I no longer feel like a human being. I beg you with all the strength that remains to me to do what is necessary to free me. I am chained up like an animal, unable to see or hear and in dreadful pain. By law, the magistrates will freeze our assets but you can get round this with the help of my friends and, in any case, you can never be prosecuted for ignoring it whereas if you don't get round it I will be tortured every day and then killed. This can only be avoided if you follow the instructions given you to the letter. The price of my life and freedom is 8 (eight) billion lire, and any hesitation, any false move on your part, will mean that *the price goes up*. The money must be in notes of 50 and 100 thousand lire. *They must be used and not chemically treated in any way*. The amount to be paid will not be bargained over and you have two months to get it together. If you refuse to pay the whole amount, on the last day of April I will be executed. If you pay up and don't try and bring the police with you when you do it, everything will go smoothly. If you collaborate with the law it will do you no good and I'll pay for it with my life. They have so much blood on their hands already that one more death will only serve to satisfy their bloodthirsty instincts. When you have the money ready you must publish a notice for three days running in the Lost and Found column of *La Nazione*. It must say: LOST in Piazza Santo Spirito, bag containing important personal documents. Reward. Tel (give the number of one of my friends). As soon as they see the announcement you will receive another letter from me telling you how to deliver the money and giving you proof that I am still alive in the form of a Polaroid photograph of me holding the day's paper with the headlines clearly visible. Once you have paid I will be released within eight days. I will telephone you, telling you where to pick me up once I am freed, so don't expect any calls until you have paid up. Don't come to the appointment without the money or attempt to bring anyone with you. Anyone appearing without the money will be executed on the spot. The person delivering the money according to instructions has absolutely nothing to fear. Rich people become rich by treading on the poor and stealing from them. This transaction is intelligent, fair, and justified.

Leo – block payments to all our suppliers. They trust us and know they will be paid when this is over. Ask my dear friend E. for help. She is in a position to help us without any hardship. The rest Patrick will do. He knows who to ask. I have to ask you and Caterina to give up your inheritance temporarily. Patrick will deal with it. You can transfer it from your accounts to his. The Italian law has no influence in the States. You know I will earn it all back for you. We have survived worse in the past and I will deal with everything once I'm free. If necessary, borrow on the house. The bank will be more than willing and your two signatures will be valid without mine as you constitute a majority. The loan will be overtly to Patrick and you will be guaranteeing it so nobody will be breaking the law. Don't wait until the last minute but do everything as fast as you can because I am suffering too much to survive very long in these conditions. Everyone will be paid back somehow to the last lira.

I send you all my love and I think of you day and night despite my suffering. Tell Patrick I love him and think of him. My life is in your hands and I trust you. Don't abandon me.'

Eight

People often maintain that they can sense when a telephone is ringing in an empty house or when someone is about to answer. This is not subject to proof but Marshal Guarnaccia, who wasn't the sort to make any such claims, nevertheless sensed that something had changed inside the Brunamonti house between the moment when he rang the bell on that Friday afternoon at his usual hour and his being admitted. He gave the matter very little thought but he did sense a change in the time he was left waiting and the nature of the footfall approaching through the marble vestibule, rapid and loud instead of leisurely and soft.

The door was opened by a woman he had never seen before and who certainly wasn't a servant. She wore no make-up or jewellery and her clothes had a secondhand look to them but she had an air of confidence and authority which the Marshal responded to, excusing himself for the interruption as he would to the owners of the house and not to an employee.

The woman ignored his remark and said in a loud confidential whisper, 'Are you the one from Palazzo Pitti? If you are I want to talk to you – not now. I'm just so worried . . . Come in, come in . . .'

He followed her into the white drawing-room and all the faces there turned to stare at him. Their expressions were anything but welcoming and he was left there, hat in hand, conscious of a silence as thick as the cigarette smoke circling slowly above Patrick Hines's head and full of the echoes of the intense conversation his arrival had interrupted. Well aware of the fact that silence was going to unnerve these people rather than himself, he examined them in turn. The woman who had let him in had seated herself on the very edge of a big armchair, her feet close together and her back as straight as a ramrod. Her hair was the same grey as her dowdy grey suit, her eyes dark, her expression just about bursting with all the things she wanted to talk to him about, but not now. Patrick Hines and Leonardo Brunamonti were seated together on the white sofa. After taking in the Marshal's arrival their eyes avoided him. The sister was perched on the arm of the sofa next to Hines, her arm along the sofa's back, her diamonds glittering. She was looking at the Marshal with that sideways stare of hers over the cascade of fair hair on her shoulder. Her mouth was widened as if in a tight smile. She was not smiling. The only member of the group arranged in an attitude of complete ease and with an expression that betokened absolute control over the situation was the English detective, Charles Bently, by which the Marshal understood him to be the most put out at his arrival, which was acknowledged with a brief nod.

'Leo,' murmured his sister, reaching to touch his shoulder, 'we should ask the Marshal to sit down.'

The Marshal, seeing Leonardo's eyes as blank as the day he had collapsed, considered this remark an adequate invitation and seated himself on a solid-looking straight chair right next to the detective. Then he waited. As he waited, his big eyes registered everything within view without his ever turning them on anything in particular. He was very aware of the dog basket not far from Leonardo's feet, aware, that is, of its being empty. The grey-haired woman spoke with sudden loudness.

'I think you should bring Tessie home. Whatever's wrong with her she'll heal better at home.' She seemed to be addressing Leonardo, and when he didn't answer she leaned forward and raised her pitch.

'Leonardo!'

'Caterina's seeing to it.'

Caterina said very quietly, 'She had to be put on a drip, she was so dehydrated, and it may have to be done again. It's not fair to a sick animal with all those injuries to keep moving it about. It's too painful. The vet's keeping her this week.'

'You can't leave her there for a week! She'll die.'

'It's the best place for her and it might need to be for longer.'

'Leonardo! You can't do that!'

There was no immediate answer. Leonardo leaned forward and dropped his head into his hands. Then he seemed to make an enormous effort to sit upright and speak.

'I'd rather have her here but that's just me being sentimental. She needs constant expert attention, which we can't give her.'

It was odd, the Marshal thought, that this remark was clearly offered in good faith as to its content but that every word sounded false.

The detective's hard-edged voice brought the subject to an abrupt end.

'I'm sure the Marshal will understand, Hines' – emphasis on the NCO rank, remark made across the Marshal's head – 'that there is a meeting in progress here and that, since we are discussing the financial situation of the family, it's by way of being a personal and private meeting. In fact, I feel bound to say that, for the moment, it would be better if these visits of his were discontinued since there's a possibility that they could be endangering the Contessa Brunamonti's life.'

'I don't agree,' declared Caterina, giving Bently a hard, bright glance. 'It's his job. He's involved, and I—'

'Please don't worry,' said the Marshal blandly. There was no point at all in his staying since they would say nothing in front of him. Better to let them talk and see what the daughter came out with later. He got to his feet and hoped that the unknown woman would show him out. Tense as she was, she was up and moving in a flash. At the door, that fierce stage whisper again; 'Did you know about the maid's being sacked?'

'I . . . no. I thought she'd gone to visit her sister. She seemed so upset . . .'

'She was. Upset about Olivia, I mean, but now she's even more upset. Sacked. That's why she's gone to her sister's. I don't think her Italian was that bad – do you think it was that bad? – oh, by the way, I'm the Contessa Elettra Cavicchioli Zelli. I know your name, that's all right. And, besides, you have to teach these Filipino girls to wait at table. Do you realise that some of them come from such poor families they're lucky if there's any food on the table at all, never mind worrying about which wine glasses are which, can you imagine? I feel so sorry for that girl I'm going to take her in and give her some work until Olivia—' She stopped.

'We're doing our best, you know.'

'*You're* doing your best? I'm not worried about what you're doing! Unless you've got eight billion lire! I'm doing my best but it's not going to be good enough and Patrick's a darling but he doesn't have a bean. I have to go. They're listening. Bye.'

The door was practically slammed in his face. He was going to need time to recover from the impact of the Contessa Elettra Cavicchioli Zelli and he paused a moment down in the piazza to make a note of her name and then dab at his eyes as the sunlight started them watering. He put away the handkerchief and fished for his dark glasses. It was really quite warm, a remarkable jump in temperature of the sort which Florence specalises in and which, every February, sends half the population down with flu. Fat grey clouds gathering behind the sunny yellow façade of the church were a reminder that warm meant wet but for the moment it was pleasant to be out. The Marshal was glad of this regular afternoon walk between Piazza Santo Spirito and Borgo Ognissanti Headquarters and never more so than today . . . Elettra . . . . well named. The woman was like a bolt of lightning and clearly in a temper, but with whom? The little dog seemed to be the chief provocation . . . and the weeping maid . . . Eight billion. Hm.

Captain Maestrangelo was in a meeting with the Colonel and had left a message for the Marshal saying that if there was nothing of note to report he would see him at the usual time tomorrow. The Marshal sent a carabiniere to knock at the Colonel's door and stood in the polished corridor next to a rubber plant, waiting.

When the Captain appeared, he looked expectantly at the Marshal but there was nothing to be read in his expression. There never was anything to be read in the Marshal's expression. He had received the Captain's message and had presented himself, just the same. He was standing there. It was enough.

'Contact?'

'Yes. A request for eight billion accompanied, I imagine, by the usual instructions but I'm afraid I can't tell you anything other than the sum. I've lost them. I'm sorry.'

'Don't assume that too quickly. The first contact is always a shock, frightening, but that's all the more reason why they should turn to you once it's sunk in.'

'No. There's that detective. He'll be able to help them.'

'Is he talking to you?'

'No.'

'But the ransom demand?'

'A friend of the family let it slip. I think she'll let plenty more slip if the detective doesn't bully her.'

'Does she seem liable to be bullied?'

'Oh no. Then there's always the daughter. She wanted me in on it but the others wouldn't have it so I came away. She must appear to agree with them or they'll keep her in the dark. I just hope the damage hasn't been done. She shouldn't have spoken out as she did today.'

'Not very bright, I gather . . .'

'I don't know . . . Of course she's upset, so . . .'

'What's the friend's name?'

The Marshal consulted his notebook. 'Contessa Elettra Cavicchioli Zelli.'

'Ah yes. Fusarri mentioned her as a likely contact. A very rich woman. Will you wait for me up in my office until I finish here? I've got some names I want to give you. We need to concentrate on finding the planner.'

*

174

There could be little doubt about the author of this kidnapping once Salis had been eliminated as a suspect, and Salis was too clever and too experienced to permit the discovery of a hide-out before the completion of a job, or even after it except in the case of an imminent raid and consequent hurried flight. There was good reason, however, to wish it had been otherwise. With Salis there would have been no need to look outside the Sardinian community for his associates, and members of enemy clans reduced the possibilities even further. But Puddu had not only lived long on the mainland, he had lost sight of his origins and traditions. His criminal associates were legion and enemy clans the only element that could be eliminated with the exception of such of his sidekicks who happened to be in prison. The Captain's men had come up with a list. Given the importance and high risk of the job, they had included only those men who had worked for Puddu before and who had experience of the kidnapping business. The resulting list had been shortened by the elimination of anyone currently serving a sentence, out on parole and reporting in regularly, or known to be elsewhere. The remaining men were under discreet surveillance as were all access points to the acres of woodland and scrub where Puddu might be hiding his victim. This last was the most difficult aspect of the job because the investigators were altogether at a disadvantage, knowing neither exactly for whom they were looking nor precisely where to look. There had to be traffic between the hide-out and the outside world for the provision of food and water and the passing of information but, should a feeder be spotted, any action at this stage could only result in risk to the victim. The only person it was safe to arrest was the planner, the contact between Puddu and his victim. Safe because he would have fixed his percentage and made his deal through an intermediary and would never know, unless things went wrong, who had done the job. He was, nevertheless, a valuable element to the investigators because someone with access to the Brunamontis could only make contact with Puddu's world during a prison sentence and that contact was at the centre of a web which would reach out to some of the names on that list.

Up to this point, neither the investigators through their informers nor the Marshal through his talks with the family had come up with even the vaguest of possibilities by way of a planner.

'Frankly, Guarnaccia,' the Captain admitted, 'I had more hopes of you than of them. What about this Contessa Cavicchioli Zelli? I have it that she's a close friend of the victim's and if she was in on the meeting you described then she's going to be providing a good part of the ransom. She'll be put on her guard by the London detective . . . what's his name? Bently . . . so I'd prefer not to make any formal approach. She might well come up with a past boyfriend of the daughter's, a resentful ex-employee. What do you think?'

'I'll go and see her if you'll give me her address. The employees . . .'

'Yes?'

'Your men have questioned them.'

'Of course. Except for a young designer from America, straight out of art school, they've all been there for years and are clean. We got nothing. Why are you insisting on this? Have you found out something?'

'No, no . . . I only looked in there on my first visit to ask directions . . .'

'If you think we've missed something, Guarnaccia, say so. Go and question them, by all means.'

'No, no . . . Me . . . no. I'm no investigator . . . treading on people's toes, no . . . There was just something. There was something.'

'So you said before. Then you did suspect somebody?'

'No.' The Marshal examined the hat on his knee, his left shoe, the window. 'I had a feeling they were all united, all loyal – just a fleeting impression, of course. You've talked to them all . . .'

'And got exactly the same impression. So, what's wrong?'

'I don't know . . . yet. And now I've lost the son.'

'You're quite sure about that, are you, Guarnaccia?'

'Oh yes. He'll try and pay without us.'

'You must try and convince him to let us mark the notes in return for non-intervention during the drop.'

'This Mister Hines . . .'

'What about him?'

'He doesn't say much.'

'Some people don't.' The irony was lost on Guarnaccia. This was the moment when any investigator would push him aside as hopeless and it was the most critical moment of all. The most nerve-racking. Just when the pressure was on, when the journalists were waiting outside every day, and the Colonel was growing increasingly annoyed at each morning briefing, Guarnaccia would slow to a stop. He would mutter something about being more used to snatched handbags and distressed old ladies and say he was hardly competent – which few but Maestrangelo would contest – and any attempt to get near him or question him was doomed to failure. He would settle down like a bulldog with a bone between its paws, silent and unaggressive. If you got close he emitted a faint but unmistakable growl. The Captain knew he must control his impatience, try and help him without either of them knowing what he needed. If he would only ask . . . or had he asked?

'You think I should speak to Hines again?'

'He doesn't say much. I see him as a wealthy man. Compared to me . . . the Contessa Cavicchioli Zelli said he hasn't a bean.'

'As I said, she's a very rich woman.'

'Yes. As I told you, they don't want me going round there any more and I can't force them . . . I need to talk to the sister alone.'

'She came to your office once. Wouldn't she—'

'No. In the house. I want to talk to her in the house. I've lost them . . . I think the planner . . . I must talk to her in the house . . .'

The Captain was there now. 'All right, Guarnaccia.

Let's assume that Prosecutor Fusarri is going to need to speak to Leonardo Brunamonti and Mister Patrick Hines in his office tomorrow – shall we say at four p.m.?'

'And that detective. Will you excuse me?' And at the Captain's nod of release he was gone.

ITALO-AMERICAN CHIC

The Contessa label is the brainchild of Olivia Birkett, top model of the sixties, top designer of the eighties and nineties. After years of solid success in Europe, Olivia Birkett is now branching out. This year Tokyo, next year New York, and in the wake of that, she hopes, Los Angeles in her home state of California. What is her style secret?

'History, I suppose. I married into a six-centuries-old family and found inspiration in the clothes of my predecessors – adapted to our modern way of life, naturally.'

And her success secret?

'I'm good at clothes, yes, but what makes our clothes different is the input of my son, Leonardo, whose historical and art historical knowledge are the basis of each year's collection. This is what defines the detail of our collection and its presentation, architectural setting, music, lighting, and so on.'

Olivia's beautiful aristocratic daughter is also to be seen in the *Contessa* workshop.

'Caterina has an elegance all her own, a fourteenth-century beauty, a twentieth-century style, ideally suited to our clothes. I love to have her model for me but her interest in the firm at the moment is more on the managerial side.'

Facing page: Pearls on a gold lace web form the collar of a *Contessa* evening gown from the winter collection.
Above: Olivia Birkett and Tessie in the white drawing room of the Palazzo Brunamonti.
  Photo by Gianni Taccola, Florence.

The Marshal let the copy of *Style* fall into his lap.

'Dad? Can we stay up to watch the match?'

'Ask your mother.'

'We have and she said to ask you.'

'All right.'

And the two boys dashed back to the kitchen, suppressing their giggles.

'Mum! Dad said we can stay up and watch the match with him if it's all right with you. Can we? Go on!'

They settled one on each side of him and he hugged them close, pleased. The players rushed about on the green background to the rise and fall of the crowd's noise, a comfortable background to the slow untangling of the more vivid images in his head.

'Batistuta won't really be transferred, will he, Dad? Giovanni says he will but I don't believe it. Dad? What are you reading *that* for?'

'Reading what? If you want to watch the match, watch it. If you start making a racket, your mother . . .'

It must have been a couple of hours later when he remarked aloud, 'I've seen that name and I think I know where . . .'

'What name? Salva?'

He stared at her. 'Have the boys gone to bed?'

'I should think they have. What were you thinking of, letting them stay up when it's school tomorrow?'

'Is it?'

'Salva, what's the matter?'

'Nothing.'

'You look exhausted. Let's get to bed.'

He fell at once into a deep sleep and imagined he'd been asleep for many hours when he heard himself say loudly, 'Dogs and photographs.'

'Dogs are what?'

He opened his eyes. Teresa's lamp was still on and she was reading the *Style* magazine so it wasn't so late. 'Photographs . . .,' he repeated, reminded as he saw it. 'It's all a question . . .'

'A question of what? Salva?'

He was asleep again.

He fell asleep convinced that in the morning the mists would have cleared, allowing him to see clearly what was in front of his nose. He awoke refreshed. The mists had indeed cleared but what he was to see clearly had yet to present itself. He started his day with quiet deliberation, sitting in his office and calling Headquarters on the internal line.

'Certainly, Marshal. Can you give me his place and date of birth? It will help me to find the file if it's here.'

'No, I can't, but I'm betting he has a record, and since he lives and operates in this area his file must be there in the archives. Urgent, yes. The Olivia Birkett – yes. I'll be here.'

Dogs and photographs. He must sit still and wait. Dogs and photographs. He sat still. Inertia at the centre of the web . . . pearls on a gold lace web . . .

The phone rang.

'Marshal Guarnaccia.'

'Maestrangelo. I have the address and phone number of Contessa Elettra Cavicchioli Zelli. Will you take it down?'

He took it down. Then he sat still.

The phone rang again.

'Marshal Guarnaccia.'

'I have that file for you. Do you want me to send it over there?'

'No, just give me the gist and when he served his last sentence. He is out?'

'Oh, yes, he's out. Didn't serve that long. Art thefts, villas around Florence – well, you knew that already, I imagine . . . released a year and a half ago, more or less. Anything else in particular that you want?'

'His address.'

'Current address Via Santo Spirito, number seventeen. Anything else?'

'No, but don't send the file back down to the archives, give it to Captain Maestrangelo, as from me. I'll be in touch with him later. Thanks.'

To be truthful, his recollection of the case was more than a little vague but it hardly mattered now. There would be plenty of time to look into that, and better people than him to do it. Besides, where was the proof?

'There is no proof,' he agreed when Maestrangelo called him. 'I'm just trying to understand.'

'And you have understood. A dangerous character, that one. I arrested him myself.'

So he, unlike the Marshal, did remember the case

clearly. A freelance photographer whose speciality was photographing fashionable people in their own homes. He chose the settings, examined all the suitable rooms, chatted to his subjects, putting them at their ease. The thefts were carried out after a discreet passage of time by professional housebreakers who were instructed in detail about what to take and even provided with photographs. Between the photo shoot and the theft, commissions were taken, using the photographs, from the discreet clients of equally discreet antique and art dealers. Until the photographer's cover was blown on his arrest.

So, why not steal the householder? One big job and set for life.

'But,' the Captain added, 'according to the information I'm getting on the family, it wasn't a good choice. Oh, there's the property, of course, and the business, but the business is expanding and temporarily overstretched, and property's hardly ideal. Kidnappers want quickly available cash, discreetly invested hidden cash that leaves no traceable hole. His information about antiques might have been expert but his information on these people must have been wide of the mark. What do you think?'

'I think somebody lied to him,' the Marshal said.

'I don't follow you. Why tell him anything, in that case?'

'People say things . . . for other reasons. Even the Contessa herself might have wanted to seem richer than she was. Perhaps photographers, like hairdressers . . . get women chatting.'

'Didn't you say there was just the one photo session?'

'Just the one, yes. As far as I know.'

Arrangements were made for Leonardo Brunamonti, the detective, Charles Bently, and Patrick Hines to be summoned to the Prosecutor's office at four in the afternoon. It was made clear to them that there was no idea of attempting to press them for information about their actions, that instead they were to be informed of the state of the enquiry and any action planned on the part of the carabinieri in the interests of the victim's safety.

'Not quite true, of course,' Fusarri confessed to the Captain, 'but it should produce them.'

Unfortunately, it produced only two of them. Hines cried off with the excuse of a headache and the reasonable assumption that the other two would update him.

Fusarri phoned Maestrangelo.

'Blasted man's keeping the daughter under control. I don't see what we can do about it short of arresting him!'

Maestrangelo phoned the Marshal.

'I'll go anyway,' the Marshal said. 'He doesn't say much, as I told you. I'd be glad to see him without that detective chap, and I imagine I can organise a minute to two alone with each of them.'

'Well, if you think it could be useful.'

'I'll try. I've lost the son, you see. That's very bad. I'm sorry . . . I'll go round there and try . . .'

He set out, on foot as usual, at a quarter to four. As he came out under the stone archway he fished for his dark glasses but the sunlight was intermittent today as fluffy white, grey, and black clouds gathered in the windless sky.

'We're in for rain, Marshal.' It was Biondini, the curator of the art gallery, ready for the downpour with raincoat and umbrella on his arm. 'I suppose you've heard the news?'

'I'm sorry?'

'The Corot stolen from the Louvre. I worry myself sick about our inadequate security arrangements but, you see, other museums have problems, too – and, of course, we have you on our doorstep and your Art Heritage Group down at the other end of the gardens to recover stolen paintings for us, so I shouldn't complain. You're looking blank – didn't you see it on the lunchtime news?'

'I wasn't paying much attention, to tell you the truth . . . Where did you say, the Louvre?'

'That's right. The new part, you know. A lovely Corot landscape.'

'A stolen landscape . . . Good. Something like that a bit nearer home would be just . . . good. Good . . .'

'Marshal?'

'Good afternoon. Thank you. Good afternoon. You're very kind . . .'

Biondini always was very kind but if he got started he'd tell the Marshal more than he could manage to ingest about the stolen picture, and all the Marshal wanted was to know it was stolen. Very kind of him, that. Something nearer home, though. Still, that was for later. Piazza Santo Spirito first.

*

185

It was a shock to find the great studded doors of the Palazzo Brunamonti shut fast. There was a porter's bell but he remembered the porter's lodge as being disused. Puzzled, he rang the porter's bell.

'Yes?'

'Marshal Guarnaccia, Carabinieri.'

The doors clicked open and he began pushing. Little wonder they had been habitually left open. They were a terrific weight, and there must be a lot of to-ing and fro-ing all day with the workshop being in there.

'Who was it you wanted?' So, there really was a porter now, and in uniform, too.

'Ah, the Signorina Caterina Brunamonti. She's expecting me.'

A lie but this man could have been employed by the son or Hines. He didn't want the fellow calling up to announce him. 'I come by every day at this time. There's no need to announce me and I know my way.'

'Suit yourself, Marshal.' Thank goodness, he went back to his newspaper. The Marshal took the lift.

As he stepped out on the second-floor landing, the apartment door was flung open and Patrick Hines rushed out, slamming it behind him. He stopped dead when he saw the Marshal, speechless, white-faced, his eyes horrified.

'Oh God!' He fled down the stairs as if pursued by devils.

The Marshal stayed still, staring after him, then approached the door. Hines could be found easily enough. If no one answered the bell, he would call for help and break in. He rang and waited. He heard no approaching footsteps but an almost imperceptible rustle made him go on waiting.

The door opened very slowly and before he saw anything the voice began, equally slow and cold as death, 'I *knew* you'd change your mind.'

And then he could see her, barefoot, her long thin body naked where the frothy white transparent gown hung open.

When she saw who it was, her glossy red lips tightened and she slammed the door in his face.

Nine

The Marshal went down the stairs in the wake of
Patrick Hines. He avoided the lift, preferring to go
slowly. This was not because he wanted time to think.
There was nothing to think. Apart from the physical
shock of the young woman's nakedness, it was only a
question of recognition, of looking straight at what he
had not felt up to seeing, much less naming. Her still,
upright stance, her long pale neck turned as she fixed
him with one bright eye. The poise of a snake fixing its
victim.

But what did she want with him? What use could she
make of him? And for that matter, what did she want
from Hines? Not affection, not sex for its own sake. The
chill that he had felt emanating from her thin white body

made him shiver even down in the sheltered warmth of the courtyard.

The fountain was playing and the spring flowers smelled fresh in the warm air. Signora Verdi came out from the glass-fronted workshops. She must have spotted his arrival and had been watching for him to come down. He walked towards her. He needed to talk to her but not now.

'Have you heard? Little Tessie's had to be put down.' She was crying, the tears rolling unchecked down her cheeks and under her collar. 'It seems like such a bad omen. It gave us such a lift when she came home alive, and now—'

'I understand how you feel. It's a shame after the little creature had struggled so hard to get home. But it isn't an omen. You mustn't torment yourself like that. The Contessa—'

'Is there some news of her? Is there?'

'No – that is – there is news, information. Try to be patient. These things go on a long time. Concentrate on looking after things for when she gets back. You must have a lot of work.'

The woman's face hardened. 'You needn't worry about that. Olivia will find everything as it should be as far as *we're* concerned.' She shot a black look at the porter's lodge.

'Yes, I believe you. I'd like to come and talk to you tomorrow – you didn't see which way Mister Hines went as he left, did you?'

'He mumbled something about getting a drink. He looked very upset. I suppose he felt the loss of Tessie as a bad omen, too. I needed to talk to him but he said he'd be back in a minute. He'll only be next door at Giorgio's . . .'

And who could blame him? The Marshal found him at the far end of the back room where all the other white tables and grey plush chairs were empty except for a couple of elderly lady tourists taking tea just inside the door.

Hines had what looked to be a large glass of brandy in front of him, but he wasn't drinking it. Cigarette smoke eddied around him and he was lighting up again with trembling hands. His face was still ghastly.

'May I . . .?' The Marshal sat facing him. The two men stared at each other for a moment and then Hines's face suddenly flashed dark red.

'You surely couldn't imagine—'

'No, no . . . Not for a moment.'

Hines tried a sip of the brandy. 'I feel sick, to tell you the truth . . . That she should have tried it at all I can understand. You hear of these things, and she's strange – a lot stranger than Olivia wants to admit. But now . . . to do such a thing now, when . . . it's inhuman! I suppose, in your job, you see weird things all the time . . .'

'Yes. I do. But I can't say I've altogether understood. What do you think she wants?'

'She wants me in her bed, surely that's obvious – in her mother's bed, to be precise, which made it even worse. Marshal, she's cleared out her mother's room, been through all her private papers, thrown out some of her clothes, sold her jewellery with the excuse of – my God, I even found a rubbish bag ready to go out with her favourite records in it! She's burying Olivia alive! She's a monster! You saw that she'd sacked the maid?'

'Yes . . . it's an enormous house to run, too . . .'

'Good Lord, Silvia didn't run the house. She's an affectionate little thing but all she was up to was looking after Olivia, especially when I was away. Cared for her clothes, made her coffee in the morning, a hot drink at night, looked after her when she had flu, massaged her neck when she was tense and overworked. There are cleaners to look after the house and also a non-resident cook, a local woman who's been with the family forever. Silvia used to like to wait at table because she liked seeing the company but she wasn't much good at it, poor thing. Olivia's always treated her like a daughter, and on more than one occasion I've heard Silvia call Olivia "Mamma" by mistake. No doubt Caterina hated her for that. So now she's been kicked out, and the Palazzo Brunamonti has a porter instead, the way a Palazzo Brunamonti should have.'

'And the doors are kept closed. I see, yes.' How many times had she said, 'She might be dead already . . .' and he had muttered something he thought would be comforting. 'That's why, then. Having you would be another nail in her mother's coffin, another way of attracting to herself all the attention her mother got. I wish it were as simple to understand why she wants me around.'

'That's a good point. Why does she? She's working out some plan of her own and nobody's taking any notice. According to Caterina, nobody ever does take any notice of her. Poor Olivia's always fallen over herself trying to give her attention.'

'And her son?'

'There's never any need for her to worry about that sort of thing with Leo. They're alike, they're close, they're both very talented. There's an understanding there that doesn't require any special attention and Caterina hates it. She'd do anything to make them quarrel. I used to try and tell Olivia, you can't pretend these things. It doesn't work and it can make things worse. All his life she's insisted on Leo's treading around his sister as though she were a land mine ready to blow.'

'It seems to me she was right.'

'Well, she was, but I still think Caterina should have been made to face reality, that all this protectiveness has only encouraged self-delusion.' He sipped at his brandy. 'I've never needed a drink so badly in my life. I'm sorry, can I offer you—'

'No, no . . .' The Marshal was glad to have arrived at such a moment. Under the influence of his private detective it was unlikely that Hines would ever have talked to him if he hadn't had such a bad shock. He thought now of those unconvincing words of Leonardo's about the little dog. *That's just me being sentimental. She needs constant care and attention, which we can't give her.* They weren't his words but his sister's. Hines, asked for his opinion, agreed.

'Word for word, you're right. And what worries me is that after years of never contradicting her just to keep the peace, he's now so distressed by what's happened, so disorientated by the absence of Olivia, the rock on which everything was built, that he's in a weakened state and, seeing her opportunity, the wretched girl is taking advantage of that to manipulate him. Her story is that Olivia is guilty of potentially causing their financial ruin. She omits to mention that they'd have been ruined years ago but for Olivia. She's using this catastrophe to try and drive a wedge between them and persuade Leo not to part with what she calls Brunamonti money. I'm glad you saw what you did today because she's our biggest problem as regards saving Olivia. I can't imagine what she might do, other than not helping, but I don't mind telling you I'm afraid.'

He drank off the brandy in one gulp and breathed deeply.

'God, she frightened me today.'

'I'm not surprised. But surely her brother will react, surely he'll understand what Caterina's doing.'

'He's an intelligent, sensitive person. He'll understand, but he saw what happened to his father, saw him reduced to a starving, crazy tramp. He won't dare turn on his sister because she's weak like her father. He loves his mother but sees her as strong, indestructible.'

'Does he have any idea of what she'll be suffering, of the conditions she's probably being kept in? People don't, in my experience, ever recover completely after a kidnapping. And besides,' the Marshal reminded him, 'nobody is indestructible, and jealousy is very, very destructive.'

'You're right, and Caterina's eaten up by it. Let me tell you something, Marshal: I often took us all out to dinner at a little restaurant we're fond of, quite near here. Always the same place, almost always the same waiter, and every time the same thing would happen: he'd address Leo, myself, and Olivia by name – Olivia never used her title – and ask if we wanted our usual choices, then he would turn to Caterina: "And the signorina?"

'She would be white with fury. "They remember your names and never mine – and they should know by now that I don't eat pasta!"

'It was extraordinary, really, because they did try to remember and were always embarrassed, and, of course, the angrier and nastier she got, the more they failed to remember her, except as in impending embarrassment.'

'I must confess,' the Marshal said, 'that I had great difficulty remembering her name and eventually had to write it in my notebook.'

'Olivia has always suffered because of it. Her children are too old for me to play at being a father figure to them. I love her very much – I hope to persuade her to marry me – and I have a very relaxed, friendly working relationship with Leo. But Olivia is protective of Caterina, and though I don't really have the right to interfere – I *don't* interfere – I have tried to convince her that it doesn't help.'

'If it's jealousy,' the Marshal said, 'nothing helps. I've seen murder committed for it.'

'You don't think – you're not saying—'

'No, no . . . She's not involved in this, not deliberately. No. But given her . . . weakness . . . she might have been an unwitting source of information. Not very accurate information, if you understand me.'

'Making herself out to be richer and grander than she is, you mean?'

'Yes. It may be, you see, that she takes after her father, who had, they say, not much grip on reality. And if she's also greedy for attention . . .'

'Marshal – what *is* your name?'

'Guarnaccia.'

'Oh dear – after what we've just been saying. I'm sorry.'

'That's all right. People aren't expected to notice me.'

'Hm. Very clever.'

'No, no . . . I'm not clever at all.'

However, he was not so stupid as to ask any questions about the communication they had received and how they intended to respond to it, or to let on that he knew where Leonardo Brunamonti and the detective were. He took this opportunity to try and explain something of the business logic to today's kidnappings, of how a professional kidnapper was only too glad to deal with other professionals, whether private mediators like their detective or the State, instead of emotional, unreliable relatives. If their detective acted as drop man, he would deliver unmarked money and have no interest in capturing the criminals. He was being paid to save Olivia so his job was simple. He facilitated the success of the kidnapping. That of the carabinieri was to cause the kidnapping to fail, capture the kidnappers, and save the victim's life.

'In that order?'

'Officially in that order, yes. But . . .'

'I'm grateful for the "but." I'll take the rest of the sentence as read. I realise there are things you shouldn't say.' They were nearing the river. Before them was the rising span of the Santa Trinita Bridge, flanked at this end by the marble figures of autumn and winter. Huge fluffy clouds, some a menacing dark grey, some pure white, touched with pink and gold highlights, drifted on an uncertain wind to brighten and darken the stucco and stone of the great houses on the opposite bank.

'I've always loved this city,' Hines said, stopping to gaze at this scene, 'but when I get Olivia back I'm taking her home to America, away from anything to do with the Brunamontis, their city, and their "accursed ditch," as Dante called this river. We can work out of New York and Leo can hold the fort here.'

He didn't mention Caterina, and the Marshal kept his doubts to himself. He also kept to himself where he was intending to go next after walking part of the way to Hines's hotel with him. Clearly, Hines would not return to the house without the protection of the others. Caterina was well on the way to making people remember her name. She had become what potentially she had always been: manipulative and dangerous. She wasn't clever enough to be very successful at it but, without achieving anything for herself, she was likely, in the present tragic situation, to cause terrible grief.

'Up there? We should have brought the jeep.' The Marshal's driver paused where the steep drive led up from the avenue. 'Oh well, we'll give it a try . . .'

It couldn't have done the small car any good but the Marshal didn't seem interested. He was staring out the window at the vineyards and olive groves dotted here and there with blossoming almond trees. The house at the top was big but not imposing. Ochre stucco, a dovecote, a generous central arch with a flagged floor. A real country house, looking down a green slope to the dome of the cathedral and a tapestry of red tiled roofs. When they stopped in front of it, the Contessa Cavicchioli Zelli appeared, escorted by a massive brown dog and with a sea of smaller dogs flowing around her. And if the Marshal wasn't mistaken, surely that little one there – he wasn't mistaken. The tiny dog was round the back of the car in a flash but there was no mistaking the stitches on her upper lip, the limp . . .

He got out. 'Good afternoon. I hope I'm not . . .' The little sandy bitch was there again, right in front of him now and standing on her hind legs, applauding his arrival, a tiny scrap of cheerfulness.

'Did you see her? Did you see my little Tessie?

Sweetheart!' The little dog leapt into the Contessa's arms and licked her face madly. 'She was a poorly girl but she wasn't going to stay in that dreary place and die, was she? No, she wasn't. No, she wasn't! Good girl! Now you go and play with the others while I talk to the Marshal. Go on! Tessie went, limping and leaping, yapping with joy, up onto a low stone wall, through a bank of crocuses and away after the other dogs. They all raced up the green hillside where a grey pony looked up to see what the fuss was about, gave a token buck, and lowered his head to graze again. For the first time since this business began, the Marshal felt better. But how on earth . . . ? He looked his question at the Contessa.

'Oh, for goodness' sake, there wasn't that much wrong with her. A few cracked ribs that will mend themselves, a couple of hours on a drip, two or three stitches, and a vitamin shot. I've brought dogs round from worse than that.'

'But . . . I heard this morning—'

'That she'd been put down? Yes, well, so she would have been if Caterina had got her way but the vet had the good sense to ring me. He's my vet, too, you see, and he knows Tessie always stays here when Olivia's away for any length of time so he told me to come and get her. She's such a little darling – not a drop of decent blood in her – I always say her mother ran away from a circus and got laid by the first stray male she laid eyes on. What do you think?'

The Marshal was speechless.

'You know, you have a look of an absolutely darling English bulldog I once had. Died of distemper, poor bugger. Do you know much English?'

'No, none, I'm afraid.'

'Pity. Could have shown you an article about him in an English magazine. It's worth reading. Sit down. Do you mind sitting out here? It's such a pleasant day. I love winter sunshine and just look at the crocuses. I don't think they've ever made a better show. If only Olivia were here.'

They sat on wrought iron chairs at a rustic table with a fine view of the dogs' unsuccessful attempts at distracting the grazing pony among the olive trees. It was indeed a pleasant day. Every so often, a big grey cloud blotted out the sunshine and the Marshal took the opportunity to blot his eyes before replacing his dark glasses.

'Must you wear those things?'

'I'm afraid so. It's an allergy I have.'

The huge brown dog came bounding back to them and stood panting before the Marshal with a hopeful gaze fixed on him.

'No, Caesar. We're not going. We have to talk. Go and play with the others. Go on! What sort of allergy?'

'I – ah, the sun. The sun hurts my eyes.'

'That must make life difficult. Sicilian, aren't you?'

'Yes. From Syracuse.'

'Ah. Still, you don't seem a bad sort.'

'Thank you. Can I ask you about Caterina Brunamonti?'

199

'Poisonous bloody girl. Never say so in front of Olivia, would be more than my life's worth. What about her?'

'Well . . . that, I suppose. Do you feel she's jealous of her mother?'

'If you like. Lot of girls are, if the mother's successful – and of course, Olivia's a beautiful woman, too. But Caterina's problem is she's barking mad like her father. Have they told you she won't part with a penny?'

'For the ransom? No. I've just been discussing the problem with Mister Hines but we . . . we didn't discuss money.'

'Why not? Money's what this is about. Those two kids have got twenty thousand dollars each invested in the States – I shouldn't be telling you this but somebody's got to speak up and I'm giving every lira I can lay my hands on in the time to save Olivia, so to hell with it. Leonardo's already offered what he's got but she won't cough up a penny. Do you know she sold Olivia's jewellery? Everything Patrick gave her – most of the Brunamonti stuff went years ago to pay off Ugo's debts but the few bits that remain the little madam will keep herself – have you seen those diamonds she's wearing? That's her mother's engagement ring from Ugo and it was his mother's. Nor will she give her signature to a mortgage on what she calls her father's house. Can you believe that? *Her father's house!* The family inheritance shouldn't be touched for someone who is, after all, an outsider. Olivia's business should be borrowed on or sold up instead – it's so shaming to have the family name dirtied by trade. You follow?'

'And a Brunamonti wife doesn't go out to work . . . someone told me that's why her husband left her.'

'Quite right. And since Caterina has no talents, no qualifications, and no skills, it has been decided that a Brunamonti daughter doesn't go out to work, either.'

'And university?'

'I should have added "no brains". Won't last the year out.'

'I'm afraid you're right. She told me she's already left . . .'

'Blaming Olivia's kidnapping?'

'Yes. Yes, she did say—'

'Barking mad. Olivia tried to fit her into the business in a dozen different ways but it was always a disaster. So she decided it was beneath her dignity. She'd like to push the fashion workshops out and shut herself into that great house and play the Contessa Brunamonti for all it's worth. It's all she's got.'

'But how would she survive?'

'How did her father survive? He didn't and neither would she. I must say, though, that dear old Ugo was adorable as a young man. Mad but fascinating. I was a bit in love with him myself when we were teenagers.'

'You didn't marry then?' She wore no rings.

'Four times. Tedious business. Most men are boring. No time now, not with the dogs. Besides, I have much more fun with my women friends like Olivia. Olivia's a wonderful woman and I really admire her. That's why I'm lending them money but it's not enough. I'd like to know where they got the idea that Olivia was worth eight billion lire!'

The Marshal told her.

'That dreadful man!'

'You know him?'

'I don't know him, but Olivia dragged me to that ghastly exhibition of his with all those weird pictures of Caterina. That girl's so stupid she thought he'd pay her for modelling but all she got was a signed picture of herself in a ballet frock.'

'Yes. I saw that.'

'You did? Well, that's all you'll see her doing in a ballet frock. Posing. And poor Olivia spent a fortune on her dancing lessons – five days a week and enough fancy outfits for a prima ballerina – until the crunch came and she was politely asked to remove herself. Can you imagine her dancing? Could never sit a horse, either. Groom I had years ago was supposed to teach her to ride here. Drove him mad. You should have seen the fancy riding outfits Olivia bought her! She'd arrive here and while the groom was riding Pegasus in for her she'd sit there criticising his riding! Then, as soon as she was in the saddle, it was "I want to get down! Get me down!" Pegasus eventually obliged, dumped her in a ditch, and we were saved any further nuisance. No doubt, you've been shown the photograph of her on horseback, too.'

'Yes. Yes, I saw it on her wall . . .'

'Looking like she's got a broom handle stuck up her ass – isn't that what Americans say?'

'I don't really—'

'I married an American once. Fun while it lasted but then he would insist on going back to America so we had to part company. He liked sailing. Drowned. Pity, really. It's getting chilly out here. Can I offer you something in the house? Whisky? I'll call Silvia.'

'Silvia?'

'Olivia's maid. I told you I was going to bring her here. I'm keeping her until Olivia's home. She's pretty useless, as a matter of fact, but I have her help me wash the dogs. Whisky? Or something else? Do you prefer red wine?'

The Marshal refused the wine but he went away as cheered and warmed as though he'd drunk it. The woman alarmed him a bit but he trusted her, trusted her heart and her intelligence. After a word with the Captain, it would be worth trying to convince her to let them treat the banknotes she passed to the family, in the hope of tracing them afterwards. It did happen, though much depended on the recycling possibilities of the kidnapper, which, in the case of Puddu, would be legion, given his contacts in every part of the criminal fraternity. Yet again he had reason to wish that the kidnapper had been Salis.

At home that evening, he showered and changed out of uniform before appearing in the kitchen. Teresa was relieved. He had been absentminded and low-spirited for about as long as she could bear without losing her temper. And if she asked him what was wrong, all she got was the usual repertoire of how was he to manage if his men kept being taken for duties not rightly theirs and Lorenzini running the place single-handed . . .

She began cautiously, 'You look well. Good news?'

He gave her a hug from behind but no news.

'I'm hungry.'

'Well, that's certainly not news. It's just a slice of steak and tossed beets but I got you some of those nice floury rolls you like so much.'

He ate his supper with relish and, after it, allowed himself to be propelled into the boys' room to give the long-promised lecture to Totò about studying more and improvising less. He thought he did it rather well. It was very solemn, about three lines long, and accompanied by a ferocious stare.

Totò said, 'Oh, *Dad* . . .'

The only snippet of news he told Teresa at bedtime was about Tessie, believed dead, found living happily in a country house.

'Oh, Salva, let's hope that poor woman will soon be safe at home. Is there no news of her?'

'The Captain feels sure she's still alive. The family is intending to pay up, I think, but they don't seem to have the full amount and they've cut us out, which may put the victim in danger.'

'But can't you do anything?'

'Not until we know exactly where she is, and even then it would be very risky.'

If he didn't talk to her about the Contessa Cavicchioli Zelli, though he knew she loved to hear about such characters, it was because it would be bound to lead to their talking about Caterina Brunamonti. The question of Caterina Brunamonti had blocked his vision of the facts in the case up to now because he had been unable to acknowledge what he suspected. Now he was unable to speak of what he had acknowledged.

Nevertheless, he slept better than he had since the case had begun. No muddled dreams of dogs and photographs tormented him, and, however unpleasant a morning awaited him, he faced it with the quiet determination that comes with clarity of vision. He had to start all over again, listening to the people he had already listened to, but this time fitting the words to the subtext and understanding them. Though he was in no way obliged to do it, he took things in their original order, so getting the worst over first.

He rang her from his office and, as he waited for her to answer, he thought of that first sight of her, sitting bolt upright in the empty chair that faced him now, her head turned a little to one side, tense and watchful, the diamonds shining softly on her pointed hands.

'Hello?' As she spoke, her long white body in the doorway superimposed itself. '*I knew you'd change your mind.*' The memory of the chilly, sneering voice made him shiver again. 'Who's speaking, please?'

He pulled himself together. He must keep a grip, tread carefully. The one thing that wasn't yet clear was what she wanted from him. Barking mad, the Contessa had said.

He felt afraid because he understood now how difficult it must be for her brother to defend himself or his unfortunate mother from someone so weak. Weak and demanding as an infant. The trouble was, she wasn't an infant, she was big enough to do damage. He talked to her briefly, every sense prickling, alert, trying to work out what she was using him for.

'Since they don't want you coming here, I can come to your office, can't I?'

Why? *Why?* 'It might not be a good idea to be seen—'

'I don't mind being seen. I've told everyone I'm the only person cooperating with you. Nobody can say it's my fault if Olivia isn't saved.'

So there was his answer. Keep the money and ostentatiously help the carabinieri so 'nobody can say it's my fault.'

The Marshal felt his stomach turn cold. In an expressionless voice, he advised her not to ask the others questions but only to observe and report what she found out.

'I'm going to,' she said. 'You'll see.'

'I'd like a word with your bro—' But she had hung up.

He tried to get the brother again at intervals throughout the morning but the telephone was always answered by the sister and he never succeeded in getting past her.

'He's busy with other matters so I'm vetting all the calls. You've no idea how many people are pestering us all day long.'

'I imagine they're concerned about your mother.'

'Well, there are far too many of them. The phone's never free when I need to use it. It's ridiculous. Some people have no common sense.'

He gave up.

He talked to Captain Maestrangelo in the Prosecutor's office. Fusarri was alert and interested and smoking his tiny cigars at an incredible rate.

The Captain looked worried. 'If you've lost the men and you don't trust the daughter, what are our chances of marking those notes?'

'Good,' the Marshal said.

'Who?' asked Fusarri. 'Cavicchioli Zelli?'

'Yes.'

'I thought as much. Why do you say so?'

'Because I trust her. And . . .'

'And?'

'Because it's her money. It's the only hope of ever getting any of it back.'

'How many times have you seen her, as a matter of interest?'

'Twice.'

Fusarri stubbed out a cigar and threw up his hands. 'Maestrangelo, I don't know how you discovered it but this man's a genius!'

The Marshal frowned. He was accustomed to being made fun of but this was no time for levity. Fusarri got up and started pacing up and down his elegant office, stretching his legs and arms with relish as though ready for some interesting action.

'I've known Elettra all my life and you have understood her perfectly. I'll get her to let us treat the notes. Go on. The planner?'

'If it's the man I think it is . . . well, I thought perhaps you or the Captain—'

'No. Too heavy. Don't want him skipping town. What do you say, Maestrangelo?'

'I think that's true – that it would be too heavy, though I don't think he'd leave. I arrested him for the villa art thefts. He's cool and very, very arrogant. Guarnaccia suggests we go in on a routine check about a stolen painting, just take a look around.'

'A stolen painting?' Fusarri raised an eyebrow. 'And do you have a stolen painting in mind, Marshal?'

'No, no . . .' Guarnaccia, deeply embarrassed, examined his shoe. He had expected the Captain to have carried on from here and felt put out. With any normal prosecutor he could have expected to be absent from this conversation entirely or waiting immobile in the corner, camouflaged by the solid antique furniture. Nobody helped him and there was nothing for it but to go on.

'There was a painting stolen in Paris . . . that was what suggested . . .'

'The Corot? I see, I see. Well, we can't accuse him of that, since he's here.' He stopped dead and faced the Captain. 'He *is* here?'

'Oh yes. I put someone to watch his house as soon as Guarnaccia had his file sent to me. We've checked with our Art Heritage Group and there are only two possible art thefts and one of those isn't in his league. Which leaves us this one.' He slid a sheet of paper from the file on his knee and Fusarri examined it.

'Two landscapes . . . Hm. No chance of his really being involved?'

'We have no reason to think so.'

'Well, they'll serve our purpose, anyway. A routine check, given his previous conviction, and who more apparently innocuous to do it than the Marshal here? Excellent. Right, Maestrangelo, tell me how you're discreet inquiries into what's happening out in the hills are going.'

The Marshal relaxed as their attention turned to matters beyond his competence and he was left in peace to listen. A feeder had been spotted taking a bag of provisions each evening by moped and leaving it inside a ruined farmhouse in the foothills. It was presumably retrieved during the hours of darkness. The feeder was a shepherd boy and had been identified by the local force as a fourteen-year-old relative of Puddu. Nothing could be done with this information at present. The boy would know nothing and could lead them no further. The number of possible guards had been reduced by following the movements of suspects over a three-day period. One was a meat humper at the central market and frequently failed to arrive home in the mornings when he could be expected to go to bed. Another had his own business, gas cannisters and firewood, and was likewise missing for long periods, often at night. These two had both worked with Puddu before, the latter as a feeder and later as a guard, the former as a feeder. Both had prison records. The third suspect had no recorded kidnapping experience but had worked on and off for Puddu for years and had a long record of minor offences. He had recently served a sentence for a knifing incident after the bar fight between the Salis and Puddu clans, according to Bini. Any attempt to close in on these men at present would endanger the victim. They were unlikely to have been involved in removing the Contessa from her palazzo, the greater likelihood being that this would have been organised by Puddu's city contacts, whether Tuscan or Sardinian. Neither they nor the planner would have had any direct contact with the actual kidnappers, except possibly at the moment when the victim was handed over to masked and unnamed men. They would have been paid off as soon as their part in the job was over.

Once the carabinieri had made sure of the identity of the planner, against whom there would probably be no usable evidence, they would have put names to almost the whole band. Until the victim was safe or some unexpected development occurred, no arrest could be made. When the victim was released, the culprits would either go to ground or leave the country. All they could do was to be ready.

The Marshal paid a visit to the photographer. He went in uniform and took with him a man from the Art Heritage Group, which was housed at the opposite end of the Boboli Gardens from his own station in the Pitti Palace. His feeling was that the specialist should do all the talking, leaving him free to look. The studio in Via Santo Spirito was fairly tatty but filled with some very expensive-looking equipment. The Marshal knew nothing about photography but it was clear, even to him, that this was way beyond the class of studio you usually found when you needed passport photos or first communion pictures. Artistic, he supposed, remembering the 'ghastly exhibition' story. Definitely not your weddings and christenings outfit.

Gianni Taccola was exactly as the Captain had described him, cool and arrogant. His black hair was fashionably short and sleek and he wore a collarless black shirt under a blue suit. When the two missing landscapes were introduced into the conversation his expression was derisive.

'You'll find them in Sotheby's next New York catalogue. Not stolen, quietly exported.'

'That,' said the Marshal's colleague, 'was a thought that had crossed our minds but we thought a respectable family wouldn't be caught doing it themselves . . .'

'Nor would I.' Taccola whipped round, thinking to catch the Marshal staring at a set of enlargements showing Caterina Brunamonti, naked and holding a glistening snake. He didn't. The Marshal never squared up to the things he wanted to examine. He let them flow around his peripheral vision while centring his gaze on something else, in this case, a close-up of a dusty stone effigy.

211

'You prefer dressed stone to naked flesh?' Taccola inquired, unable to control his arrogance, inviting the Marshal to turn to the pictures of Caterina.

'No, no . . . ,' the Marshal said blandly, forced now to let his glance sweep over the whole set of enlargements, which covered most of one wall. They were in black and white and so dramatically shadowed that there was nothing pornographic or even erotic about them. They were just sinister. 'Very striking . . .' In his peripheral vision now was a battered old chaise longue with a length of black silk draped over it.

Taccola shrugged. 'To be honest, I prefer boys myself, but you know how it is. A client is a client. Perhaps I should adapt one of those signs they put up behind the counter in bars where they don't want to give credit. "Please don't ask for sex as refusal often offends." Couldn't offend the rich little lady, could I? She financed my exhibition. Besides, she turned out to be a virgin, which made it rather more piquant. Almost but not quite as good as a just pubescent boy. Now, if there's nothing else I can do for you . . .'

As they went down the stone staircase, the Marshal said, 'Squalid enough place . . .'

'Isn't it? You should see the sixteenth-century villa he lives in. Filled with art treasures legitimately bought with his illegitimate gains. Marble swimming pool surrounded by statues in the garden.'

'How long did he go down for?'

'Not nearly long enough, Marshal. Not nearly long

212

enough. I sincerely hope you get him for this kidnapping but I don't give much for your chances. He's a clever bastard.'

The two parted company in the street, and the Marshal cut through into Piazza Santo Spirito from behind the church.

'Blast!' He had momentarily forgotten about the porter and the closed doors. He was about to press the porter's bell when he noticed *Contessa S.R.L.* next to it and tried that instead. There was something of a wait, then footsteps. Signora Verdi was dragging one of the huge doors open. He helped her and she put a warning finger to her lips.

'This is not allowed,' she whispered. 'All visitors report to the porter's lodge, and he calls up to her ladyship to find out if they're allowed in. I don't know whether you are.'

'Don't worry about it.'

She hurried him inside the workrooms. 'No friends of Olivia's are allowed in except those likely to cough up money. We've worked that one out. Is there any news?' Every pair of eyes in the room watched for his response.

'Nothing I can tell you. I really came to talk to you for a moment. I won't keep you long.' The truth was she'd already told him what he wanted to know in her first remark but he went through the motions anyway.

'Do you have one of your labels handy?'

'Of course . . .' She took the box from a shelf. Over half

of them had gone. They were going on with their work then, which pleased him. He picked up a label.

'Do you remember telling me you'd discussed using the name Brunamonti rather than just *Contessa?*'

'Did I? I forget. We've all been so upset. It's true anyway, because of pirating, but her ladyship—'

'Yes, you said that at the time. You meant the Signorina Caterina?'

'Of course I did! "I am a Brunamonti," she says to her mother in this very room, "and *you* are not." Olivia's heart was broken – not because of the labels, you understand. Well, all I can say is that, except for her mother, we all breathed a sigh of relief when she took against the business and we saw the last of her down here. Criticising the designers, sneering at the machinists, nothing being done that she couldn't do better. We had to put up with it for Olivia's sake but you can imagine how people with thirty and more years' experience felt about being sneered at by an ignorant chit of a girl – and Brunamonti or no Brunamonti, that's what she is. Anyway, we were saved when she decided she'd be better than the professionals at modelling. At the Milan show, it was. There she stood, all dressed up and the music playing – bridal gown, Olivia's pièce de résistance, and the blasted girl wouldn't set foot on the catwalk. Stood there paralysed. What a scene. Anyway, that was the last we saw of her, thank God. She can't help not having her brother's talent but it would help if she only had his good manners, not to mention a bit of common sense *and* a bit of respect for other people.' Her face was red with remembered anger. 'It's incredible how different they are.'

'I know what you mean. I have two boys myself and they're as different as chalk and cheese . . .' He talked on until she cooled down and then left her with the one bit of good news he realised he could give her, that the little dog was safe.

'You've made my day! Does Leonardo know?'

'Probably not. I've been trying to phone him but . . .'

'I know. Well, I'm going up there right now. It'll give him new life. Little Tessie home and safe!'

The Marshal went next door and ordered a coffee in Giorgio's bar.

'I'll make it for you myself. How's it going?'

The Marshal shook his head. 'What do they say in the piazza?'

'Nothing you can believe. Like the papers. If there's no news they make it up. Talk of the devil . . .'

The Marshal looked round to see plump, slow-moving Nesti coming in the door.

'Give me a coffee.' He had an unlit cigarette dangling from his thick lips, which meant he was trying to give up smoking again. To the Marshal he mumbled, 'If you can't find your kidnappers, why don't you at least arrest that cow of a daughter, whatsername, and keep her out of my office.'

'She's been visiting your office?'

'Visiting? She's a fixture. She's round there now

chewing somebody's ear off. I escaped when I saw her coming. I told you how it'd be. She's more interested in getting her picture in the paper every day than getting her mother back and it's the only way she'll ever make the news, unless one of my colleagues bumps her off, which is getting more likely by the minute. For God's sake, get this case solved, can't you? I've got to get back – look at this, I've taken to hiding behind dark glasses like you.' He drank off the last of his coffee and rambled out into the busy piazza, unlit cigarette still dangling.

'What's up with him?' Giorgio asked. 'Not that I've ever seen him in a good mood – not sober, anyway.'

'Oh, he seems to have taken a dislike to the Contessa Brunamonti's daughter. What do I owe you?'

'Oh, nothing. On the house. Taken a dislike is right . . . Don't know her personally. Never comes in here. What's her name again?'

'Caterina.'

'Ah. D'you know something? It's too warm. It said on the news last night. Far above the seasonal – What the . . .'

The glass door of the bar slammed shut, making the whole place vibrate. One of the waiters went and opened it again and wedged it more firmly.

'You see,' said Giorgio, 'far too hot. Must be a storm brewing. Blast of wind like that.'

But it wasn't a blast of wind.

Ten

Because of the earthquake, felt in Florence but with its epicentre in the next county where it caused enormous damage, Caterina Brunamonti failed to make the first page next morning. Nevertheless, on the basis of the interview she had given, almost three pages were given over to the kidnapping itself and to a polemic surrounding kidnappings in general. From Sardinia, a Prosecutor General launched heavy accusations against the magistrate considered responsible for the escape of Puddu. Prisoners are given periods of freedom, sometimes hours, sometimes days, in return for good behaviour. Long-term prisoners who have served half their sentences for serious crimes can be released on parole. Good behaviour in prison is the speciality of professionals who know how to manipulate the system and of the most dangerous, child molesters and murderers, whose everyday behaviour is excessively meek and obedient. The latter are usually recaptured if they fail to return, sometimes having committed another murder; the former, like Puddu, vanish.

The sentences given for kidnapping are extremely heavy, heavier than those for most murders, but this is mere show if prisoners are then released on parole after serving half their time and allowed to escape. Each time a kidnap victim is freed, cheers go up. Naturally we are all relieved to see the victim alive and well and in the general chorus of joy no one wants to be the first to put in a more sombre and critical note. But every successful kidnapping – the victim released at the kidnappers' leisure, the ransom paid – is a defeat, not a victory. Like so many laws, that on the freezing of assets is a drastic and rigid one in theory, punishing even those who fail to pay taxes on money known to have been paid as ransom, money whose existence has usually been well concealed until then. In reality, we then hear of ransoms paid, under the protection of clause seven, paragraph four, as 'Controlled payment of ransom for investigative purposes.' And yet, not only do the 'investigative purposes' fail to result in any arrests on the release of the victim, we even see two government ministers on television consoling us with the thought that the law freezing assets is really quite flexible. A flexible law is a law which is not applied. The popular saying about the law being something you apply to your enemies and interpret for your friends comes to mind. I am as relieved as the next person when one of these victims is released but there is no question in my mind that, at least in Sardinia, the frozen assets law has only decreased the number of small-time amateur kidnappings. Not only this, but a number of victims have failed to return home and the time of imprisonment has inevitably been lengthened. Professional kidnappers are by no means discouraged. Families are told that if their assets are frozen they must make other arrangements. And when they fail to make such arrangements, malign rumour has it that, if they know the right people, the State does it for them. This is not victory. This is, at best, defeat; at worst, collaboration, and, as a judge, I consider myself rendered impotent and even ridiculous when I think of the successful kidnappers taking their ease in the Bahamas at the taxpayers' expense. Given such an example, kidnappings of wealthy people with influence in government circles are bound to increase. However, for the moment, all we can hope is that as long as this law is in existence it is enforced, and vigorously so. Otherwise, it must be changed, as must the law that allows dangerous professional criminals freedom, so giving Puddu the chance to kidnap the Contessa Brunamonti. I, and I think most Italians, have had enough. I would like to see the frozen assets law suspended. I would like to see the forces of law and order taking a serious stand against kidnapping by assiduous patrolling of the territory, the capture of those bandits known to be on the run, and the setting up of specialist forces in high-risk areas. Only then would I address myself to the rewriting of the law on kidnapping, first of all making it a crime of violence against the person, not just an aggravated form of robbery.

On the same page, in heavier print, was an article which defended the existing law on frozen assets but which criticised heavily the one allowing a known kidnapper, serving a thirty-year sentence, to be allowed out on parole.

In principle, the law should remain because it ensures that ransom is paid under police control, marked and traceable. Ransom paid in secret could compromise an investigation. Let's be careful then, not to throw out the baby with the bathwater at this point. The law requires modification, yes, but, more importantly, we should be thinking about preventing those kidnappers who have been successfully captured and imprisoned from walking free.

The rest of the page was taken up with statistics and rundowns of recent kidnappings. Overleaf was a double-page spread with photographs of Leonardo and Caterina Brunamonti. The picture of Leonardo was the one previously published in this same paper. The one of Caterina was new, glamorous, with a touch of show-business tragedy in the form of dark glasses to suggest eyes ruined by shed tears. An interview accompanied the pictures. The Marshal read it in his office and the frown on his forehead was not of concentration but apprehension. The interviewee was referred to as 'a spokesperson for the Brunamonti family.' The Marshal's worst fears were realised.

Your feeling, then, is that this kidnapping was based on false information?

It must have been. The amount of the ransom request is way beyond our means. Their information must have been false.

And where do you feel such false information could have come from?

Obviously, no one can say for sure. We may never know.

But you have a suspicion?

Not of a particular person but, unfortunately, the Contessa's running her business from within the Palazzo Brunamonti meant that a great many more people frequented the building than would have been the case otherwise, and, of course, anyone working there permanently would have an unusual amount of contact and, inevitably, of information.

What is your opinion of the law freezing your family's assets?

I think it's an intelligent law, protecting us and helping in the apprehension of the kidnappers.

You're not afraid of its causing prolonged imprisonment of the victim and even the risk of the victim's death?

I don't see why that should necessarily be the case. We are cooperating with the State, and the State must cooperate with us in return.

And what form do you feel this cooperation should take?

I know of a number of cases in which the ransom was paid by the State using marked notes as a way to further the investigation.

So you hope the State will come to your aid?

It's the only thing I can hope since we don't have the means to pay ourselves. I'm well aware that we don't have the sort of political contacts to guarantee first-class victim status. We can only collaborate and hope that even a second-class kidnap victim has a chance of survival.

Before Marshal got to the end of the page the phone connecting him to Headquarters rang.

'Guarnaccia.'

'Have you read it?'

'Yes . . . yes, I'm reading it now.'

'Don't talk to any journalists.'

'No. Will you call a press conference?' His eyes, still scanning the paper, caught sight of a headline about first- and second-class kidnap victims.

'Not if I can help it but the Prosecutor will be the one to decide. I'm certainly not answering any questions about those ransom payments. Apart from anything else I don't know the answers. What I'm concentrating on is saving this victim.'

'Do you think there's any hope?'

'Not much, but if they don't kill her today when they read this article there's a faint chance that something might change. The son might be sufficiently frightened by it to come for help. I'm assuming this is the daughter's handiwork, though there was a bit of an attempt to cover her tracks by saying *the Contessa* instead of *my mother*.'

'She never does call her *mother*, she calls her *Olivia*.'

'Really? Well, unless she's extremely stupid she must want her dead.'

'Yes . . . a bit of both, perhaps. She's very dangerous. I think, with your permission, Captain, I'd prefer that what she refers to as collaboration should occur in the presence of the Prosecutor. She's threatening to come round here, you see . . .'

'No, no, no, absolutely not. Don't receive her or God knows what we'll see in the papers next. I'll warn the Prosecutor. He's going to work on the Contessa

Cavicchioli Zelli. I'm concentrating on the known contacts of the feeder we've spotted.'

'Is there anything further I can do?'

'You can only hope that some element in this story changes because otherwise its conclusion can only be that poor woman's death.'

Nothing changed. The daughter never did turn up at the Marshal's office. Once, he spotted her in the street, coming out of a fashion house shop with two beribboned dress bags, but her eyes slid away from his and she walked quickly on. The Captain's men watched on the hills and scrutinised the Lost and Found columns in the paper, the most common place for the exchange of messages. Nothing likely appeared. All possible informers were contacted with no results but then, as the Captain pointed out, they knew who the kidnapper was but at this stage they couldn't act on the information since any attempt to search for the hide-out carried the risk of the victim's being killed if they unknowingly got too near. Their arrival would be spotted at a distance of kilometres in such territory.

Elettra Cavicchioli Zelli told them she could not let them mark the notes she passed to the Brunamonti family.

'I don't know what's best but they made me promise and I did promise so I can't go back on my word. I know you want to catch these bandits but I just want Olivia home. Do you think she's still alive?'

No one knew what to answer. Weeks of silence passed.

When a change did come it was as unexpected as it was unhelpful. The English detective, Charles Bently, presented himself at the Public Prosecutor's office and announced that he was dropping the case.

'We had rather thought,' said Fusarri, 'that by this time you'd be dropping the Contessa Cavicchioli Zelli's *unmarked* ransom payment.' Just to let him know they weren't completely in the dark.

'I know my business, Mister Prosecutor,' Bently said, 'and I don't consider it any part of my business to get myself killed.'

'I appreciate that,' Fusarri said, 'and Elettra – the Contessa – did warn me that she would be unable to provide the whole amount and no one could expect you to run such an obvious risk to your life. I also appreciate your correctness in coming here to tell us of your decision. If you felt able to tell us what time limit we're dealing with on this, it might help to avoid an equally great risk to the Contessa Brunamonti's life.'

'I'm glad to know you appreciate my correctness.'

The Prosecutor put his hand up. 'Of course, of course. I can't expect you to break the confidence of whoever is paying your fee. I beg your pardon.'

'Thank you. And you're wrong. I only take a fee when I can do the job. Until I make that decision I'm on daily expenses. I can't do this job without the ransom money.

Nevertheless, I will not betray a confidence. The family must decide about the extent they wish to cooperate with you. All I can tell you is that I have myself advised them to collaborate. If they drop a wholly inadequate sum of money, after that article in the paper, she's dead. As long as they delay and the kidnappers imagine they are trying to scrape together the whole amount, then even if they pass or have passed the deadline, there's hope. As long as that hope exists, they must keep her alive or get nothing. If they decide to make do with less, cut their losses, they might as well kill her as not. They won't want to put future jobs at risk. My opinion is, they'll wait, and if the family collaborates with you, you can use the waiting time for your purposes. It's only a question of the right informer, I imagine. Your Special Operations people are good, I know that.'

'Oh, indeed they are.'

'So, the right informer then. In our recent talks you told me of an attempt to inculpate an enemy clan. No hope of their knowing something?'

'Every hope of their knowing everything, but not of their telling us about it. They come from Orgosolo, a place where it can take three weeks for an arrested man to admit to – not give – his name. The Orgosolese idea of an effective defence is total silence. You can't trip him up in a contradiction or a lie if he doesn't open his mouth. What they say is "Nothing comes from nothing".'

'Sounds like something from Shakespeare. *King Lear*, if my schoolboy memory doesn't deceive me.' The

Englishman stood up. 'But I see their point – and your problem. Well, I must leave you. My plane leaves in little more than an hour. Mr. Prosecutor. Captain.'

The Captain, who had witnessed this exchange in silence, rose to shake his hand after Fusarri. The Englishman's cool correctness was impeccable. Only for a moment was it shaken when Marshal Guarnaccia appeared, apparently from nowhere, and offered his hand, too, to this exotic personage.

'Ah! You're here, too. I beg your pardon. Didn't notice you in that corner – I mean, thought you were a guard of some sort . . .'

'Yes.'

Only a question of the right informer.

As the door closed, Fusarri dropped back in his chair, took a deep, noisy breath, and then leaned forward to fix the Captain with a bright stare.

'Every Sardinian up there will know where she is, won't they?'

'More or less.'

'But more or less won't meet the case, will it? More or less would kill her. We have to know exactly, don't we?'

'Yes.'

Fusarri leaned back again and there was a moment's silence. Then he turned his head slowly to where the Marshal sat, bulky and silent.

'So who will know *exactly*? Marshal?'

The Marshal shifted uncomfortably under his stare, looked at his hands, his hat, his shoe. 'Bini would be the man to ask.'

'Bini? Maestrangelo, who on earth is Bini?'

'Local force.'

'Ah . . .'

'Bini,' the Marshal said, 'knows Salis. And his wife. Salis's wife disapproves of kidnapping.'

'I'm delighted to hear it,' Fusarri said, still at sea. 'You're not telling me she'd turn informer, even on a rival clan?'

'No, no . . . She wouldn't do that.'

'I assume she's from Orgosolo, too?'

'I expect so. Bini would know for sure.'

'Well then, Marshal' – Fusarri tried to catch the Captain's eye but couldn't – 'you'd better pay a visit to your colleague Bini.'

'I'll do that,' the Marshal said. 'If you'll excuse me, I'll do it right away. After that article there might not be much time.'

Bini had the flu. Either that or the reason for their journey kept him unusually quiet as the jeep's wheels sprayed up dust and grit along the country lane. The Marshal looked out of the window to his right at the high, dark hills whose flat tops were slowly being obliterated by banks of cloud. A few drops of rain spattered the windscreen but it hadn't begun to rain in earnest. Every so often Bini sneezed and said, 'Sorry, this wretched flu.' Every so often, the

Marshal shivered as he looked up at those hills and he said nothing.

The sliced-up car was gone from the yard when they arrived. The dog kennel was still empty, a dirty bowl overturned near its entrance. Washing hung on the line, motionless in the grey air. Despite the gloominess of the day, there was no light to be seen through the glass panels of the kitchen door, but its outer shutters were open.

'She's in.' Bini got down from the jeep, and the Marshal followed him with a glance towards the sheepfold on the left, where the shepherd boy had slept with his ears cocked for danger like the sheepdog. Now the guilty boy was buried and the dog was still in the morgue fridge. Salis dealt with his problems alone. As yet, he only knew that he had been set up by Puddu, that his land and his people had been subjected to a search. He certainly knew what had been found. The only thing he didn't know was that by now the trick had been understood by the carabinieri. Bini tapped on the glass and opened the kitchen door.

'May we come in?'

She didn't answer, having no words to waste on a foregone conclusion.

The kitchen stove was lit and she turned her back on them to feed wood into it and drop the cover back into place.

On the plastic tablecloth lay a pile of sheets of paper-thin Sardinian bread, pale and crisp.

'Can we sit down a minute? You don't make this bread yourself, do you? It must take hours to get it that thin . . .'

'You haven't come here for a cookery lesson, I imagine.'

'No. And we won't waste your time or ours telling you what you already know. You know what we found on your land. Your husband's going to have this kidnapping on his file.'

'He didn't do it.'

'So you say. And what difference do you think that's going to make with his record and the evidence we've got?'

Silence.

'It's real evidence, you know. That hide-out wasn't faked. She was really there, and we have proof. If you're interested, she wrote something on the wall of that cave that her son recognised as something only she could have known. What do you say to that?'

'Nothing.'

'Whether we find him or not doesn't matter. He'll be convicted in his absence.'

She would probably have gladly seen them both dead but, in accordance with the rules of hospitality, she placed a flask of her own wine and two glasses in front of them. The Marshal's mouth was dry with fear at what they were doing. The wine was strong and sour. He wished she'd switch the light on. He wished he were at home with his wife and children. The thought invoked Caterina Brunamonti, the article, the pall of cloud settling on the dark hills. He took another sip of wine. He felt the heat of the stove and shivered.

'Of course,' Bini continued, 'if we should find out that somebody else did it, he'll be off the hook, but I'm afraid it could be too late. We think she might already be dead, in which case . . .'

Both of them watched her face closely on these words but she looked as little as she said. Bini had no alternative but to carry on.

'We've no hope of finding an informer. Puddu's lot wouldn't dare, and we have every respect for the Orgosolesi. We just thought your husband should know. We respect him but evidently Puddu doesn't. Maybe because your husband's getting on in years Puddu thinks he can—'

'Come back the day after tomorrow.'

'Remember, there isn't much time. If you're telling me to come back, I'll come back, but nobody can guarantee the victim will still be alive the day after—'

'Come back the day after tomorrow.'

They followed the instructions exactly, driving up a cart track in the jeep, which bounced them every which way as they clutched the overhead handles for safety. At a certain point, very high up, a branch lay across their path. Bini stopped the jeep and they got out. They walked forward from there without speaking. Only once, Bini, stopping to blow his nose, murmured, 'I've got a temperature. I shouldn't be here . . .'

230

Neither of them should have been there. What was worse, they couldn't be sure what Salis would decide to do and, whatever it might be, they were responsible. They had put themselves in his hands. Despite the height and the faint cool drizzle, the Marshal's back was sweating, and he prickled all over at the thought of eyes and rifles maybe being trained on them. Among all his other worries was that of their finding their way back down in the dark. The light was already waning.

Could it be so far? Had they missed the next signal? No, it was there, not far ahead: a white rag tied to a thorny bush. They took a footpath to the right and walked on for over half an hour until another white rag signalled a turn to the left. This was no longer a path but a way through the brush, sufficiently used to be visible but difficult and thorny. They were dressed in old thick clothing and the brambles tore at it and dragged as they pushed on. Every so often they had to stop and untangle themselves. When at last they reached the clearing which was marked by the fourth and last signal, it was getting very dark. They stood waiting in silence. There was no reason not to talk to each other but they couldn't manage to do it. They stood until the darkness enveloped them and they could no longer see each other.

The voice, when it spoke, seemed to be very near but there was no point in looking towards it. They were risking a great deal but not their lives. They could be certain that Salis's word was his bond but certain, also, that a stupid move, a torch, a third person following, would mean death. They stood still and listened.

'Tomorrow evening, a woman will telephone your station to report the attempted theft of a moped. She'll tell you it happened right in front of her house. She'll say a man jumped out in the road, causing the moped to swerve and the boy riding it to skid and stop. She'll say the rider, who had a shopping bag on his handlebars, was attacked and a long struggle took place. During the struggle she will have seen a second man approach the moped and bend over it as though to take it. He will be there for some time, inserting powdered sleeping pills into the much-used wine flask which the shopping bag always contains, but the woman will say she didn't notice exactly what he was doing. She'll say she was watching the fight. When it's over, the second man will be gone. The boy will break free, get on his moped, and ride away. The next morning at dawn, you can fly over the Monte della Croce and the place where the victim is held will be marked by a white signal. You'll find her alive. You'll find the men who are holding her dead.'

'No! My God, Salis, don't do that! I can't deal with that!'

'Please yourself. In that case, you'd better be there before the two who go up at dawn. If they get there before you and find they can't wake their guards up it won't matter whether they cotton on to the wine or not. They'll know the job's screwed up and they'll get rid of the woman. The choice is yours. Now go. You needn't be afraid of not finding your way down. You're under my protection here.' The voice stopped. They could hear nothing apart from their own loud breathing. Salis wouldn't move until they were away. They would not hear one sound from him that he hadn't decided they should hear, not so much as the cracking of a twig.

The Marshal felt, rather than heard, a slow, deep intake of breath before Bini decided to speak.

'Have you thought . . . you could give yourself up. Now that you've collaborated with us on this, you'd—'

'I'm not collaborating with you. I'm using you to settle my own business.'

'Of course. I realise that. Even so, it might be the best chance to come your way. You might think about it—'

'So you could stage a big capture scene for the television cameras? How much?'

'I can't – I'm not authorised to deal. I was only wondering—'

'Forget it. I was curious to know what I'm worth. My family's well provided for. I can afford to die a free man.'

'No offence meant, you understand . . .'

'None taken. Now go.'

They turned and started to feel their way back. Brambles tore at their faces now they could no longer see to avoid them. Only below knee level was the way clear, adapted to men who could move crouched double, invisible below the brambles; impossible for upright people. They knew when they had gone wrong because

233

their boots would become entangled in uncut brush. Then a voice would come out of the blackness.

'Turn back. Stop. Go on to your left.'

It wasn't always the same voice, and they were too disorientated by the thick, damp blackness to be sure which direction these instructions came from.

It was a relief when they felt themselves back on the footpath but their relief was short-lived and they were soon stumbling through a void which offered no clues to give them direction or balance.

'Jesus, Mary, and Joseph . . . !' gasped Bini in relief as they hit against the friendly solidity of the jeep.

On the road back to the village, cheered by their own headlights, the sound of the motor, the sight of the first farmhouses, they found their normal voices again, or at least Bini did.

'I heard tell they put adrenaline in those nose spray things they give you for a cold. Did you notice I haven't sneezed since we got out of the jeep up there?' But even then he didn't tell any jokes. 'Salis . . . he's his own man. Living on the continent hasn't touched him. I wish I hadn't said what I did . . .'

The Marshal, filled with apprehension about the possible consequences of this night's business, didn't speak at all.

Teresa, when he got home, bathed the stinging scratches on his face to an accompaniment of cross remarks on the lines of, 'I can't see why you don't leave this sort of thing to your young carabinieri who are fitter than you and think nothing of being up half the night.' But her voice came out more frightened than angry and she didn't ask him just what 'this sort of thing' was.

His written report to Captain Maestrangelo was brief and contained no mention of the previous night's activities. It stated that their colleague, Marshal Bini, had referred to him an intimation, presumed to be from an unnamed informer, that an indication of the position of the hide-out, etc . . .

Verbally, he referred to the matter of the expected report of a stolen moped and the drugged wine, adding his private worry that the feeder might suspect something.

'We've been watching him for weeks. He can't be more than eleven or twelve. Besides, there'll be nothing missing. He will only worry about his precious moped. He's underage for riding it and couldn't report it stolen. No. Salis knows his business. We need to concentrate on ours. It's time to get the experts in.'

The Captain telephoned at once to the Special Operations Group in Livorno. They were alarmed by the risk involved in such close timing but rose to the challenge with a suggestion: that the parachute regiment should create a noisy diversion by flying helicopters low over Salis's nearby territory, under cover of which their own helicopter would go in over the area of operations, and at first light drop nine men with directional parachutes into the nearest clearing to the signal.

The Captain asked the Marshal no questions about the

previous night's business, confining himself to an expression of relief that he hadn't been tempted to arrest the young feeder. The temptation to make an arrest when such an investigation went stale was considerable. Such a gesture might be made in the hope of gaining or regaining the confidence of the family but might just as easily make them nervous about the investigator's priorities. It would keep the press busy for a day or two. The public might imagine that the feeder would talk, not knowing that such a minor player knew nothing other than that he left a bag of food in a given place each day and never saw who retrieved it or knew for whom it was intended. When their conversation was over it was tacitly assumed that it had never taken place.

The Marshal's feelings, as he crossed the river to go back to Palazzo Pitti, were an incomprehensible muddle of apprehension about what he had done and irritation at having failed to live up to the Captain's faith in him. After all, it might not have been necessary to do what they were doing if he had succeeded in keeping the trust of Leonardo Brunamonti. Some part of the blame must be attributed to the Captain himself, who overestimated the Marshal. Young Brunamonti was well bred, intelligent, and would surely have been more likely to trust the Captain himself than a dull-looking NCO. And yet, thinking back to their first long talk, Leonardo had been disarmingly open and trusting. Except, of course, that he hadn't told the truth about his sister. Now there was the biggest source of irritation! There was his real failure.

How could he have let himself be taken in when all along he had known something was wrong? He had listened to her endless compliments to herself and her endless criticisms of everybody else, especially her mother, and, if he hadn't been wholly taken in, it wasn't for want of trying. He'd been afraid to see what she really was.

How, then, could he blame her brother? The brother who had stroked her arm so softly once to restrain her with an almost painful gentleness, willing her not to become what their father had become. It would be unreasonable to expect him – in such traumatic circumstances, too – to see the necessity of overcoming his fear, his affection, his shame.

And yet, how many other people had rung alarm bells which the Marshal had failed to respond to? Signora Verdi, on that first day, with 'her ladyship wouldn't have it.' Nesti with his disgusted remark about whether this was a case or a career opportunity, the maid's sobs, and her all too justified fear, 'What will happen to me now?'

Not to mention the alarm bells Caterina herself had set off. A lot of the time she lied, but what about when she told the truth? What about her avoidance of the word *mother* when she used the word *father*? Saying a model was nothing more than a coat hanger? So many things that had made him so uncomfortable that he had refused to think about them.

If he thought at all about the operation soon to take place on the hills it was with a deep-felt wish for a safe outcome but without any detailed thoughts about how it would be achieved. There, he felt on safe ground. The job was in the hands of experts now and was their responsibility. His only contribution had been to act as a connection between Bini – whose years of experience, goodwill, and carefully cultivated contacts made the operation possible – and the men capable of carrying it out. A bit part which he considered adapted to his station and capabilities and which would be ignored in case of scandalous failure, forgotten in glorious success.

But it would be a long time before he would stop being irritated with himself about 'that poisonous bloody girl,' as the Contessa Cavicchioli Zelli called her. Now there was a woman who called a spade a spade. There'd been no more fooling himself after meeting her. If only the others had been so explicit.

The Marshal climbed the sloping courtyard in front of the Pitti Palace and turned left to go under the stone archway. His idea, at this point, was to retreat into his own space and apply all his concentration to the little everyday tasks which were normally his lot. First he would have a talk with his second-in-command, Lorenzini, and get himself up to date on what was going on in his Quarter other than a kidnapping, then he would see anybody who was in the waiting room and give any time left after that to his backlog of paperwork. If he achieved nothing else, he would so fill his mind with details that there would be no crevice through which the thought of the Brunamonti girl could worm its way. It was this same quest after normality and sanity that inspired him to telephone his own quarters and ask Teresa, 'Can we have pasta?'

She laughed at him. 'You sound like Giovanni!'

'I am like Giovanni – or, rather, he's like me.' He was offended. 'It doesn't matter, it was just a thought.'

'You are a comic. I'll put the water on. It'll only be tomato sauce, I hadn't planned—'

'That's all right.'

This system worked until five o'clock. Then a twinge of anxiety twisted his stomach at the thought of what the sister might be up to that could in some way damage tonight's operation. She had shocked him with the Patrick Hines business, surprised him with the closed doors, the sacked maid, the new porter, alarmed him with that newspaper interview. He couldn't afford to seek his own comfort by forgetting her. He mustn't talk to her, the Captain had agreed about that, but he had to keep a check on what she was doing.

Fifteen minutes later, he was holding on to the handle above his head as the jeep bounced violently up a rocky tractor path, Lorenzini at the wheel.

'I didn't believe you when you said we'd need the jeep to get to a place two minutes away from the city centre but – hell! You all right?'

'I'm all right. I've been up here before. Stop here and turn round and then wait for me. I'll not be long.'

The bank where the crocuses had flowered was now a forest of Florentine irises, some of which were opening their first pale blue frills. Nothing else had changed.

Elettra, as the dogs yapped the news of the jeep's arrival, burst out the door, accompanied by Caesar and surrounded by her chorus, wearing the ancient grey suit and running a hand through her unruly wisps of grey hair.

'Oh, I'm so glad to see you! And so is Tessie – just look how she's greeting you! She knows the nice Marshal is trying to help her mummy, doesn't she? Yes he does, yes she does, the little sweetheart!'

They had sat in the February sun last time, but now, although the season was more advanced, they went indoors to escape impending rain. The drawing room was lit with small lamps. There were flowered sofas, a polished stone floor, and a wood fire burning in a large grate. They sat facing each other near the fire on a sofa each and, as the sofas filled up with dogs, the Marshal told her his fears.

It wasn't easy. This was a very bright lady and he couldn't expect to fob her off with an invented story, assuming he were capable of inventing one, which he doubted. He had to convince her with something that was less than a lie but not the whole truth. He didn't know whether the partial ransom had been paid but he thought not. He had to convince her that, if not, it mustn't on any account be paid now.

'That article in the paper would become her death warrant. They would be sure no more was forthcoming. They would know that there are no powerful connections who might intervene. To release her for so much less than the requested sum would ruin their business. You do understand?'

'Of course I understand. I also understand that you're up to something that makes it suddenly so important not to pay up and that you're not going to tell me what it is.'

He looked at the wall. 'I can't . . . I'm not – it's a matter that my superiors—'

'Virgilio Fusarri, the old fox. I like him. He can't boss me around, wouldn't dare try. So he sent you. Tell me. Does it look as if, because of the two photographs, the "spokesperson" – blast her – was really speaking for Leo and perhaps even Patrick as well?'

'The message is all that matters. A small payment would confirm it. It doesn't matter to them who the messenger is.'

'It's going to matter to Olivia! You don't think they'd show it to her?'

'They might well. If they intend to make her write another appeal they will. Don't you think, though, that she'll recognise her daughter's handiwork, even the words she uses?'

'Of course she will – Caesar, get down off the Marshal! You're too big to sit on people's knees! Sorry, he's a Rhodesian Ridgeback, bred to hunt lions, but he doesn't know. He thinks he's as small as all the others. Get down, Caesar. All right, well sit next to him quietly.'

The dog subsided and fell into a deep sleep leaning heavily on the Marshal. He was a very powerful leaner.

'She'll recognise Caterina's poisonous voice in that

article – who wouldn't? But Leo didn't stop her, that's the point. He let her do it. He knows she's crazy. He should have kept her locked up till this was over.'

'He could hardly—'

'He should have warned the papers. And how come they printed such a thing if you say it's so dangerous? Why didn't you stop them?'

'We can ask them to cooperate, but their job is to sell more newspapers, and we can't stop them doing their job. The article contains nothing that infringes the law.'

'There must be something you can do!'

'We are doing what we can. We must prevent any payments being made.'

'That's what that detective fellow said. Do you have any real information about Olivia?'

It was risky but he needed her help.

'Yes.'

'You're not going to make some futile gesture that will make you all look heroic and risk Olivia's life?'

'No, no . . . Her life is already at risk. We have a chance of saving it. It's only a chance but if that incomplete payment is made we won't have that.'

There was silence between them for a moment. The Marshal listened to the settling of the wood fire, a sound from his childhood. The many dogs on the other sofas snored quietly in the fire's warmth.

'All right!' The Contessa announced her decision: 'I'll help you. That money won't be paid.'

'You're sure you can prevent it?'

'Damn sure. It's my money.'

'Anything I've told you, of course . . .'

'You haven't told me anything. Don't worry. I know exactly what you mean. I'll keep what you haven't told me to myself.'

The Marshal could do no more. This whole venture depended on two people keeping their word. Two people, each in a hillside fastness, each with a strict code of honour. The Marshal trusted them both absolutely. His part was over.

Caesar escorted the jeep as far as the gates on the avenue below, then turned and bounded back up the hill.

It was raining.

Eleven

'There must be thousands of people in the world who are suffering constant and terrible pain. You stare at me with those big, watchful eyes of yours and I know you must be wondering why I'm so calm, happy even. To tell you the truth, I was never very brave about pain. As a child I cried at the dentist's, and vaccinations were a tragedy. And yet, the violent pain that pierced my ears and seemed to penetrate my brain and which terrified me so much at first because I thought I would lose my mind over it became a normal part of my life. I suppose if agony is prolonged and constant, our brains somehow adjust our threshold. The fixed pain becomes the norm and it takes a much greater or more acute attack to make any impression. I know I used to be afraid of pain and of illness, especially cancer, but I'm not any more. I trust my body to deal with it now. If anything, I was more aware of the lacerations caused by the chain on my ankle and wrist, which worsened despite Woodcutter's efforts. The chain was so very heavy, and every movement hurt and damaged me. What was even worse was the psychological pain because there was no reason to keep me chained up except cruelty. The cruelty of "the boss" I never saw.

'Yet, the tiniest joys could obliterate it all. The fresh sun touching my forehead as I sat at the opening of the tent. Sat waiting contentedly for cool water and crunchy bread but perhaps receiving instead a rare cup of wonderful coffee, the smell of it mixed with sweet wood smoke on the pure morning air. I will always appreciate coffee more now than I used to, but never as much as I did then.

'I had begged Woodcutter for, and obtained through good behaviour, the few privileges I needed, the most important of these being the use of the bedpan outdoors in the mornings. I had also been given a change of clothing, a bag full of very cheap-feeling cotton under-wear, and a green tracksuit. I also had plastic slippers instead of my boots because it was getting warmer. The bag of underwear was sometimes taken away and washed. Was it Woodcutter's wife who did this? I tried to imagine what she knew, what she thought. I remembered Woodcutter's words about how you could never get out. Perhaps she didn't think anything, ask anything, just did as she was told out of fear.

'I organised my day around their arrivals and departures, their changes of shift, the serving of my meals. I divided up the interim periods and developed one train of thought at a time – my children, my work, my lover, my parents, and the past. Friends, too. I allotted them each a space and thought about them. You know, when you live in another country, your friends assume the importance of family. I learned that I had to be careful in organising this timetable of contemplation, avoiding any pathway that might upset me just before it was time to sleep. Sadness becomes overwhelming in the lonely night. It didn't keep me awake – the rhythm of my days was too regular to allow my old insomnia to plague me – but it could cause distressing dreams, even nightmares.

'So, after each meal, I placed my tray carefully on the ground, retreated into the tent, pulling my chain in with me, and settled down to think. In a way, I've been privileged to have this quietness, this thoughtfulness, forced upon me, though I don't expect anybody to believe that. They won't envy me for it either, will they? I'll probably never tell anyone.

'I feel the need to tell you things, though, as if this is the one stop, the halfway house where two worlds meet and you're the keeper of it, the only person who knows and understands both. I'm sure that nobody out there will understand where I've been. For them I've only been absent. I believe that once I'm back in my own world I'll never talk easily about this again.'

The Marshal, well aware of it, sat still and silent,

memorising what he needed, not daring to make a note.

'My mother seemed all right after my father's death. She appeared to be going along as usual, but it was only a façade. I felt such anguish when I was in the house that I hated going home and spent all the time I could at the homes of my friends. I was thirteen and didn't understand what was wrong until she was taken away to a clinic to dry out. I remember my aunt opening the wash-house door and finding all the bottles. I think she was the one who said, either then or later, "Remember you'll have to stand on your own feet from now on. It's a hard world and you're alone in it. Nobody will help you." I spent a few years in a boarding school, passing the vacations with one relation or another, and then went to college, against my aunt's wishes.

' "Nobody will help you." Do you know that my whole life has turned on that one cruel phrase uttered at my most vulnerable moment. What the hell did she mean by it? I was thirteen years old and a virtual orphan. Why couldn't I be helped? From that day I saw life as a battle I had to fight alone. I became tough, at least I managed to appear so, but before this happened, I had reached such a point of inner exhaustion that I knew there was no way forward for me. At night I sweated with years of accumulated fear, by day I tried to reason it out. Should I give up the business because it was too stressful, leave it all to Leo? Should I marry Patrick, dear man, who did understand and tried to help me. "Nobody will help you." That was the rule I lived by. Patrick would cradle my aching head on his chest when I was reduced to tears by anxiety and exhaustion and say, "Listen to this poor turnip of yours pounding away. Give it a rest. Lay down your sword, I'm here now." And I did. With him I rested. Then next day I'd grab my sword again. Years of habit, you see. Besides, apart from Patrick, who saw through me, everyone believed I was invincible, tough as nails. "Olivia will sort it out somehow. Olivia always knows what to do. Olivia's a fighter."

'The only way I could alleviate my orphan's distress was by offering comfort to others. When my husband went, I became a father as well as a mother to the children. They would never hear the words "Nobody will help you" just because their father was dead. I found it odd, thinking of all this, that the one person I ever allowed to do anything for me was my son, Leo. Perhaps because I recognised myself in him, perhaps because he was the one person I knew had a mother who loved him and would always be there for him, the one person I didn't need to be afraid for. Leo was always my early evening thought, before Patrick, my father, and sleep. It was such a joy to scan his life. I loved his deeply solemn gaze as he sucked with quiet determination at the breast. Such concentration he had as a small child! At three he made careful wobbly drawings – almost always of insects. He wasn't old enough to know how to scale a larger object down to the size of his paper. Later, at seven, he painted delicate watercolours out on the loggia. The palaces and trees down in the piazza, bats and swallows in a red sky at sunset, painting for two or three hours at a stretch until the fading light forced him to stop.

'The migraines began when he was fifteen. The pain was so terrible it filled the whole house, weighed like lead in every room so that I could barely breathe. I wanted to comfort him, do something to help, but he would beg me in the faintest whisper, "Just leave me alone in the dark . . ." I had to sit in the dark myself, outside the just open door, so that no crack of light could disturb him. Caterina hated it because she felt neglected. She couldn't understand, a child of ten, that her brother didn't lie there still as death because he was sleeping but because of a pain so terrible he couldn't move. When it was over it left no trace and he never talked about it.

'There was such a stillness about him, such an unfathomable intensity, and, every so often, a bubbling up of thoughts and dreams or of stored merriment. He would suddenly burst out into astonishing imitations of the teachers in his Liceo Artistico, especially the local artisans who came in to teach their skills – casting, printing, and so on – with their loud Florentine dialect and scathing jokes. And I suppose much of the astonishment came from the contrast with his habitual silence. How he made me laugh! You must think I'm crazy, unbalanced after my terrible experience, though your face gives nothing away, because I tell you of dreadful experiences with a calm smile and now I'm telling you of joyful things and I – I can't – I'm sorry. It'll stop now. I'm sorry. I've missed him so much . . . Oh dear, this dreadful noise I make because I'm still afraid to cry, although the plasters are gone. I'm not crazy, I promise you . . . Thank you. Just a sip and I'll be all right.

'They used to change the plasters once a week – Woodcutter did that. Thank God it was always him. He told me it was once a week. I didn't count in days and weeks, only in seconds and minutes, dripping slowly in time to my thoughts . . . Each time he came to change them, tugging gently twice on my chain so I would know who it was, I'd hope for news, developments, another newspaper article, anything. Well, I got what I wished for and I will never wish for anything again as long as I live, I swear to God. I knew that morning that something was wrong. When I was still sitting in the doorway of the tent with my breakfast tray – only bread and water that day, but I didn't mind. The air was damp with impending rain and all the sweet smells of new grass and spring flowers were accentuated. There had often been rows before, though I could never hear or understand well enough to know what they were about. Perhaps their shifts, the food, their boredom and nervousness about how long this was going on. After all, they probably wanted to get back to their lives as much as I did to mine. I couldn't follow their arguments but, like a small child, I was immediately aware of tension, a quarrel among the "grown-ups" which would often result in some unreasonable punishment for me. As I sat with my tray, raised voices penetrated the waves of my undersea world and I tensed up, careful not to turn or lift my head

250

because sweat had loosened the plasters across my nose and they might think I was trying to look at them. I had only felt this edginess before on Sundays when there were so many hunters' guns going off around us and the risk of discovery was at its greatest. Because of my blocked ears, the shots reached me as a far-distant *plaff* but they were hearing them sharp, clear, and near so it was bound to get on their nerves.

'It wasn't Sunday. It was the day for changing my plasters and that was never done on Sunday but on one of the two days a week when hunting was forbidden. And yet, something was very wrong. Woodcutter himself was rough with me, ripping the tray from my hands and ordering me in an angry whisper near my face to get inside and be quick about it.

'I crawled into the tent and pulled in my chain.

' "Are you going to do my plasters?"

'He didn't answer and I heard the zip swish down, a fast, angry movement.

'Trying to appease him, my only ally, I said, "You should change them. They're coming loose over my nose. I promise you I haven't touched them, it's just sweat, and I haven't tried to lift my head and look—"

' "Shut up!"

' "Please don't be angry with me. You said I should tell you, for my own good, if they—"

' "Shut up." He began ripping the plasters off himself instead of letting me do it slowly so it wouldn't hurt. He tore some hair out by the roots near my temple and I

cried out. I sensed his arm lift as though to hit me and I
cringed. The plasters were off and he threw a newspaper
onto the sleeping-bag, telling me to read it. My heart
pounded as I saw Caterina. Caterina in dark glasses. She
never wore sunglasses, she hated them, and I imagined
her beautiful brown eyes, wide and childlike, ruined now
with tears. And Leo, Leo in his old ski jumper, turning to
look over his shoulder at me, the same as last time. Only
this time I must force myself to keep control of my emo-
tions and read about what was happening. Woodcutter
wouldn't leave my eyes unbandaged for long. I began to
read. Stopped. Started again, unable to understand. I was
stumbling, tripping over the words that danced around
on the page so that I could make no sense of them.

'"Have you got the message?" yelled the agitated
Woodcutter into my face. "They don't want you back,
your fancy educated rich children, do you hear me?
They've decided to keep the money and do without you –
well, it's what would happen in the long run, isn't it, so
what's the odds? This is the result of those stupid farts
taking you instead of your greedy bitch of a daughter –
you'd have paid up, wouldn't you? Mothers do. You can
never risk taking a woman like you without even a
husband who wants her back. A husband, even if he'd
prefer to keep the cash and set up with his mistress, would
be ashamed to do it so publicly!" He flung the newspaper
at me. "That's what you've been bringing up all these
years. Like the Florentines are always saying – the trouble
with having children is you don't know what sort of

people you're letting into the house. Well, you do know now. Your children want you dead!"

'I sat staring at the paper and felt my stomach turning colder and colder, a coldness that spread upwards. When it reached my head I passed out, and only the pain as my stone-hard ear block hit the floor caused me to come to. I managed to grab the bedpan in time to vomit undigested bread and water into it. The sour smell of vomit mixed with the bleach and made me retch again and again but to no avail. Woodcutter took the bedpan and put it outside, closing us in again with the smell still there. He shunted close to me and, giving me the pads to hold against my eyes, said, "It's over for you. The boss has decided. There are only a few days left to the deadline and they haven't contacted us. If they don't pay, or try to fob us off with less than we asked for, you'll have to be killed." His anger seemed less as he said this, his fingers gentle as he moulded new strips of plaster over my nose. Then he whispered, "Give me your hand."

' "Why? Why?" This unnecessary cruelty was as much as I dared register and react to. "You never chain my hand in the daytime. Why? Please don't! It hurts me."

' "It's for your own good. It's so I can leave the tent flap open, get rid of this stink."

' "But I promise not to move. I'll lie in the sleeping bag. Please."

' "Give me your hand."

' "At least don't do it so tight. It doesn't need to be so tight."

'He did try it on the next link, only to pull it tight again. "It's too slack like that. If the others see it, they'll only tighten it even more than I do." He snapped the padlock shut and I heard him crawl out backwards, leaving the flap unzipped.

'I sat where he had left me, rigid, barely breathing, as if I could suspend life by not going on with it, keep at bay the tidal wave of grief that menaced me. My slightest move would loose the catastrophe. As long as I sat still, blind and deaf, I was safe. Movement, habitual movement, touch, would set life in motion again and I would be overwhelmed. But, perhaps because of my fainting spell, I was icy cold and was soon forced to seek the warmth of the sleeping bag. I had no choice but to take up my habitual thinking and sleeping position, the prop under my neck to relieve the pain in my ears, and let it come. An annihilating flood of despair, drowning me, destroying me, a litany of grief that tore at my brain and issued forth as rhythmic groans.

'Caterina! Don't let it be true. I'm trying to be strong. I want to live and I can do it but only if you stay with me. Don't abandon me. Don't . . .

'And Leo, the greatest joy of my life – I fought your father and all his family who wanted you aborted rather than have a Brunamonti marry a foreigner. And I never told you because you'd say, as the young and unknowing always say, "I didn't ask to be born." But you did. I heard you. Hear me, Leo! Hear me, please. Don't leave me alone in the dark . . .

'Patrick, where are you? What's happening?

'*Nobody will help me.*

'I was too crushed to form these words. As I said, they came out only as the rhythmic grunts and gasps of an animal in pain. I don't know how long it went on because it continued even as I slept. I know that because somebody – I think Fox – unzipped the tent and woke me by hitting me because I was making too much noise. It must have gone on until next morning because I remember no more meals that day. The next thing I remember was breakfast again. It had rained in the night and I felt the earth and grass wet when I put down my tray. The fresh damp sunshine stroked my forehead, and I heard a bird singing. I felt very quiet. The decision had been made. I was going to die and that meant I could lay down my sword. My battle was over and I had nothing more to worry about. I could concentrate entirely on being alive. Nothing mattered except the little piece of bread softening in my mouth, the sun's warmth, the bird's song. My only regret was that I hadn't known how to live like this before, giving proper value to all manifestations of life, all its griefs and problems. It wasn't a battle you had to win but a privileged state to be savoured.

'I remained calm despite the fact that my captors, especially Fox and Butcher, were in a state of extreme agitation, which they took out on me. One day, I felt for the food in my bowl and found a number of smooth metal objects. They were bullets.

' "Thought you might like to choose your own."

'I drew my face away, hating the acrid smell of Fox, who had spoken close to my cheek. So they were going to shoot me. They would probably do it on Sunday morning when the noise would pass unnoticed. That would be safest for them. I had accepted their killing me but, until then, I hadn't thought about how. I waited until Woodcutter came, and when he was undoing my padlock in the morning I asked him if there wasn't some other way.

' "I've always been so frightened of guns. Can't you do something else to me?"

' "I asked the boss specially. He was against it because we can only do it on a hunting day. I persuaded him for your benefit. It's quick and sure. You won't suffer."

' "I'll suffer fear, horror. I don't want to be shot like an animal."

' "You won't even see the gun. Your eyes are covered."

' "But I'll hear it. I hear the hunters, just about. I hear your voice if you're close to me."

' "You'll not hear a thing because the bullet will be in your brain. You'll be dead before the noise."

'I believed him but I went on protesting until he agreed to hit me a heavy blow to the head and then, when I was unconscious, to strangle or suffocate me.

' "It will be you? Nobody else will touch me?"

' "It's bound to be me. I'm responsible for you."

' "When will you do it?"

' "Probably the day after tomorrow."

' "Will you take my bandages off first and unblock my ears so that I can see you and say goodbye to you?"

' "No."

' "Don't you have the courage to do it if I can see you?" I remembered how he'd called me Signora whenever I was unbandaged. Now he didn't answer me but said roughly, "Get in the sleeping bag. I've got things to do."

'I zipped myself up as far as I could, and he did something he had never done before. Very gently, he tucked my arm with the chain well into the bag and zipped it up to the top for me.

' "It's still raining. It'll be a cold night." I could feel his breath on my cheek as he spoke.

' "Why do you feel sorry for me? Is it because I'm going to die?"

' "No. Don't think too much about that thing in the papers. They twist things. It's all the same to us. They don't pay, you die. But you shouldn't believe everything that's in that article." He was sorry for me because my children didn't want me. I heard him shuffle backwards out of the tent and I wanted to cry out to him to stay with me, comfort me, touch me. I could still feel his breath on my cheek, his sweet, wood-smelling breath. He was going to kill me and I wanted him. I don't think I've ever desired a man so much. It was a stab of pain, a torment. I'm sorry if I'm shocking you.'

'No, no . . . you mustn't be afraid of that. It's only natural.'

'Do you think so? The need for comfort seemed to me

257

to be natural enough but the desire shocked me. Perhaps it was a reaction against having to die . . . well, it hardly matters now, does it?

'I slept just as always and the next day I found his words were still with me. How could I lose faith in my own dear children because of a newspaper article? They could have been delaying the payment because there's a law of some sort about not paying kidnappers, isn't there?'

'Yes. Yes, there is.'

'I remembered that – and then, maybe the bank was causing difficulties – or you had set up the article to help in some way in your investigation. After all, you rescued me. You had plans which the payment could have spoiled and so you asked for Leo's collaboration.'

'Yes. I personally asked him to collaborate . . . these things are very complicated. All that matters is that you're safe. Let other people worry about the rest.'

'Woodcutter was right then. It couldn't be true. The others went on tormenting me because they must have been furious about the ransom's not being paid but I had nothing to fear since I was to die anyway and Woodcutter had promised me that he would be the one to kill me. I wasn't afraid to die. All that mattered to me was to die loved by those I loved. I began to think about preparing myself. I asked Woodcutter if he would also bury me. He said not. He said that all trace of the camp would have to be removed and I couldn't be buried. He didn't explain any further and I asked no more questions. I knew the wild boars in the woods leave no trace.

'So there would be no burial. No one would cleanse my body and say a ritual goodbye to it. I decided to do this myself. I had thought so much about my life in the past weeks but never about the body which had served me well all those years. On my last day I convinced Woodcutter to bring a bowl of precious water into the tent and asked him if he had a comb. I think he understood me, and I was not disturbed by Butcher, who was on duty with him. I washed my body as best I could with swabs of rolled-up toilet paper, putting my dirty clothes back on over my damp skin. It felt odd, my skin, rough where it had always been smooth, especially on my arms and legs. My skin must be very dry and is flaking. Dehydration, I suppose. And my nails – undoubtedly long black claws – but Woodcutter had no scissors or he would have helped me. My hair was impossible to comb, being so long and, by now, badly matted. I did what I could with it but a great deal of it must already have fallen out and remained tangled with the rest so that the comb brought away thick strands and clumps of it. I gave up and smoothed it over with my wet hands. My fingers were hugely swollen. I didn't recognise them as mine. I remembered Woodcutter taking off Patrick's ring "for my own good." He must have known this would happen. He wasn't stealing it. He would have given it back to me if he hadn't been forced to run away. I lay still then and felt my body, curious about it after so long an estrangement. I felt my

259

breasts, my hips, my sex, and thought of them making love, giving birth, giving suck. I felt my arms and long legs, thin and flabby now, despite my little efforts at gymnastics. Still, I no longer needed muscles. I felt very peaceful and thought that dying was a great deal easier than living.

'After I had been fed at midday – the usual hard bread, a piece of Parmesan, and a miraculous juicy tomato which I savoured for as long as possible – Woodcutter took my tray and whispered near my face that he was leaving and would be back tomorrow at dawn with the boss. I knew what that meant. The last words he said to me were, "Go in. It's going to rain hard."

'I could smell it. There were rumblings of thunder, too. I crawled inside, got into my sleeping bag, and pulled in my chain. I thought about Woodcutter tucking me in and zipping me up. I wished he were here to do it now. Even inside the tent the air was heavy with the approaching rain and I shivered. Both the sleeping bag and my skin seemed damp. I didn't think about my usual things. There was no need to think any more. For my last hours I could just be. However much I had enjoyed my precious thinking time, it was a relief. I was very tired and the pain in my ears seemed more violent than usual, though I could see no reason why it should be. Tomorrow Woodcutter would come and it would be over. I could trust him. He was responsible for me. Somebody had to be responsible for me because I was too tired . . .

'I fell asleep. I don't know for how long, only that the

rain woke me. How hard could it be raining for me to be able to hear its whispered pattering on the roof of the tent? I extracted my arm from the sleeping bag to feel the canvas and was amazed at the vibrations. There was thunder, too, which must have been directly above me because not only could I hear it loudly, though distorted, its rattle even caused my ears to hurt more than ever. I tried to cover them with my hands but to touch those great hard lumps was agony and only made things worse. I reached upwards and felt the roof of the tent sagging under a great weight of water, which soaked through and ran down my arm the moment I touched it. How could that happen? As I scrambled out of the sleeping bag, pulling too quickly at my chain so that the pain made me gasp, I felt that the ground below the tent was awash and one side of it had come loose so that it was sagging inwards, heavy with water. I called out. Nobody answered me, and I remembered with dismay that Woodcutter wasn't there. He had told me once that there was no need to be afraid of being left with the other two at night because once they had eaten and fed me, they settled down to play cards and drink themselves into a stupor. I called out again very loudly, remembering that my blocked ears tricked me into thinking my voice was loud when it wasn't. Nobody came. Was anyone there? I hadn't been fed since Woodcutter left at midday. How long had I slept? Could it be night already? Were they too drunk to hear me? I was completely disorientated and I began to panic at the thought of being trapped in the tent, drowned in it. I gave one last loud cry. If there had been anyone there I would have been punished for making half that noise. Nothing. Just more vibrations of thunder, water dripping onto me in my darkness. I searched for the zip, thinking as I found it that if it was night, not only should I have been fed, my wrist should have been chained. I opened the zip and knelt there, afraid to get out, calling for help. No one came.

'Unfortunately, my plasters were relatively new and well stuck down over my nose. I didn't dare rip them off. I must have forgotten in my panic that I was going to be killed anyway, so the rules didn't matter. I couldn't overcome my habits of submission. Even at such a moment it cost me to do the unforgivable thing I had promised Woodcutter I would never do: I picked at the strips of plaster over my nose and loosened them so that I could lift my face and peer down below the eye pads. I put my head near the tent opening and peered. I was pelted with rain but the world was black. I could see nothing, nothing! What was happening? Why did nobody come? I got hold of my chain and crawled outside, my hands slipping in swirling mud and water. I had never seen the world outside my tent. Inside it didn't matter because I knew exactly where everything was, which was as good as seeing. Out here was a void. I only knew one thing: my tree. If I followed the chain on my ankle I would find my tree. I lifted the chain, my breath noisy inside my head, and pulled it towards me. When I reached my tree I hugged its soaked trunk. I held on to it for a long time with my forehead pressed against its wet bark, for the comfort its presence gave me. My chain and my tree were all I had left of a whole world that was swirling away in the storm, leaving me stranded. Had they decided to abandon me here instead of killing me? It could make little difference to them. If there was going to be no money they might as well get away as quickly as possible.

'As to the difference it would make to me . . . I would perhaps be attacked by wild boars and eaten alive instead of dead but that made no impression on me since it was impossible to imagine. The real difference was that Woodcutter had lied to me. He had promised to come back. "I'm responsible for you." He had promised me and let me down and that was unbearable. Hugging my familiar tree, abandoned by my captors, my children, my trusted executioner, I sank down in the mud and let my tearless groans loosen themselves and rise from my stomach. Their rhythm was loud in my head, and the noise kept me company, like my tree, for many hours.

'Then something changed. The rhythmic animal groans in my head were accompanied by other noises. I couldn't stop my noise, which wasn't under my control, more like breathing than anything, but I tried to understand what else it was I was hearing. Not thunder, a muffled *phut-phut-phut* from far away and a nearer drone. Something else. Below my forehead, still pressed painfully hard against the tree trunk, there was a sliver of light. Keeping one arm around my precious tree, I poked at the plasters, lifting them more. It had stopped raining and it was dawn.

'I found it difficult to stand up but my tree helped me. I held on tight and raised my head to peer out below the loosened plasters. There was someone there! Big brown rubber boots, greeny brown trouser legs, the shining muzzle of a machine gun. He must have seen me with my head raised! I had done the unforgivable – seen the man, seen, behind him, the shelter, the mattresses, the table, the others asleep. Woodcutter had come back for me and I had let him down. I turned away, sticking the plasters down like a child caught with its fingers in the jam pot. "My eyes were shut! I didn't see anything, I didn't. Please, please, forgive me!"

'I didn't fight against him when he got hold of me, only bowed my head and begged, "Please . . ."

' "Contessa Brunamonti."

'I could smell by then that it wasn't him. He got away . . .'

It was a question though she tried to make it sound like a statement.

'Yes, he got away. He's still up there somewhere with Puddu.'

'Puddu?'

'The one you call the boss.'

'I never saw him.'

'No. He would never have let you see him. We know that. You don't need to be afraid.'

'I never saw any of them.'

'No.'

'The man I saw this morning was one of your people?'

264

'Yes.'

She seemed relieved. Perhaps, now she had her other senses, that of smell didn't reassure her as it had before. By the time she had passed a few days in hospital, the civilised world would have reasserted its claim on her and what she recounted afterwards would be told from a false viewpoint, filtered through the channels of other people's expectations. Nevertheless, the Marshal refrained from asking any questions.

She said, 'I'm warm now, in these blankets . . . Whose is this tracksuit I'm wearing?'

'Bini's wife lent it. Bini is the marshal of this station. Don't you remember? She dried and changed you when we arrived, in their quarters.'

'I don't remember . . .' Because she had caught sight of herself in a mirror, a staring-eyed, haggard face in a tangle of straggling grey hair, she who a few months before had been mistaken for her daughter. She had fainted. 'Will you thank her for me? What's that noise?'

'The siren? That will be Captain Maestrangelo arriving with the Prosecutor in charge of the case. They will have to ask you a few questions because you may forget things later. If you've already told me the information I'll give it to them. Then we'll drive you to the hospital. Do you feel all right? Do you need anything?'

'I need to use a bathroom.'

'Of course. Can you wait just one moment? They're all men here. I imagine Bini would like to check that everything's as it should be.'

265

'What could it matter after all that . . .' But the Marshal got up and went out of the small office. Bini was opening the door, ready for the new arrivals.

'Bini, she needs to use the bathroom.'

'There's one right here.'

The Marshal opened the door and peered into the little room. It was raining heavily again, beating against the tiny high window through which filtered gloom and dampness.

'The light switch is here,' Bini said, then watched, puzzled, as the Marshal went in and carefully, reaching up over the mirror, unscrewed the light bulb.

Twelve

Rome –

The Minister of Justice was about to leave Palazzo Chigi when we stopped him to ask:

Are you pleased, Mr Minister?

'About what?'

About the outcome of the Brunamonti kidnapping.

'Naturally, I'm happy that we've saved the victim. The Contessa Brunamonti has returned to her family.'

And the polemic about how this was achieved?

'What polemic?'

Some people are saying that the kidnappers would not have released her unless the ransom had been paid. It has also been reported in the newspapers that a spokesperson for the Brunamonti family had declared only days before that they couldn't pay.

'I can't comment on what newspapers choose to put about.'

The same person also said in a published interview that they were collaborating with the State and that the State should, in turn, collaborate with them.

'I don't know what you mean by collaboration. We have rescued the victim and arrested three members of the gang. Our business now is to find and arrest the two men on the run.'

Excuse my insistence on the point, but how was the rescue achieved? Was some arrangement made to exchange money for the victim which then turned into an arrest? Did the captured men talk?

'I'm sure you're well aware that I can't give that sort of information at this stage.'

Kidnapping is evidently still a profitable business since it still goes on. People are concerned, not unreasonably, about kidnappers being allowed out of prison. Isn't something wrong here, Mr Minister?

'This case has been solved. The victim is free. A number of arrests have been made and we have every reason to hope that the information we hold will lead to the arrest of the remaining culprits. Any change in the legislation must be discussed at the appropriate time and in the appropriate place. We are already discussing corrective measures to the prison benefits system, which must, of course, respect the indications laid out by the Constitutional Court, as regards the perpetrators of this particular crime, particularly since it invariably involves a group of criminals and can therefore be considered as organised crime.'

So the same rules should apply for Cosa Nostra?

'That may well be. Kidnapping is organised, professional crime as is Mafia crime. Professional criminals go back to work if released.'

And in the meantime?

'In the meantime, the Contessa Brunamonti has been saved. Naturally, I am delighted.'

'Naturally, he was furious.' The Captain passed the article across the desk to the Marshal. He knew that the Minister had already answered these same questions a dozen times to as many journalists and on two occasions had lost his temper and said the wrong thing. Had the accusations about the State's having paid the ransom been true, he would have been prepared and kept his cool. Since they were not, he was at a loss. The only story he had been given was of 'information received leading to the pinpointing of the hide-out.' Who was going to prefer that to a nice bit of scandal? Who would even believe it –

that and the conveniently heavy sleep of the guards, who hadn't so much as opened their eyes when they were handcuffed? It had been decided that this part of the story should be omitted since, without recounting Salis's part in the affair, it would not be credible. Nobody believed the rest, anyway. Not the newspapers, not the opposition, and not the public either. The Minister had said as much to the Colonel in command in Florence, who took it out on Captain Maestrangelo. Captain Maestrangelo was unhappy about the irregularity of this affair but at least he wasn't unprepared. Prosecutor Fusarri, relaxing behind a cloud of smoke in the Captain's leather armchair, was as satisfied by the irregularity of the affair as by its success. Suddenly he leant forward and jabbed towards the Marshal with his cigar.

'Now I've got you. Yes, the Maxwell kidnapping. I can't remember precisely what it was you did but you did something that . . .'

'No, no . . . ,' the Marshal said, shifting his gaze from the newspaper cutting to the painting behind the Captain's head. 'It was Captain Maestrangelo here who dealt with it.'

'Hm.' Fusarri raised one eyebrow, pursed his lips in a half-smile, and murmured, 'Maestrangelo, call a press conference.' The Captain did so and brought in someone from the Special Operations Group and they concentrated on the operation itself. It went down well, especially the helicopter decoy. This story was being worked up into a TV documentary with a reconstruction of the rescue. The Captain saw the necessity for this shift of focus but, being an honest and serious man, he regretted that as much of the true story as could have been made available would have been of no interest to anyone. The fashion was for Special Operations Groups, dangerous midnight shoot-outs, camouflage outfits, and expensive weapons. 'Information received' wasn't much of a headline. You couldn't work up a television documentary about a dull NCO in a country village who told bad jokes and spent his days quietly attending to the problems of his people. What could you add to that? That an equally unimportant marshal from a small station in Florence had listened to him? So the Captain did what he had to do. The journalists were happy. The Captain was put out and said so when he recounted all this to the Marshal, who had waited the press conference out in the Captain's office. The Marshal only said, 'As long as the poor woman was saved . . .' and, as soon as he decently could, asked permission to get back. Something about an urgent appointment.

The Marshal was more than put out, he was very disturbed. When Teresa caught sight of his looming black shape out of the corner of her eye she was a bit sharp with him.

'Salva, get changed. We've to be there in ten minutes.'

'It's only round the corner.'

'Get changed. It'll look bad if we're late.'

The looming black form retreated.

They walked down the slope in front of the palace and

waited to cross. It was six-thirty and the traffic was heavy but there had been rain that morning and now that the sky was clear the scent of lime blossom on the evening air overpowered even the exhaust fumes. Further on, the narrow pavement was blocked by a mother having trouble with a small girl.

'That's enough. I said that's enough!'

The little girl screamed and hit out at her mother with clenched fists. 'I hate you and I'm telling my dad on you! I hope you wet your knickers! I *hate* you!'

'Will you stop that? And mind you get out of the way. There are people trying to pass.'

The mother pulled her child aside and smiled at the Marshal and his wife apologetically. 'They get too much,' she remarked, quite unperturbed by the small girl's red-faced rage.

Teresa had always wanted a little girl. She smiled at the woman as they squeezed past. 'Small children, small problems, as they say.'

When they were past, she laughed and repeated, ' "I hope you wet your knickers" – did you hear her? That must be the worst disaster she could think of wishing on her mum.'

The Marshal wasn't amused.

'What's the matter with you? You were just as bad at lunch-time.'

'Nothing. It's nothing . . . bit tired.'

'Well, if you weren't up to it I could have come by myself.'

'No.' They reached Via dei Cardatori and went in at the school entrance.

How could you know what was right for your children? Nobody told you. You just muddled along, doing your best, inventing solutions to one problem after another. There was a time when parents just followed age-old rules which nobody had ever questioned. He couldn't imagine his own mother ever having been in doubt about what to do, fully occupied as she was with keeping her children clean, fed, and respectable. And she saw their future in terms of getting a safe job and so continuing clean, fed, and respectable. What did he know about whether Totò would have done better in the English language stream with his friends than he had without them, doing French in less crowded classes? He was frightened and angry at the thought of his son's being held back a year and, in his anger, continued to say, 'It'll do him good, teach him a lesson.' How did he know? And more difficult decisions loomed ahead about which he had no information, no experience, no confidence. How did Teresa take it all in her stride the way she did? Did it never occur to her that her child might one day in the future turn on her and accuse her of some unfathomable wrong?

'Salva!'

'What?'

'Sit down.' Then, as the teacher turned to answer a question from one of her colleagues, Teresa whispered, 'At least try and look as if you're listening, for goodness' sake.'

That morning he had been at the hospital where Olivia Birkett had been kept for two weeks because she had developed bronchial pneumonia. There had been photographers in the Contessa's room and he had found himself waiting in the corridor. There he saw Elettra Cavicchioli Zelli in furious conversation with Caterina Brunamonti. Their fury was such that he could hear every fiercely whispered word long before he was near enough for them to notice him. Elettra's voice came to him first.

'It isn't a question of it's being none of their business. It's only natural that they would look around for some flowers to include in the photos. Damn it, even her doctor was asking where they were. So where the bloody hell are they, starting with mine, which were freesias, her favourites?'

'The nurses complained. There were far too many. This is a hospital, not an opera house. She can't be playing the prima donna here.'

'I can't believe this. And Patrick's orchids? You're not going to tell me you threw a whole basket of orchids away?'

'I didn't throw them away. I took them home for her.'

'For her? Or for yourself?'

One of the photographers put his head round the door. 'Signorina. Could we have one with you by your mother's bedside?' Her smile already in place, Caterina hurried into the room.

'Marshal! Oh, I'm so glad you're here. Can you believe what's going on? Listen, Olivia's out of danger. The fever's gone and the doctor says she'll recover better at home now, but he says Leo has asked him to keep her in here another week!'

'Her son asked that?' His eyes followed in the wake of the daughter, the more likely perpetrator of this betrayal.

'I know! But it wasn't her, it was Leo. He asked for an appointment, said he was worried about her and would feel happier if she stayed in here longer. He'd feel happier! Never mind what Olivia feels if she finds out.'

'You're sure she doesn't know? Wouldn't they have told her first of the decision to discharge her?'

'I don't know and I daren't ask. We're not supposed to upset her. You've got to talk to Leo.'

'Me? Wouldn't it come better from you? I mean, as a friend of his mother's . . .'

'I've been trying for two days but there's no getting past that little pot of poison who's in there now smiling for the cameras.'

'Even so, they can't prevent her going home.'

'She's changed the locks! Did you notice? The closed doors, the porter, that whole business? She's taken over. Olivia doesn't know it yet but she can't even get in. A nice homecoming after what she's been through. Listen, I'm going to suggest she comes to my house for a week or so with the excuse that Tessie's there and recovering better in the country than she would in the city. If you want Olivia to do anything, you've got to tell her it's for somebody else's good. She has no sense. And you must talk to Leo. He doesn't talk to anybody much but he talks to you, doesn't he?'

'Well . . . he did, but the circumstances were extreme then . . .'

'They're extreme now. Olivia's tough. She's come through this business like nobody else could and now the fever's gone she's quiet and happy. But nobody can defend themselves from their own children, especially not when they love them as much as Olivia does. If she finds out what's going on it will break her. You don't think she could ever get to see that ghastly interview that was in the paper, do you?'

'She has seen it. The day it came out. They showed it to her.'

'But, knowing Olivia, she didn't believe it. She's always defended Caterina, though she must know in her heart . . . Leo, though! If she thinks he doesn't want her home it'll be enough to kill her!'

The photographers came out, Caterina firmly attached to them, telling them what a terrible experience she had been through and how she was working night and day to help her dear mother. The photographers, with the exception of one small ginger-haired one who continued to take shots of her as they went, looked slightly dubious and extremely bored.

'Good God!' was Elettra's only comment, and they went into the room. A nurse was coming away from the bed after measuring the patient's blood pressure. She frowned at these new arrivals and murmured, 'She's very tired.'

Olivia looked more than tired. She seemed to have collapsed into her pillows, her face drawn and haggard. She looked like an old woman. However, she lifted her arm to accept her friend's embrace.

'Olivia! You look so upset!'

'I'm all right. I am really.' Her voice was weak and scratchy but she attempted a smile which looked more like grimace.

'The Marshal's here – I don't know what for – what are you here for?'

'Just to bring a rough copy of the Contessa's statement so she can check it and add anything more she remembers. Then I'll give her the corrected copy to sign.'

'I can't . . . not now. I . . . I'm sorry . . .' Her chest began to heave and she seemed to be trying to cough.

'I thought your cough was better. Shall I call the nurse?'

'No. Please don't, Elettra. It's just the ulcer on my ankle . . . it's still so painful . . . I'm sorry. I want to sleep.' She closed her eyes.

They looked at each other and left.

Elettra marched off down the hospital corridor at such a pace that the Marshal had his work cut out keeping up with her.

'Sorry. Got to run. I've left three dogs in the car. Her ankle's not that bad, you know. It's probably quite painful, but I've seen it and it's almost healed. I think she's upset because she's found out.'

'Yes.'

'The ankle thing's just an excuse.'

'Yes. I wouldn't let on that you know. It must be a relief to her to have a ready explanation for her distress. There's not much privacy for her between the hospital, the journalists, and us.'

'I think you're right. The ankle it is then. I have to go. Thank you.'

What did she thank him for? She always seemed as glad to see him as he was to see her. He walked, more slowly now, to his car, wondering whether to go straight to the Palazzo Brunamonti and try for an interview with the son, or whether it would be wiser to have a talk with Patrick Hines first. The trouble was that he was quite certain Hines would be very wary of interfering between Olivia and her children and particularly wary – if not downright frightened – of crossing the daughter, who would be quite capable of coming out with a doctored version of the events of a certain afternoon. And if she called him as a witness? What could he tell other than that he had seen Hines leaving the house and found the daughter pretty well naked when he went in. No. It would have to be Leonardo. But how—

'Marshal?' He was standing right there by the car. 'I hope you don't mind. I saw you going in when I arrived and I've been waiting for you. Can we talk a moment?'

'Of course.'

They walked slowly on to the end of the line of cars and then began circling the edge of the car park. They had almost completed two circuits before the Marshal permitted himself to prompt his silent companion.

'I'm sorry . . .' Even then there was another long pause before he said, 'My mother has talked about you. I feel that she trusts you.'

'I was the first person she really had contact with. It's probably nothing more than that.'

'Still, she does trust you so . . . Please help me to persuade her to stay here a little longer. There are things I need to put right at home. Things – some at least that you already know – that I mustn't let her find out about.'

The Marshal had to remind himself of Leonardo's shock and grief, his devastating pain, in order to check the urge to say it would have been better not to have let them happen.

'I know what you mean but you can't do it. It's more than likely that she'll find most of it out anyway. What's more important to think about now is that she's in a very weakened state, and nothing, absolutely nothing on this earth, could damage her more than your trying to prevent her going home. It would confirm everything in that newspaper article. Confirm the suspicion hovering in the air all around her that the two of you chose to abandon her in favour of your inheritance.'

'But that's not true. It's not what I wanted: I was ready to give up everything I had but Caterina . . . I even thought of selling the business – there's a competitor who'd buy us out tomorrow – but Patrick said it was out of the question. She'd built it up from nothing and we mustn't lay a finger on it. He suggested a mortgage on the palazzo but Caterina wouldn't sign because it was Brunamonti property and not my mother's. My money and Elettra's wasn't enough. What was I to do? I should have dealt with it better, I know, but it's not true that I wanted to abandon her and keep the inheritance.'

'If you say so. I have to give you the benefit of the doubt. I imagine your mother would rather have died than live to face such an idea. Many people do die during kidnappings. Those who survive have only a slim chance of complete recovery. If you don't go in there now and tell your mother you want her home – and then get her there by tomorrow – if you don't behave like a son should, you'll destroy that slim chance for ever.'

'But it'll work so much better if I can sort these other problems out first. After that—'

'There is no "After that." There's only now, the one moment in her life when she is not the strong, competent person you imagine but a damaged, vulnerable woman whose only hope of recovery depends on you.'

He knew he had no right to talk to this man in such a way but he couldn't stop himself. The fear that churned in his stomach drove him on. The broken woman in the hospital bed took on Teresa's face. He was pleading for her as if to his own sons because he couldn't live forever. 'Besides' – he was clutching at straws now as he felt his lack of effect – 'the doctor has discharged her. Hospital beds can't be taken up for no reason.'

'I've already talked to the doctor. It can be arranged. We are paying for the room.'

Horrified, the Marshal tried to look Leonardo in the eyes. He had felt from the first that this was a candid person, and his honesty shone out in his eyes. Only now the eyes were blank and darkened as they had been on the day he'd collapsed in the courtyard. The Marshal felt he was staring into the windows of a roofless house. He was unreachable.

'You don't know how difficult my sister can be. She's very jealous.'

'Yes.' The Marshal knew a great deal more than her brother did about the extent of her jealousy but neither he nor anyone else would ever tell it.

'She'll calm down, given time. If my mother came home now and saw . . . the rows, the tension would be unbearable . . .'

Unbearable for you, presumably, thought the Marshal, but he didn't trust himself to speak.

'There's her missing jewellery and clothes and I don't yet know what else. And I can get the maid back but I can't sack the porter . . .'

'Yes' – the Marshal tried to keep his voice free of expression – 'she might wonder at the reluctance to part with ransom money coupled with the expense of a porter, I agree.'

'I released everything I had, but I've told you it was nowhere near enough! Caterina said they would have killed her. She said they might well have killed her already. Why not?'

'That's not how kidnappers work. An inadequate

281

payment, it's true, does sometimes result in some evidence of violence to the victim so as to extract more money.'

'Elettra blames me. I couldn't force Caterina to sign away the house.'

'Did you try?'

'I didn't insist. She becomes hysterical when crossed. My mother and I always tried – my father's death . . . my father . . . I can't explain, it's too complicated. Besides, it's true what she said – the State has paid up for well-connected victims in the past. She thought we were being treated as second-class citizens and that's not right. Everything my mother worked and struggled for all those years would have gone. I wanted to save it for her if I could. And I have. When she does come home she'll have everything she had before.'

Except a son, the Marshal thought, because however hard she tries to believe you, however much she loves you, she'll never trust you again because of this moment.

All he dared say was, 'Please take your mother home. Do it now.'

'I think Elettra – my mother's closest friend – might ask her to go and stay with her for a week or so. If she won't stay here, that would be the best thing, I think.'

'It would at least be better than the hospital, but please—'

'I think Elettra will manage to convince her, if only because Tessie's there.'

'Yes. I only hope she never finds out why Tessie's there.

I don't know your mother well but from the brief contact I've had with her, I think your failure to protect her little dog could well do more damage to your relationship than your protection of your heritage could mend. She has been a very good friend, the Contessa Cavicchioli Zelli.'

'Elettra's all right, but she knows nothing about kidnappings and it wasn't her business to tell us what we should or shouldn't do, even if she was helping. Caterina said—'

At the completion of their third turn around the car park the Marshal's patience was at an end. 'Your sister,' he said firmly, 'has no knowledge or experience of kidnappings either, and she wasn't helping. She was hardly the ideal person to take advice from in the circumstances.'

'I don't think that's true, Marshal. She was all the family I had left. She was the person most deeply involved. Who else should I have consulted? You? You couldn't have done much to help, could you?'

'No, no . . . Are you going in to see your mother now?'

'I don't think I will. The way she looks at me . . . I did what I could . . . it really hurts, I don't mind telling you. I'll come back another day.'

'Salva!'

'What?'

'You haven't heard a word I've said, have you?'

'Of course I have. You just said we should talk to Totò's teacher another day.'

'I said *you* should. You might as well not have been

there! I don't think you're interested in that child's future at all.'

'I am. I know I tend to leave things to you. I know that.'

'I just don't understand you. You insisted on coming when I could see you were tired and upset.'

'I didn't say I was upset.'

'What's that got to do with it? Wait here a minute, there's a bit of a queue.'

'You're not shopping now? Can't we get home? The children . . .'

'I'm going to buy some strawberries. It's the first time I've seen them this year. Totò will be waiting there, worried sick. I'm not having any more upset today. Enough's enough. We'll have a nice supper and watch a film or something. Wait there. And for goodness' sake don't block the entire pavement.'

Like that woman with the little girl. Small children, small problems. But then they grow up . . . If he wasn't to go inside the shop because it was crowded, how could he help blocking a pavement that was less wide than he was? Cars hooted at him when he stepped off it so he walked on a bit to the corner of Piazza Santo Spirito, where he could get out of everybody's way near the newspaper kiosk. The headlines advertising all the papers were more or less the same.

ANOTHER ARREST IN BRUNAMONTI CASE

There he waited, tired and, as Teresa had said, upset.

Why had Totò got himself into this mess when he had brains enough to prevent it? It's such an impossible task to understand other people. How did Teresa do it? Sometimes, when he came in after work, she had sized up the mood he was in without so much as turning round to look at him. So, she would know what to say to Totò. Wouldn't she? 'Brunamonti case another arrest' . . . The Contessa, her head sunk in the pillows, her dry eyes filled with pain . . . Her answer to all her children's problems seemed to have been more help, more love . . . but it hadn't answered at all. No one could tell you what was best to do for your children. So much of it was luck and guesswork. He was grateful, as Teresa came along and slipped her arm through his, that he didn't have to guess alone.

'Salva! Look at that headline. You didn't tell me they'd made another arrest.'

Nobody had nursed any illusions about capturing Puddu and his accomplice, presumed to be the one the Contessa called Woodcutter. The two guards captured in their drugged sleep were the ones she called Fox and Butcher, who, she said, had been on duty that night. The network of tunnels through the brush, coupled with Puddu's intimate knowledge of the terrain and the help he could demand from other Sardinians in the area, gave the men still up in the hills too big an advantage. There were only two of them. They were silent. They were invisible. Their pursuers were many, visible, and audible. The search went on for days but the Captain's hopes were pinned on night surveillance of places where they could safely seek food and of the motorway running below the hills where they might be picked up by other members of their clan. They weren't high hopes because these men who still had the centuries-old skills of the bandit also had twentieth-century technology. There was no need to risk a near approach to a farmhouse if you could use your mobile phone to summon food, clothing, batteries, money to a well-hidden cave. For weeks, the only sign of life from them was a package posted to the Contessa Brunamonti containing a valuable ring wrapped in a piece of brown paper torn from a bread bag. The Contessa informed them of its arrival but claimed she had thrown away the envelope it had been posted in. It hardly mattered. The posting must have been done by some collaborator, and the postmark would be useless information.

Then, one day, they inadvertently came near enough to their quarry to cause them to move off in a bit of a hurry, and the small covered clearing where they had been eating still bore traces of their presence: a half-full flask of wine, some rinds of sheep's cheese, and, most valuable of all, a polythene bag containing a dirty T-shirt, treasure for the dogs. The Captain was well aware that Puddu wouldn't have been fool enough to leave the T-shirt, no matter what his hurry, and that on discovering his accomplice's mistake he would split off from him. This proved to be the case. The dogs were racing towards the accomplice when he boarded a car driving south on the motorway. There was a chase during which the car's tyres were shot at and their quarry injured in the shoulder. From a prison hospital bed, he apologised to the Contessa Brunamonti and her family in front of TV news cameras. Under interrogation, he remained silent as to the likely whereabouts of Puddu. Of the three men who had taken the victim out of the city, no trace had been found, and against the photographer, Gianni Taccola, there was not, nor was there ever likely to be, a trace of evidence.

A year had passed and the lime trees were in flower again before the Marshal happened to see Olivia Brunamonti. It was a sunny Saturday afternoon and he was strolling through Piazza Santo Spirito with Teresa's arm through his. They were on their way to a discount store in San Frediano to buy a new fridge. The old one was on its last legs and they had decided to replace it now rather than risk having it breathe its last in the August holiday when they would be unable either to do without it or to replace it.

He was the one to notice the wedding group outside the church. He was soppy about weddings, according to Teresa, who disapproved of the excessive expense and mundanity of them.

'But it's still a nice ceremony,' he said, as he always did, 'and that's a lovely girl. Just look at her.'

Teresa looked. 'That's the Brunamonti girl.'

'No!'

'Yes, it is.' It was. 'She does look nice. White suits her.'

'Marshal! I'm so glad to see you again!' The Contessa Cavicchioli Zelli, smiling, breathless, and dogless, was hurrying away from the wedding group to join them.

The Marshal introduced his wife. 'You remember, I talked to you about her and all her dogs.' He had been slow to recognise her as she approached because she was so beautifully dressed, though the wispy hair was tucked anyhow into the brim of a most elegant hat. They talked for a while and she brought the Marshal up to date on the latest developments in the Brunamonti family. Olivia and Leo kept reaching out to each other, as she put it, and missing.

'At least Olivia's got her ghastly daughter married off but she's not rid of her. He'll be moving in. That one will never step outside the Brunamonti house though she'd get Olivia out if she could. She's already got her to move the workrooms out, did you see? Olivia converted the ground floor and first floor the other side of the bar when they came free. A typical Olivia job. She didn't much want to do it but saw it as another possible way of giving Leo a chance of getting back to feeling easy with her by asking him to design and set it up for her. She thought once they were busy on a project the tension would melt and their relationship fall into its usual habits of cheerful goodwill.'

'And did it work? It sounds like a good idea.'

'It was a good idea and no, it didn't work because Leo had just decided to move up to Switzerland with his girlfriend in the hope that his mother would get on better with Caterina without him there to cause jealousy and that Olivia might even be more likely, in his absence, to marry poor Patrick – I feel so sorry for him. Well, he's gone now. So she was left to sort the move out for herself, causing more resentment on her side, more guilt on his. The only concrete result, apart from Olivia's exhausting herself, was that that poisonous snake dressed up as an angel over there got her own way again. Oh, well, Leo still comes down to design Olivia's shows so maybe one day they'll get themselves sorted out. How do you like the bridegroom? That little chap with the ginger hair.'

'That's not—'

'Oh yes, it is. Half her size and twice her age. Hasn't a bean. Dreadful snob and marrying her for the name. Hasn't a saving grace.'

'She must think he has.'

'Yes, well, the fellow's a photographer on some newspaper or other. She picked him up during Olivia's thing. He was the only one who kept photographing her when all the others were flocking round Olivia. It was the wedding she wanted. All dressed up – and you must admit she looks stunning – and at the centre of all the photographs, plus a permanent court photographer at her service. I wouldn't give it a year. Have you seen Olivia? That suit! Caterina chose it. Nearest thing to putting a black cloth over her. She should have married Patrick. She's a damn fool.'

'Why didn't she?'

'She's still all taken up with that bandit fellow. Visits

289

him in prison. Didn't you know?'

'No, I hadn't heard . . .'

'There's a wife and a little boy, too. Olivia's rescuing them all. And, do you know, she told me that if things had gone wrong he would have killed her? What do you make of that? She just says she wants to understand. She can't rest until she understands why. Why he should destroy someone he barely knew and who had done him no harm. I said to her it might be more to the point to find out why her own children behaved the way they did but she said, "I can't think about that or I'd go mad. I want to be well."'

'She could get help. There's the National Association of Kidnap Victims. They're used to dealing with the problem—'

'They're not used to dealing with Olivia. She doesn't know how to be helped, she only knows how to help. Hence the bandit. She says he's going to study for a degree in prison. Well, he might turn out to be very grateful to her, which is more than can be said of her children. Look at that! The groom's behind the camera and Olivia's very carefully standing where she's been placed, at the back on the very edge of the group. She never complains, you know. She gets agitated if Leo's name comes up and sometimes I've thought I heard her crying but I was wrong. She's tough, is Olivia. I've never seen her shed a tear. I've got to get back over there. I'm so glad to have seen you!' She hurried back to the church, holding on to her hat.

The Marshal and his wife turned and walked among the groups of small children and grandmothers near the fountain, leaving the Palazzo Brunamonti behind them, enjoying the sunshine and the scent of blossoming limes.

Death of an Englishman

Magdalen Nabb

Introducing Marshal Salvatore Guarnaccia of the Florentine Carabineri, a Sicilian stationed far from home. He hopes to return home for Christmas to spend the holiday with his family, but he is frustratingly laid up with the 'flu. Reports come in of the death of a retired Englishman. Who has shot Mr Langley-Smith in the back? And why has Scotland Yard felt it appropriate to send two detectives, one of whom speaks no Italian, to 'help' the Marshal and his colleagues with their enquiries? Most importantly for the Marshal, ever the Italian, will he be able to solve the crime sufficiently quickly for him to be able to join his family over the holiday season?

This is the first of Magdalen Nabb's acclaimed Marshal Guarnaccia mysteries, now reissued in Arrow. With dry wit, an all-to-human detective and an evocative depiction of the Florentine setting, Nabb does for Florence what Donna Leon does for Venice, showing us the shadowy realities lurking behind the glittering tourist façade.

'Guarnaccia continues to impress as the most convincingly human of modern detectives and his creator as a writer of deep and rare dimensions'
Observer

'Guarnaccia is one of fiction's most satisfying detectives, a man whose domestic life is as fascinating as his cases . . . the series began with *Death of an Englishman* and is distinguished by its superb sense of place'
The Times, 'One Hundred Masters of Crime'

arrow books

Some Bitter Taste

Magdalen Nabb

When it comes to motives for crime, the past can never be forgotten.

Sara Hirsch is a nervous elderly spinster who still lives in the flat above the long-standing Florentine antique shop in which she was raised. Frightened, she calls Marshal Guarnaccia for help, sure that strangers have been in her apartment. The Marshal knows she is a lonely old woman but he is preoccupied with an investigation into an Albanian prostitution ring. Before he can respond to her latest alarm, she is found dead.

The Marshal's search for the villains who caused her death brings him into confrontation with the past, with Jewish refugees from fascism, and with English expatriates, including the ailing heir to the elegant Villa L'Uliveto, Sir Christopher Wrothesly . . .

'Pleasure from beginning to end'
TLS

'A perfect example of crime-and-pleasure . . . so cunningly plotted that it is only at the end that you realise that not one strand of the intricate tapestry has been superfluous . . . [*Some Bitter Taste*] will at one and the same time surprise, amuse and finally sadden'
Spectator

'A wonderfully satisfying read'
Daily Mail

arrow books

ALSO AVAILABLE IN ARROW

The Marshal Makes His Report
Magdalen Nabb

When the body of Buongianni Corsi is found lying face down in the courtyard of the Palazzo Ulderighi there seems no doubt in the minds of his family that his death was an accident. The Marchesa, wife of the dead man, will entertain no other possibility and her power and status in the city means that Marshal Guarnaccia questions at his peril. But question he does.

The death could have been suicide, or even murder. Guarnaccia knows something is not quite right, and resents being expected to go along with any possible cover up. The Palazzo is a maze of passageways, darkened corridors, locked rooms and something else, a family secret. Can he ignore his instincts and his integrity? Should he press on with the case, risk his job, and maybe more? As he paces the courtyard of the Palazzo, he is haunted by the strange piano and flute music that filters down from above, as well as by the irresistible conviction that something truly sinister has happened there . . .

'Magdelan Nabb's books are set in Florence so vividly brought to life that I long to go back there after reading each one'
Susanna Yager *Sunday Telegraph*

'He shares with Maigret a rounded solidness; strong reactions to weather, a sense of small community relationships and a readiness to relieve the plod of routine by intuitive flashes.
Sunday Times

arrow books

Doctored Evidence

Donna Leon

When the body of a wealthy woman is found brutally murdered, the prime suspect is her Romanian maid, who has fled Venice. As she attempted to leave the country, the maid runs into the path of an oncoming train and is killed, carrying a considerable sum of money and forged papers. Case closed.

But when the old woman's neighbour returns from abroad, it becomes clear that the maid could not have been the killer and that the money on her was not stolen. Commissario Brunetti decides – unofficially – to take the case on himself.

As Brunetti investigates, it becomes clear that the motive for the murder was probaby not Greed, rather that it has its roots in the temptations of Lust. But perhaps Brunetti is thinking of the wrong Deadly Sin altogether . . .

'Leon's talent for sketching Venice with equal measures of affection and exasperation is undermined, and Brunetti and his serious, thoughtful wife Paola remain subtle and pleasing creations'
Sunday Times

'Elegant, unflashy fiction . . . sharply intelligent and reassuring in its insistence that integrity is what really matters'
Literary Review

'[An] enjoyable addition to a fine series.
Susanne Yager in the *Sunday Telegraph*

arrow books

**Order further Michael Palmer titles
from your local bookshop, or have them delivered
direct to your door by Bookpost**

☐ **Death of An Englishman**	Magdalen Nabb	0099443341	£5.99
☐ **Some Bitter Taste**	Magdalen Nabb	0099443368	£5.99
☐ **The Marshal Makes his Report**	Magdalen Nabb	009944335X	£5.99
☐ **Doctored Evidence**	Donna Leon	0099446758	£6.99

Free post and packing

Overseas customers allow £2 per paperback

Phone: 01624 677237

Post: Random House Books
c/o Bookpost, PO Box 29, Douglas, Isle of Man IM99 1BQ

Fax: 01624 670923

email: bookshop@enterprise.net

Cheques (payable to Bookpost) and credit cards accepted

Prices and availability subject to change without notice.
Allow 28 days for delivery.
When placing your order, please state if you do not wish to receive any
additional information.

www.randomhouse.co.uk/arrowbooks

arrow books